THE DEVIL'S TEMPTATION

TAROT FANTASIES SERIES

BOOK ONE

JAX WILDER

THE DEVIL'S
TEMPTATION

Tarot Fantasies Series
Jax Wilder

RAINBOW QUARTZ PUBLISHING

The Devil's Temptation © 2024 by Jax Wilder

Published by Rainbow Quartz Publishing

Edmonds WA, 98026

ISBN: 978-1-961714-41-0

First Edition: 2024

Cover design by Miranda Townsend

Interior design by Miranda Townsend

Tarot Card description by Lorelai Hamilton from the book Teenage Tarot – used with permission.

For permissions or inquiries, please contact:

Rainbow Quartz Publishing

rainbowquartzpublishing@gmail.com

❀ Formatted with Vellum

Happy Birthday, Mom.

May all your wildest fantasies come true.

Jax Wilder

15. The Devil

"We all have darkness inside of us, but acknowledging it is the first step to breaking free," The Devil.

Materialism and excess
Addiction and unhealthy attachments
Ignorance of one's true self
Feeling trapped or powerless
Shadow aspects of the psyche
Chains of illusion and deception
Lust and desire
Self-imposed limitations
Breaking free from oppression and bondage

The Devil card is all about temptation, and feeling stuck. Sometimes we get so caught up in our desires or fears that we forget we have the power to break free.

Here's the thing though, The Devil card is about more than being trapped by external forces. It's also about the things we do to ourselves—like letting negative thoughts or habits hold us back. You're stronger than you think. You have the power to overcome these chains.

—Lorelai Hamilton, author of *Teenage Tarot* and *Tarot Tales & Magic Spells*

THE DEVIL .

ONE

I never believed in fairy tales.

Not the real way, anyway.

I liked them well enough as stories. Give me a cursed spindle, a tower, a beast with a tragic jawline, and I could enjoy myself for an hour or two. I owned enough fantasy novels to prove I was not immune to the appeal of a dramatic cape and a morally questionable man. But believing in fairy tales required a kind of softness I had spent most of my life kneading out of myself.

Fairy tales belonged to girls who got rescued.

I became the kind of woman who paid rent on time, made her own bread, unclogged the bakery sink with a plunger and spite, and knew better than to wait around for anyone to come fix what she could fix herself.

Still, when he touched me, my world unraveled.

Not all at once. Nothing honest comes apart that cleanly. It happened like dough giving way beneath the heel of a palm. A slow loosening. A stretch. A surrender. The kind of collapse that feels like ruin until you realize it's how something rises.

But that came later.

First, there was flour under my nails, a burn on my wrist, a man I did not want to want, and a bakery that smelled like sugar, butter, and financial panic.

Knead the Dough was supposed to be closed.

The sign on the front door said so, flipped to Sorry, We're

Closed in my own cheerful handwriting, complete with a tiny rolling pin doodle because apparently I hated myself. The lights in the cases were off. The last croissants had sold at four-thirty. The espresso machine had been wiped down. The tables were stacked with chairs, all except the one by the front window where Lea had planted herself like a small-town oracle with a tote bag full of books and opinions.

I stood behind the counter with both hands flat on the stainless steel prep table, staring at a tray of cinnamon rolls I had overbaked by six minutes.

Six minutes.

People act like baking is soft. All butter and sugar and cute aprons. Those people have never watched a batch of laminated dough decide to punish you for humidity. Baking is chemistry with a grudge. It is timing, temperature, pressure, patience, and the constant knowledge that one mistake can turn twelve dollars of ingredients into compost with frosting.

The cinnamon rolls were not ruined.

They were edible. Sellable, maybe, if I discounted them and distracted the customer with enough icing. But the edges had gone too dark, the centers less tender than I wanted. Not bad. Not perfect.

My least favorite category.

Lea watched me from her table, one boot crossed over the other. She owned Spellbound Stories two storefronts down, which meant she had the rare privilege of working retail with books instead of butter. She had wild curls, dramatic glasses, and the unnerving ability to see through people while pretending to browse.

"You're glaring at those rolls like they owe you money," she said.

"They do owe me money."

"They look fine."

"Fine is a word people use when they don't want to admit something disappointed them."

Lea leaned back in her chair. "That feels like it's about more than pastries."

"Everything is about pastries if you understand metaphor."

"Dottie."

I kept my eyes on the tray. "Don't use that voice."

"What voice?"

"The one that says you're about to care at me."

"I care at you constantly. This is a friendship."

"This is harassment with tea."

She smiled, which only made me more suspicious.

My feet hurt. My lower back hurt. My fingers smelled like cinnamon, yeast, dish soap, and the faint metallic tang from the oven rack that had kissed my wrist during the lunch rush. I had been awake since three-forty that morning. The bakery opened at six, which meant the world got croissants because I got insomnia.

There was flour in my bra.

I did not know how flour got into a bra while a person was fully clothed, but bakery ownership taught a woman many dark mysteries.

The day had been too long. Too busy. Too full of people smiling at me as if a fresh muffin was not the only thing standing between me and a complete emotional collapse. I had smiled back. I was good at that. Customer service is theater, and I had been performing the role of Well-Adjusted Local Business Owner for years.

Then Lorenzo had come in.

The universe had a terrible sense of comedic timing.

He arrived during the eleven o'clock rush, when the line wrapped past the pastry case and my assistant called in sick with what she described as "food poisoning or spiritual punishment." I was steaming milk, boxing tarts, answering a question about gluten-free options from a woman who was obviously personally betrayed by wheat, and trying not to think about the stack of invoices waiting in the office.

Then the bell over the door rang, and every nerve in my body acted like it had been waiting for him.

Lorenzo De Luca walked into Knead the Dough wearing a charcoal coat, dark jeans, and the kind of confidence that made people step aside before they realized they were doing it. He had black hair, a little too long, the sort of mouth that looked like it had ruined lives casually, and eyes that always seemed to know more than I wanted them to.

He did not look like a bakery customer.

He looked like a complication with cheekbones.

"Dorothea," he said when he reached the counter.

Not Dottie.

Never Dottie.

Most people called me Dottie because Coral Cove had a way of sanding formal names down into something neighborly. I let them because fighting it took energy, and energy cost more than pride most days. But Lorenzo called me Dorothea, the full name, every syllable set down like a hand against my spine.

I hated the way I liked it.

"What can I get you?" I asked, too brightly.

His eyes flicked over my face. "You look tired."

"A dangerous thing to say to a woman holding hot coffee."

"I brought paperwork."

"Worse."

He set a folder on the counter.

The woman behind him sighed, which saved me from having to react properly.

"I'm a little busy," I said.

"I can see that."

"Then you understand the concept of later."

His mouth curved.

Not a smile. Lorenzo did not waste a full smile unless he intended to make someone forget their own name. This was smaller. More irritating.

"I understand several concepts, Dorothea. Later tends to become never with you."

The truth of that annoyed me.

I grabbed a paper cup and wrote his name on it even though he had not ordered. "Americano?"

"You remember."

"I remember every regular's order."

"I'm not a regular."

"You're regularly in my way."

That got the full smile.

Damn him.

The espresso machine hissed behind me. Steam curled

into the air. My face went warm, which I blamed on the machine because denial is free and sometimes useful.

He leaned one elbow on the counter, too comfortable in a place I owned. "We still need to talk about the festival contract."

"No, you need to talk. I need to sell muffins."

"And the lease."

I froze for half a second.

Too long.

Lorenzo saw.

His expression shifted, the charm dimming under something sharper. Concern, maybe. Strategy. With him, it was hard to tell the difference.

"We should discuss it before the deadline," he said more softly.

"I know the deadline."

"Do you?"

I handed him the Americano with enough force that coffee sloshed near the lid. "Careful. It's hot."

"So are you when you're avoiding me."

The woman behind him made a sound that was either a cough or interest.

I smiled at her with my customer service face, the one that said no one was being strangled with an apron cord today.

"Anything else?" I asked Lorenzo.

His gaze stayed on mine.

Yes, it said.

A thousand things.

The lease. The festival. The fake relationship arrangement he had somehow turned into both a business solution and a daily threat to my blood pressure. The way he had held my hand last week in front of the Coral Cove Business Association and made it look like affection instead of strategy. The way my whole body had believed him for three disastrous seconds.

He picked up his coffee.

"I'll come by after closing."

"No."

"Yes."

"No, I have plans."

"You don't."

"I could."

"You won't."

I hated him a little then.

Mostly because he was right.

"Don't you have someone else to annoy?" I asked.

"Not at this level."

"Lucky me."

His eyes warmed. "Yes."

He left before I could answer.

Which was good, because I had nothing useful to say. My tongue had become dough, and not the cooperative kind.

After that, the day went crooked.

A child spilled hot chocolate under table three. Someone asked if my almond croissants contained nuts. The card reader froze during a rush. A tourist told me the lemon bars were "almost as good as one from a bakery in Portland," and I had to briefly leave my body to avoid committing violence. By the time I locked the door, I was running on old coffee and the thin, brittle kind of energy that makes a person dangerous near sharp objects.

Then Lea walked in with a tote bag and a mission.

Now she sat by the window, watching me watch the over-baked rolls.

"You need a break," she said.

"I'll take one when the bakery makes enough money for me to hire reliable help, replace the mixer before it explodes, pay the quarterly taxes without crying, and convince the landlord to stop treating rent increases like a seasonal hobby."

"So never."

"Exactly. I'm glad you understand."

Lea stood and came to the counter. She picked up one of the cinnamon rolls, tore off an edge, and ate it.

I stared. "That one was not for you."

"It's delicious."

"It's overbaked."

"It has frosting."

"You people are easily manipulated by sugar."

"Yes. That's your business model."

I took the roll from her before she could eat more of my evidence. "Why are you here, Lea?"

She wiped icing from her thumb. "Because you have been a clenched fist in an apron for three weeks."

"I own a business. Clenching is part of the job."

"You snapped at Mr. Alvarez yesterday."

"He asked if macarons were supposed to be chewy."

"He is eighty-six."

"He has had eighty-six years to learn texture."

Lea gave me the look.

I hated the look.

It was a bookstore-owner look. Patient. Literary. Full of themes.

"What?" I asked.

"You don't need a day off, Dottie. You need to remember you have a body."

I blinked.

The bakery went quiet around us.

Outside, Coral Cove settled into early evening. Rain darkened the sidewalk. The storefront lights across the street flickered on one by one. Spellbound Stories glowed soft and golden two doors down. People hurried under umbrellas. The ocean wind pushed mist against the window, turning the town watery at the edges.

My body.

The idea felt rude.

I knew I had one, obviously. It carried flour sacks and trays of sourdough. It stood for twelve hours at a time. It burned, ached, cramped, bled, sweated, and occasionally demanded coffee with the urgency of a hostage negotiator. But Lea did not mean that kind of body.

She meant the other one.

The one I tried not to think about.

The one that went too still when Lorenzo said my name. The one that had not been touched by anyone but me. The one that wanted things at inconvenient times and then panicked at the suggestion of having them.

I picked up a towel and began wiping a clean counter.

"Don't do that," Lea said.

"Clean?"

"Hide."

"I'm not hiding. I'm sanitizing."

"You've sanitized that spot four times."

"It might be especially dirty."

"It's stainless steel, not your soul."

I threw the towel at her.

She caught it, because betrayal was apparently one of her skills.

"I'm serious," she said.

"I know. That's what makes this unpleasant."

She reached into her tote bag and pulled out a small black card. She set it on the counter.

The Arcane Room.

Silver letters. Nothing else.

I stared at it.

"No."

"You haven't heard what it is."

"The name contains arcane. That is enough."

"It's a metaphysical shop."

"I own a bakery, Lea. I cannot afford a crystal habit."

"It's not about crystals."

"Everyone says that before crystals happen."

She pushed the card closer. "Ms. Vesper does readings. Experiences. Private ones."

I looked up. "That sounds illegal."

"It isn't."

"It sounds like something where I wake up in a bathtub missing a kidney."

"You are impossible."

"I'm healthily suspicious of secondary locations."

"The shop is three blocks away."

"Kidneys can be stolen locally."

Lea laughed, but her eyes stayed serious.

"I went last month," she said.

That got my attention.

"You?"

"Yes."

"What happened?"

Her face changed.

Only slightly, but I knew Lea well enough to catch it.

Something softened behind her glasses. Something private and a little shaken.

"I got unstuck," she said.

"That is not an answer."

"It's the only one I'm giving you."

"Was there tea?"

"Yes."

"Drugs?"

"No."

"Would you know?"

She gave me a flat look. "Dottie."

"Fine."

"Ms. Vesper is safe. Strange, but safe. And she has a way of showing people what they are avoiding."

"I'm avoiding nothing."

"You have made avoidance into an Olympic sport."

I crossed my arms. "What exactly do you think I'm avoiding?"

Lea's gaze flicked toward the folder Lorenzo had left near the register.

I hated that folder.

It sat there, smug and legal.

"No," I said.

"I didn't say his name."

"You thought it loudly."

"He is not the only thing."

"Good. Because he is not a thing."

"He is a very attractive man who makes you behave like a feral cat in a bakery hat."

"I don't have a bakery hat."

"Emotionally, you do."

I pointed toward the door. "Out."

"Go to The Arcane Room first."

"No."

"You asked me what I think you're avoiding."

"I regretted that immediately."

She picked up the card and tucked it into the pocket of my apron.

"Yourself," she said.

I did not have a joke for that.

I hated when she did that too.

"Lea."

She stepped back. "You have built something amazing here. You know that, right?"

I looked around the bakery.

The pastry case. The tables. The wall painted a warm buttery yellow. The chalkboard menu I rewrote every week. The kitchen door, the ovens, the mixer, the proofing racks, the shelves stacked with flour and sugar and chocolate. My whole life, condensed into rent and recipes.

"Yes," I said carefully.

"And you're proud of it."

"Yes."

"You should be."

"I'm."

"But you keep acting like survival is the same as living."

The words landed too close.

I turned away, pretending to check the sink.

Lea's voice gentled. "You deserve more than a business that consumes you and a man you only touch when there are witnesses."

My throat tightened.

The fake relationship had started as a solution. A bad one, but still.

The town festival committee wanted Knead the Dough and Lorenzo's family restaurant to co-sponsor the summer food walk. There were permits, vendor disputes, landlord politics, and one extremely inconvenient rumor that the two of us were dating after Lorenzo held my hand at a meeting to stop his ex from making a scene. It should have ended there.

It did not.

Because small towns feed on nonsense, and Coral Cove ate like it had not seen bread in years.

Then Lorenzo suggested we let people believe it for a while. Good publicity, he said. Helps with the festival, he said. Keeps people out of our business, he said.

A fake relationship.

A business strategy.

A disaster wearing cologne.

"I don't want to talk about Lorenzo," I said.

"That's how I know you need to."

"No, that's how you know I don't want to."

Lea picked up her tote bag. "The shop is open until seven."

"I have cleanup."

"I'll help."

"No."

"You'll go?"

"No."

She smiled.

I sighed.

"Maybe."

"Good enough."

"It's not good enough. It's a noncommittal word designed to end this conversation."

"And yet, I accept."

She kissed two fingers and tapped them on the counter, like a blessing or a threat. "Go remember your body, Dottie."

Then she left with one of the overbaked cinnamon rolls.

Thief.

I cleaned for twenty-three more minutes out of spite.

Then I stood in the middle of the bakery with the lights half off, the ovens cooling, the day's receipts waiting to be counted, and The Arcane Room's card burning a hole in my apron pocket.

My body.

I looked down at myself.

Black jeans dusted with flour. A gray T-shirt with butter on the hem. Apron stained with chocolate, raspberry jam, and what might have been coffee. Hair piled in a messy bun that had started the day cute and ended it structurally unsound. My hands were dry from washing. My feet throbbed. My shoulders ached.

This was a body built for work.

Useful. Strong. Tired.

But not cherished.

Not touched.

Not wanted in any way I trusted.

I thought of Lorenzo's voice saying Dorothea.

I hated the little pull low in my stomach.

I hated more that I had no idea what to do with it.

So I did what I always did when my feelings became too loud.

I made a list.

Count register.

Cover cinnamon rolls.

Start poolish for morning loaves.

Check walk-in.

Text Lea that she is a menace.

Ignore Lorenzo's folder.

Don't think about Lorenzo's hands.

Fail at that.

I stared at the last line.

I had not written it.

The pen was in my hand. The words were on the bakery order pad. My handwriting, unfortunately.

Don't think about Lorenzo's hands.

I tore the page off, crumpled it, and threw it away.

Then I uncrumpled it because wasting paper was expensive.

"Fine," I said to the empty bakery.

The empty bakery did not applaud.

I grabbed my coat, locked the back door, checked the front twice, and stepped out into Coral Cove's wet evening with flour under my nails and a mystical business card in my pocket.

The town looked like it had been painted in damp jewel tones. Neon from the diner bled red onto the sidewalk. Spellbound Stories glowed gold, its window full of books and little string lights. The sea was not visible from Main Street, but I could smell it under the rain, salt and cold and restless. Coral Cove always smelled like something was ending or beginning. Sometimes both.

I passed the bookstore quickly, in case Lea was watching from the window like a literary gargoyle.

She was.

She waved.

I flipped her off inside my pocket like a lady.

The Arcane Room sat on a side street I usually ignored because it mostly held businesses I could not afford to visit. A florist with impossible arrangements. A shop that sold hand-made candles for people who thought thirty dollars was a reasonable price for wax. A narrow tea house with mismatched chairs and a chalkboard sign that said Ask us about your aura, which I never intended to do.

Then there it was.

The Arcane Room.

It was smaller than I expected. Narrow and tucked between the tea house and a closed tailor shop, with a simple wooden sign above the door. The letters were carved deep and painted silver. No flashing neon. No dramatic pentacles. No mannequin in a witch hat, which frankly showed restraint.

The window displayed crystals, tarot decks, little brass bells, jars of herbs, and a black candle shaped like a coiled serpent. A small sign in the corner said Hex, Bless, Manifest.

I snorted.

It was very Live, Laugh, Love, but witchy.

The door opened before I touched it.

I stopped on the sidewalk.

Rain misted my face.

"Nope," I said.

The door stayed open.

Warm air drifted out, carrying sandalwood, smoke, vanilla, and something darker. Burnt sugar maybe. Or caramel just before it crosses the line from delicious to ruined. The smell wrapped around me, tugging at some soft place beneath the ribs I had not authorized anyone to access.

Coming home.

That was the first thought.

I disliked it immediately.

I rarely found places familiar. Admittedly, I did not like most people, and I was rarely looking to make friends. Famil-iarity was usually a trap. Familiar people asked questions. Familiar places expected you to return. Familiarity made it harder to leave when leaving became necessary.

But standing outside The Arcane Room, rain in my hair and cinnamon still under my nails, I felt something inside me loosen.

Not much.

Enough to be concerning.

The door creaked a little wider.

"Fine," I muttered. "But if I lose a kidney, I'm haunting Lea first."

I stepped inside.

The bell above the door did not ring.

It laughed.

Low and soft, almost human.

I froze.

The door closed behind me.

The shop was warm in a way that felt deliberate. Not overheated. Not stuffy. Warm like bread after it leaves the oven. Like a mug held between both hands. The walls were a deep maroon with gold trim, the kind of red that made everything inside it look a little more secretive. Shelves lined the room from floor to ceiling, filled with books on tarot, magic, astrology, spirit work, manifestation, herbalism, and at least three titles that looked like they might argue with me if opened.

There was a wall of incense in every possible iteration.

Lavender. Dragon's blood. Sandalwood. Rose. Myrrh. Something called Midnight Orchard. Something else called Ex Lover, which seemed irresponsible.

Tarot decks filled another wall, stacked and displayed like little doors. Two hundred varieties, easily. Maybe more. Angels, cats, witches, bones, flowers, art deco women, haunted houses, mermaids, saints, demons, planets. I moved toward them despite myself, drawn by the same dangerous curiosity that made me taste batter even when I knew it needed more salt.

An amethyst crystal twice the size of my head sat in the center of the shop on a carved wooden pedestal. Its purple points caught the lamplight. Beside it, a cluster of black stones had been arranged in a shallow brass bowl, each one smooth and glossy like hardened night.

The shop was a treasure trove of New Age paraphernalia, and I knew this was going to be rough on my pocketbook.

"Welcome," a velvety voice said.

I turned.

A woman stood behind the counter.

Beautiful did not quite cover it. Beautiful was for people in perfume ads or women who came into the bakery wearing white coats without fear of powdered sugar. This woman looked curated by candlelight. Long dark hair fell over one shoulder in loose waves. Intricate tattoos covered both arms, disappearing beneath soft, loosely fitted black clothing that draped around her body like fabric had decided to worship her. Her eyes were dark and bright at once, and when she looked at me, I had the absurd feeling she had been expecting me for years and I was late.

"I'm Ms. Vesper," she said. "Can I assist you in finding anything?"

Before I could answer, a familiar voice came from behind a stack of books.

"Oh, hey, Dottie. How are you?"

I turned.

Park stood near the mythology section, holding a stack of books high enough to qualify as a structural hazard. He was tall, lean, forever dressed like a man who had accidentally become charming while reaching for a cardigan. He worked at Spellbound Stories with Lea, which meant he had access to my pastries and far too much of my personal business.

"Fancy seeing you here, Park," I said.

"Is it fancy? I feel underdressed."

"You look like a librarian in a romance novel."

"That is the nicest thing you've ever said to me."

"Don't get used to it."

He shifted the books against his chest and grinned. "What are you up to today?"

"Honestly? Bakery is closed, Lea said I needed to come here, and I'm too tired to keep making responsible choices."

"That tracks."

"What about you?"

He lifted the stack slightly. "Picking these up for the bookstore. We keep a small magic section at Spellbound. Ms. Vesper has an in on all the best witchy titles, especially when someone comes into the shop asking about a subject in particular."

"That sounds suspiciously tailored."

"It often is."

"Does everything in this town conspire?"

"Yes," Park said. "Mostly with good intentions. That's what makes it unbearable."

I smiled despite myself.

Ms. Vesper watched us with polite amusement.

"Oh," I said, remembering manners. "Hi. I'm Dorothea."

I reached across the counter.

Ms. Vesper took my hand.

Her fingers were cool.

Not cold. Cool like stone in shade.

The moment her palm touched mine, something behind the counter clicked.

I looked past her.

A glass display case sat beneath the register. Inside were antique tarot cards, each one propped on tiny stands. The Magician. The High Priestess. The Lovers. The Tower. The Star.

And The Devil.

The Devil card, old and faded, had shifted slightly in its stand.

Its black lines seemed darker now.

I stared.

Ms. Vesper's thumb brushed the back of my hand once before she released me.

"Dorothea," she said, like the name tasted important.

My pulse stumbled.

It was not Lorenzo's voice.

Still, hearing the full name in this place made my stomach dip.

"Your shop is lovely," I said, because apparently I could still perform politeness while questioning whether a tarot card had just moved. "I own the bakery in town."

"Her stuff is delicious," Park said. "Lea picked up a dozen of your pastries this morning. I might have eaten most of them."

"You say that like a confession. It's more of a diagnosis."

"I accept."

Ms. Vesper smiled. "Knead the Dough."

"You've heard of it?"

"I know most places where people make offerings."

16

I blinked. "Offerings?"

"Bread. Sugar. Coffee. Comfort." She tilted her head. "People come to you hungry and leave with something warm in their hands. That is a kind of magic."

My chest went oddly tight.

I looked away first.

Park's gaze bounced between us, delighted.

"Well," he said, "I'll let you do your shopping. I need to get back before Lea notices I've been gone too long."

"Lea always notices."

"Yes, but sometimes she pretends not to for dramatic effect."

He turned toward the door, then stopped. "Thanks again for ordering these, Ms. Vesper. I'll put this one aside for that mutual friend of ours."

He held up a book.

The Beginner's Guide to Romance Magic.

My eyes narrowed. "Who is that for?"

Park's smile became dangerous. "A customer."

"Park."

"Many people read books, Dottie."

"Not that innocently, they don't."

Ms. Vesper's mouth twitched.

Park hugged the book to his chest. "Look, I don't name names. Spellbound Stories respects privacy."

"You work with Lea."

"We respect privacy selectively."

"Is it for Lorenzo?"

Why did I say his name?

Why did I open my mouth and let the devil himself stroll out wearing Italian leather?

Park's smile widened.

I wanted to throw incense at him.

"I didn't say that," he said.

"You didn't have to."

"I will simply say that certain men in town have recently shown interest in books involving romance, magical or otherwise."

"Certain men?"

"Tall ones."

"I hate you."

"Possibly. But you feed me, so I risk it."

He winked and headed for the door.

"Bye, Park."

"You too, Dottie. Have fun. Or have an emotional break-through. Around here it's hard to tell the difference."

The bell laughed again as he left.

I turned to Ms. Vesper. "Does your door always do that?"

"Only when it's amused."

"Comforting."

"Isn't it?"

"No."

She smiled as if my resistance was a perfectly normal weather pattern.

I shifted my attention back to the shop because looking at Ms. Vesper too long felt like standing near an oven with the door open. "You have a lovely collection. I work a lot, which means I don't get out as often as I'd like. How long have you been here?"

"Nearly fifteen years."

"I've lived in Coral Cove for six."

"Yes."

"And I've never noticed this place before."

"No."

I waited.

She did not elaborate.

"That's strange," I said.

"Many things are."

"That is not an answer."

"No," she agreed.

I did not know what to do with that, so I moved along the display cases and pretended to browse.

The shop was full of tiny provocations.

A candle smelled like burnt sugar and smoke every time I passed it, though the label said Clarity. A shelf of journals held titles stamped in gold: What You Refuse to Say, What You Almost Did, What You Want When No One Is Watching. A small bowl near the register was filled with brass keys, each tagged with a handwritten word.

No.

Yes.

Mine.

More.

Enough.

I looked away from that one.

Ms. Vesper came around the counter and stood near the tarot wall. She did not crowd me. I appreciated that. People in shops often hovered as if theft were the only possible reason for touching things. Ms. Vesper stood like someone guarding a threshold, which was worse, but more interesting.

"Lea sent you," she said.

"She bullied me."

"Same root system."

"She said you were life-changing."

"She is generous."

"She said I needed an emotional and mental time-out."

"She was imprecise."

I looked at her. "Excuse me?"

Ms. Vesper's gaze moved over me, not in the way people assess bodies. Not like Lorenzo's careful, heated glances that made me want to both step closer and flee to a monastery. Ms. Vesper looked at me the way a baker looks at dough. Texture, tension, readiness, what it might become if handled correctly.

"You don't need a time-out," she said. "You need a threshold."

A laugh slipped out of me. "That sounds more expensive."

"For first-time customers, not necessarily." Her smile deepened. "Would you like to see what kind of experience I can offer you today?" she asked.

Experience.

The word carried too much velvet.

My curiosity piqued, which was inconvenient because curiosity had caused at least sixty percent of my worst decisions.

"Did Lea call ahead and tell you I was coming?" I asked.

"She told me to expect someone carrying too many keys."

I glanced toward the bowl of brass keys.

Ms. Vesper followed my gaze.

"Not those," she said.

"Then what keys?"

"Business keys. House keys. Emotional keys. Keys to rooms you don't enter. Keys you use as proof you can leave."

I stared at her.

The shop seemed to quiet around us.

"I'm sorry," I said. "Do you always read people for sport?"

"Never for sport."

"Professionally, then."

"When invited."

"I did not invite that."

"No," she said. "But you walked in holding the door open behind you."

I had no idea what that meant.

I had the very uncomfortable feeling some part of me did.

"This is the part where I should leave," I said.

"Probably."

"You're not going to stop me?"

"No."

That made leaving harder.

Annoying woman.

I looked toward the door. Then at the rain sliding down the window. Then at the black card Lea had shoved into my apron pocket, now sitting warm against my hip.

"What's the experience?" I asked.

Ms. Vesper gestured toward the counter. "Come this way."

She moved behind the counter and withdrew a tarot deck from a wooden box. The box was black, carved with little flames along the lid. When she opened it, the air filled with that burnt sugar and smoke scent again.

She shuffled.

The sound of the cards was soft, dry, oddly intimate.

I stepped closer.

"Tarot?" I asked.

"One doorway among many."

"That sounds like yes with drama."

"You learn quickly."

"I own a bakery. If I don't translate nonsense fast, vendors rob me."

She laughed.

I liked the sound of it more than I wanted to.

"We offer a unique experience here," she said. "A little magic, if you will."

"Magic, magic?"

"Is there another kind?"

"Stage magic. Marketing magic. The magic of compound interest, which I've heard rumors about but never experienced personally."

"Real magic," she said.

The words were simple. No flourish. No sales pitch. That made them harder to dismiss.

"You can think of it like an immersive dream," she continued. "A private realm shaped by your chosen card, your own desires, and what you are most ready to face. Some people call it fantasy. Some call it ritual. Some call it the first honest room they have ever entered."

My skin prickled.

"That sounds intense."

"It can be."

"And safe?"

Her eyes sharpened.

"Always safe. Not always comfortable."

"Those are very different things."

"Yes."

Good.

I liked that she knew that.

"How much is it?" I asked, because even in the face of possible magic, I was still a small-business owner with invoices.

"For first-time customers, free."

I narrowed my eyes. "That is suspicious."

"Yes."

"You just admit that?"

"Suspicion is appropriate at thresholds."

"What's the catch?"

"You may tip after."

"There is always a tip jar."

"A lady has rent."

That startled a laugh out of me.

She smiled.

The Devil card in the display case seemed to warm at my

side. I felt it before I looked. Heat against my hip, impossible and insistent.

Ms. Vesper's gaze flicked toward it.

"I don't know," I said.

"You don't have to know. You only have to choose."

"That is not reassuring."

"It's not meant to be."

She spread the cards facedown across the counter in a long dark arc.

The card backs were black with a thin gold chain printed across them. Each link curved into the next, forming a loop.

A chain.

Subtle.

"Before you pull," Ms. Vesper said, "I want you to take a moment."

"I'm not great at moments."

"I suspect you are excellent at avoiding them."

"Lea has been talking."

"Lea did not need to."

I looked down at the cards.

They seemed to breathe.

No. Not breathe. That was ridiculous. Paper did not breathe. But the line of cards shifted almost imperceptibly, expanding and settling like dough under a damp towel.

I blinked.

They were still.

"Think about your deepest fantasy," Ms. Vesper said.

A blush climbed my neck so fast it was embarrassing.

"I don't have one."

"Everyone has one."

"I have practical goals."

"Those are fantasies with spreadsheets."

"I like spreadsheets."

"I know."

I glanced at her. "That is a rude amount of knowing."

She only smiled.

Deepest fantasy.

The phrase sounded pornographic and childish at the same time. Like something whispered in a dark room or printed on a cheap candle. I wanted to laugh it off. Make a joke. Say I fantasized about the bakery turning a profit, a reliable dishwasher, a landlord with a sudden passion for rent control.

All true.

None true enough.

I thought of intimacy and immediately tried not to.

That was usually how it went.

No matter how much I desired closeness, I could not bring myself to let anyone get too close. At twenty-nine years old, I was still untouched by love or the complexities of sex. Virgin felt like a word from a different century, wrapped in either purity or pity, neither of which fit. My body had known pleasure, yes. I was not a nun or a liar. My own hands had mapped me in the dark. I knew what I liked when no one was looking.

But another person?

A mouth. Hands. Weight. Want. Expectation. The terrifying possibility of being disappointing in real time.

No, thank you.

Life had not been easy, and I had spent most of mine trying to keep a roof over my head. Every spare penny had gone into Knead the Dough. Love, or whatever version of it people kept trying to sell me, seemed like a luxury item. Beautiful in the window. Financially irresponsible. Likely to break.

And sex without a connection felt impossible.

Sex with a connection felt worse.

Because if I cared, if I wanted, if I let myself soften in someone's hands, then they could hurt me in ways I would not be able to bake, budget, or joke my way out of.

My mind, traitorous and predictable, went to Lorenzo.

His hand closing around mine at the business association meeting.

His thumb brushing once over my knuckles. Not for the room. Not for the act. A small, private touch that had moved through me like heat through sugar.

His voice saying Dorothea.

His eyes when he looked at me too long.

Historically untrustworthy, I reminded myself.

A playboy.

A man who could flirt with a lamppost and make the lamppost question its boundaries.

A fake boyfriend, for business purposes only.

A complication.

And yet.

"What are you afraid you would become if you stopped saying no?" Ms. Vesper asked.

My heart lurched.

I looked up.

Her face held no judgment.

That made it worse.

"What kind of question is that?"

"The useful kind."

"I say no because no is a complete sentence."

"Yes."

"Because boundaries matter. Because I don't owe anyone access to me."

"Never."

"Then what are you implying?"

"That sometimes a locked door is protection," she said. "And sometimes it is a room you forgot how to leave."

I swallowed.

Lorenzo's face rose in my mind again.

His mouth. His hands. The infuriating softness in his voice when he stopped teasing long enough to ask if I had eaten.

My deepest fantasy was not simply sex.

It was worse.

It was being wanted by someone who saw the locked door and did not try to break it down, but also did not pretend it was a wall.

It was being worshiped fearlessly, knowing all the while I was completely safe.

It was wanting without shame.

Surrender without danger.

Heat without losing myself.

Oddly specific.

Deeply inconvenient.

I looked down at the cards.

My fingers moved before I decided.

I pulled one from the middle of the spread and handed it to Ms. Vesper without looking.

Her eyebrows lifted when she turned it over.

"Well," she said. "This is very interesting, my dear."

The card faced me.

The Devil.

A dark figure sat enthroned beneath a black sky, horned and winged, one hand raised. Two figures stood chained below him. But the chains around their necks hung loose enough that either could lift them away.

That was the part I noticed.

Not the demon.

The looseness.

A chill moved through me.

Then heat.

The card seemed to smell faintly of smoke, dark chocolate, and something animal beneath it. Something alive.

"The Devil," Ms. Vesper said.

"Cheerful."

Her mouth curved. "More honest than cheerful."

"The card is about temptation, right?"

"Among other things."

"Sex."

"Yes."

My face warmed.

"Power."

My breath caught.

"Bondage. Shame. Appetite. Excess. Illusion. The places we hand over our freedom and call it safety." Ms. Vesper tapped one fingernail lightly against the card. "The Devil is not always the monster holding the chain. Sometimes he is the part of us that refuses to notice the chain is loose."

I stared at the two figures beneath the Devil.

Loose chains.

My throat felt tight.

"You think restraint makes you safe," she said.

The words struck too precisely.

I looked away.

"It has only made you lonely."

"No," I said.

The answer came too quickly.

Ms. Vesper did not argue.

The shop seemed to wait.

I thought of the bakery after closing. The quiet apartment upstairs. The untouched side of the bed that did not belong to anyone, because it never had. The way I worked until I was too tired to want. The way I told myself I was too busy, too practical, too focused, too smart to make foolish choices with charming men who called me by my full name.

Lonely.

The word sat inside me like a stone.

"I'm not lonely," I said, quieter.

"No?"

"I have friends."

"Yes."

"A business."

"Yes."

"A life."

"Yes."

Ms. Vesper's gaze softened.

"That does not answer me."

I hated her for that.

A little.

"The Devil represents temptation," she continued, softer now. "But temptation is not always a thing trying to ruin you. Sometimes temptation is the door to the part of yourself you have kept starving."

My pulse beat hard in my throat.

"What happens in the experience?" I asked.

"The card builds the realm. You enter. A guide meets you. The rest depends on what you are ready to face."

"A guide?"

"Yes."

"A person?"

"Usually."

"Like a therapist?"

Ms. Vesper's eyes sparkled. "Not exactly."

"Like a sex demon?"

Her smile became dangerous.

"That depends on the customer."

"Oh my God."

"Not usually him, no."

I laughed because the alternative was panic.

The Devil card warmed beneath her fingers.

I could leave.

That remained true.

The door was behind me. The bakery was three blocks away. The invoices would still be there. Lorenzo's folder would still be waiting by the register. Lea would ask me how it went, and I could lie. I could return to my apartment above the bakery, shower the flour from my skin, fall asleep alone, and wake up at three-forty to make bread for people who would never know how tightly I had held myself together.

Safe.

Familiar.

Lonely.

"What if I'm not ready?" I asked.

"Then the realm will begin where you are."

"What if I want to stop?"

"You stop."

"What if I panic?"

"You breathe. You speak. You leave if you choose."

"You say that like it's easy."

"No," Ms. Vesper said. "I say it like it is allowed."

Allowed.

That word did something to me.

"Okay," I said.

Ms. Vesper stilled.

The card seemed to darken.

"I'm game," I added, because apparently I needed to sound casual while agreeing to magical shadow-work with possible sex demon components.

"Come with me."

She gathered the deck and led me behind the counter.

We passed through a narrow doorway into the back of the shop. The warmth of maroon walls and gold accents vanished at once.

The room beyond was white.

Not white like paint. White like absence. Walls, floor, ceiling, all seamless and pristine, devoid of decoration, shelving, windows, or warmth. The space felt less like a room and more like a pause between two thoughts. At the center sat a black leather chaise lounge, sleek and old-fashioned, the only object in all that blankness.

The contrast made my skin prickle.

"I'm going to be honest," I said. "This is giving sexy dentist."

Ms. Vesper laughed softly. "I've heard worse."

"It's a stark difference from the shop."

"It's meant to be."

"It feels void of life."

"It's a blank page."

"I don't trust blank pages. They expect things."

"They invite things."

"Same problem."

She gestured to the chaise. "Have a seat."

I lowered myself onto it.

The leather was warm.

I chose not to think about that.

Ms. Vesper disappeared through the doorway and returned moments later with a clipboard, a pen, and a cup of tea. Steam curled from the cup, fragrant and dark.

"Here is our consent form," she said. "Read it. Ask questions. Sign only if you choose."

That steadied me more than any mystical promise could have.

Paperwork, at least, I understood.

I took the clipboard.

The form was surprisingly clear. It stated that I consented to a magical immersive experience guided by tarot, that my physical body would remain in the room, that I could end the experience by speaking the phrase return me, that the experience might include intense emotional, sensual, or symbolic content based on the chosen card, and that no real-world physical harm would occur.

I read that line twice.

No real-world physical harm.

There was also a section about erotic content, consent, and personal boundaries.

I looked up.

"People sign this and still drink mystery tea?"

"People sign mortgage documents with less care."

"Fair."

I kept reading.

The tea will assist transition into the magic. Duration in physical time: twenty minutes. Perceived duration may vary.

"You're serious about the twenty minutes?"

"Yes."

"No matter how long it feels?"

"Yes."

"What's in the tea?"

"Herbs."

I lowered the clipboard. "Ms. Vesper."

She smiled. "Chamomile, damiana, rose, cacao husk, cinnamon, and a little magic."

"I appreciate that magic is apparently an ingredient."

"In this shop, yes."

"Any drugs?"

"No."

"Will I be unconscious?"

"Trance-state, but aware inside the realm."

"Will you be watching?"

"No."

"Can anyone?"

"No."

I looked back at the consent form.

Privacy. Physical safety. Emotional intensity. Return phrase.

My hand moved to the signature line.

Then stopped.

"What if I'm embarrassed after?"

Ms. Vesper's expression softened.

"Then you will have learned embarrassment can be survived."

"That is not comforting."

"It's true."

"Truth is overrated."

"Only by people hiding from it."

I signed.

My signature looked steadier than I felt.

Ms. Vesper took the clipboard and handed me the tea.

It was black-red in the cup, almost the color of wine held up to candlelight. It smelled like cinnamon, smoke, chocolate, rose, and the burnt sugar candle from the shop.

"The tea will help you relax into the magic," she said. "It helps with the transition. When you come out, you should feel awake and refreshed, as if you slept ten straight hours."

"That alone may be worth the kidney risk."

"No kidneys will be taken."

"That sounds like exactly what a kidney thief would say."

She smiled.

I lifted the cup.

The first sip was sweet.

Then bitter.

Then warm in a way that did not stay in my mouth. It moved down my throat and opened through my chest, spreading like heat through dough. My fingers tingled. The tension in my shoulders loosened half an inch, which was basically a miracle.

"I suppose twenty minutes doesn't eat into my day much," I said.

"That depends on what you call a day."

"I call it the period of time between one bakery crisis and the next."

"Then no."

I finished the tea before I could talk myself out of it.

The warmth settled low in my belly.

That was concerning.

Ms. Vesper took the empty cup.

"Lay back," she said.

I did, though every practical part of me objected.

The chaise seemed to hold my body perfectly. Not too soft. Not too firm. Like someone had measured exhaustion and built furniture accordingly.

Ms. Vesper stood beside me.

The white room felt larger now.

No, not larger.

Farther.

The walls seemed to pull back without moving.

"Do I need to do anything?" I asked.

"Let go."

"I run a bakery. Be specific."

Her smile was faint.

"In shadows deep, where secrets dwell," she said, her voice low and rhythmic, "I cast the Devil's potent spell. Release what binds. Unclench the soul's embrace. By moonlit heat and hidden grace, let desire find its place."

The room warmed.

The Devil card was not in my hand, but I felt it anyway. Heat at my chest. At my throat. Around my wrists, though nothing touched me there.

Loose chains.

My breath caught.

Ms. Vesper leaned closer.

"One more thing, Dorothea."

"What?"

"The Devil is not here to punish your wanting."

My eyes burned suddenly.

"He is here to show you where you gave your wanting a cage and called it virtue."

I swallowed.

"That is rude."

"Yes."

"Useful?"

"Usually."

The warmth intensified.

The white ceiling blurred at the edges.

Ms. Vesper's voice grew distant.

"If you need to return, say the words."

"Return me," I whispered, testing them.

"Good."

"Has anyone ever used them?"

"Yes."

"And?"

"They returned."

The answer was simple enough to hold.

I closed my eyes.

For a moment, nothing happened.

Then the chaise beneath me softened. The air thickened. The scent of the tea deepened until it became smoke, cinnamon, and something like hot stone after rain. My limbs grew heavy, but not trapped. My mind stayed sharp in the oddest way, as if some inner part of me had finally been given coffee.

Images flickered behind my eyes.

Lorenzo's hand around mine.

A hallway of doors.

A black card edged in gold.

A mouth I had not kissed.

A version of myself standing naked without apologizing.

Fear moved through me first.

Then desire.

Then fear again, because desire was the less familiar of the two when another person stood anywhere near it.

The white room tilted.

My body sank.

No, rose.

No, opened.

Heat spread beneath my skin. The air brushed along my arms, no longer sterile and clean, but scented with jasmine, candle wax, and velvet dust. A low sound rumbled somewhere beneath me, like thunder trapped inside stone.

I tried to open my eyes.

For a second, I saw both rooms.

White walls.

Red curtains.

Black chaise.

Four-poster bed.

Ms. Vesper's silhouette.

A shadow at the foot of the bed, tall and waiting.

Then the white room vanished.

Hell, what was I talking about?

I was no longer in Coral Cove.

Two

When I open my eyes, I'm no longer in Coral Cove.

That is the first thing I know.

Not because I see the room clearly yet. I do not. My vision arrives in pieces, soft around the edges, like looking through steam rising from a pot of sugar syrup. Shadows gather above me. Red light breathes against the ceiling. Something warm and heavy presses beneath my back. For one disoriented second, I think I'm in my apartment over the bakery, that I fell asleep on top of the covers again after telling myself I would only close my eyes for five minutes.

Then I smell jasmine.

Not bakery vanilla. Not coffee. Not butter browning in a pan. Jasmine, candle smoke, old stone, and something darker beneath it. Hot iron, maybe. Burnt sugar. The scent of caramel two seconds before it turns bitter.

My eyes focus.

A canopy hangs above me.

Not a normal canopy, either. Not the cute kind some people put over beds so they can pretend adulthood involves fewer spiderwebs. This one is huge and dramatic, carved from dark wood and hung with thick curtains of red velvet. The fabric spills down in heavy folds around the four-poster bed, creating a room inside the room. Gold thread runs through the velvet in twisting patterns that look decorative at first.

Then I realize they are chains.

Tiny embroidered chains.

Subtle. Elegant. Very normal for a magical sex castle, apparently.

I lie very still.

This is always my first strategy when life becomes unreasonable. Do nothing. Assess. Try not to make any sudden movements that might encourage the situation.

The bed beneath me is absurdly soft. Not soft like my mattress at home, which has one suspicious dip on the left side and a personality disorder. This is rich-people soft. Palace soft. The kind of soft that says someone else does the laundry and no one involved checks their bank balance before buying sheets. Beneath my fingers, the coverlet is velvet too, thick and cool, with raised patterns that brush against my skin.

Skin.

I look down.

I'm wearing a gown.

The gown is black, though not plain black. It shifts when I move, dark red glimmering beneath the surface like wine under candlelight. The bodice fits close without pinching. The sleeves fall off my shoulders in a way that makes me immediately aware of collarbones, upper arms, and the fact that my bakery clothes are gone.

My jeans.

My flour-stained shirt.

My bra with the mystery flour.

Gone.

"Okay," I whisper.

My voice sounds too loud.

The chamber answers with silence.

I push myself up.

The room around me is enormous.

Opulent grandeur is a phrase people use when they want to sound impressed by a place and avoid admitting it might eat them. This chamber deserves the phrase and the caution. The walls are black stone, polished until candlelight runs across them like water. More velvet tapestries hang between narrow arched windows, all deep red and black, all embroidered with chains, flames, pomegranates, keys, serpents, and winged creatures whose faces look almost human if I don't stare too long.

I stare too long.

One of them seems to smile.

"Nope," I tell it.

It remains fabric.

Probably.

Candles burn everywhere. Tall black tapers in iron holders. Clusters of red pillar candles on carved tables. White candles floating in glass bowls filled with dark water. Wax drips down their sides in thick, glossy trails, some red, some black, some gold. The whole room flickers, alive with flame and shadow.

And iron.

There's so much iron.

Iron sconces. Iron bedposts. Iron rings set into the stone walls as if something used to be chained there or might be again if it requests the right package. A decorative chain loops between two pillars near the fireplace, heavy and black, each link as thick as my wrist. It should make the room feel like a dungeon.

It does not.

That is the problem.

The room is gorgeous.

Dangerous and gorgeous.

A cage that hired an excellent interior designer.

I look toward the windows. Outside, instead of Coral Cove's wet streets or the back alley behind Knead the Dough, I see night. Endless night. A sky so dark it looks blue at the edges, full of stars too bright and too low. Below the window, far below, a landscape rolls out in jagged shadows. Mountains. Forest. A river shining like black glass.

I'm very high up.

Not ideal.

I turn my attention to the room again because anxiety likes variety.

On the wall opposite the bed stands a mirror.

No, not a mirror. A series of them. Seven full-length

mirrors in black iron frames, arranged in an arc. Their glass is dark, almost smoky. Each reflects the room differently.

In the first, I see myself on the bed in the black-red gown, hair loose around my shoulders, eyes wide.

In the second, I see myself standing behind the bakery counter, smiling at a customer while my body looks hollowed out from the inside.

In the third, I see myself alone in my apartment, sitting on the edge of the bed with one hand pressed between my thighs and shame sitting beside me like a second body.

I flinch.

The reflection shifts.

Now the glass shows only candlelight.

My pulse bangs hard against my throat.

"Absolutely not," I say.

My voice shakes.

I don't like that.

I slide off the bed.

My bare feet touch black marble.

Cold shoots up my legs.

The floor is veined with red stone, thin lines branching through the black like heat trapped beneath the surface. I take one step, then another. The gown whispers around my legs. It should feel ridiculous, but it fits like it belongs to me, which is worse.

"Return me," I say.

Nothing happens.

I stop.

My heart jumps.

"Return me," I say again, louder.

Still nothing.

Panic rises fast and hot.

Then I remember Ms. Vesper's exact wording.

If you need to return, say the words.

Maybe I don't need to return.

Maybe I only want to test the door.

That distinction feels like the sort of technicality magic would enjoy.

"Rude," I mutter.

The candles flicker.

I cross to the nearest mirror, keeping my distance from the one that showed me too much. This mirror reflects me clearly. My hair is loose, darker than it looked in the bakery light, falling over my shoulders. My face is mine, but softened somehow. Not changed. Not made prettier, exactly. Just seen under better lighting and less fluorescent exhaustion.

The gown hugs my body.

I immediately look for flaws.

That is embarrassing, but true.

Stomach. Hips. Breasts. Arms. All the places I have learned to assess before anyone else can. Not because I hate myself. I do not. Not most days. I have a body that works hard, carries trays, lifts flour bags, stands for hours, and keeps me alive despite my coffee intake. But being useful is different from being looked at. Being wanted is a separate language, and I have never been fluent.

The mirror darkens.

My reflection changes.

Now I'm not in the gown.

I'm naked.

Not tastefully. Not softened. Not hidden. Naked and standing in front of myself with my arms at my sides, eyes full of terror.

A chain hangs loose around my throat.

I step back so fast my heel slips on the marble.

The mirror returns to normal.

My reflection stares back in the gown.

Breathing too hard.

"Fantastic," I say. "The furniture has emotional range."

A sound comes from the door.

A click.

The chamber door opens.

I spin.

The door is enormous, arched and carved from black wood banded in iron. It swings inward without a creak. Beyond it lies a narrow strip of shadow and candlelight.

Then he steps through.

At first, I see only his outline.

Tall. Broad-shouldered. Cloaked in red dark enough to be almost black. Horned shadow behind him, cast by the ironwork above the door or by something else entirely. He moves with the kind of control that makes the room seem to rearrange itself around him.

My body goes very still.

Not peaceful still.

Rabbit-under-hawk still.

He stops just inside the threshold.

"Welcome, Dorothea."

The voice is deep.

Not just deep. Warm, rough, and low enough that I feel it in my ribs before my ears finish translating. It's the kind of voice that should belong to an opera villain, a morally ambiguous king, or a man who knows exactly how to say your name in a way that makes you question your scheduling priorities.

Dorothea.

Not Dottie.

No one here should know that name the way he says it.

No one except Lorenzo.

And that is the second problem.

Lucian steps forward, and the candlelight finds his face.

My breath catches.

He is beautiful in the unfair way fantasy men are beautiful, but not pretty. There's nothing soft-edged about him. He has a strong jaw, dark hair that falls almost to his shoulders, and eyes so deep a brown they look black until the firelight catches them. His skin is warm bronze. His mouth is full, severe until it curves, which it does slowly when he sees me staring.

He carries an aura of forbidden temptation.

That sounds dramatic.

It's also accurate.

He wears a white linen shirt open at the throat beneath the red cloak, black trousers tucked into tall boots, and a belt with a heavy iron buckle. A chain hangs from one side of the belt, decorative maybe, but my eyes catch on it anyway. The little sound it makes when he moves is soft and metallic.

I want to lick him.

The thought arrives whole and uninvited.

I have never wanted to lick someone before.

That is not strictly true, maybe. I have looked at people and thought they were attractive. I have had crushes. I have imagined kissing. I have imagined more, alone, safely, with no witnesses but my ceiling fan and my poor decision-making. But this thought is direct. Physical. Undignified.

I want to lick him.

Specifically, I want to lick the place where his throat disappears into the open collar of his shirt.

I blink.

Horrified.

He has not glanced away.

My face burns.

"Stop that," I say.

His eyebrows lift.

My brain catches up.

"I mean, hello."

His mouth curves.

Oh, good. He has dimples. Why would the Devil's fantasy realm not weaponize dimples?

"I'm Lucian," he says.

"Are you?"

"A philosophical beginning."

"I mean, are you really?"

"That depends on which answer frightens you more."

I stare at him.

No. Absolutely not. I'm not doing riddles with a man who looks like temptation got bored and built a body.

"Is this real?" I ask.

The question comes out barely above a whisper.

Lucian's expression changes.

Only a little, but I catch it. The seduction remains, yes. That slow curve of his mouth. The heat in his eyes. But beneath it, something steadier appears. A guide stepping forward under the costume.

"This is your fantasy, Lady Dorothea," he says. "In every way that matters to your senses, it will feel real. Touch. Taste. Heat. Pleasure. Fear. Relief. This world is formed from you."

"From me?"

"Yes."

"Then I have expensive taste."

His smile deepens. "You have locked yourself in a very beautiful room."

My stomach drops.

The mirrors seem to listen.

I look around again. The velvet. The iron. The chains. The dark windows. Gorgeous. Heavy. Caged.

"Did I make this?" I ask.

"Yes."

"I would like to file a complaint with my subconscious."

"It accepts complaints poorly."

"I assumed."

Lucian moves farther into the room, but stops several feet away. Close enough that I can see the texture of his shirt, the rise of his chest when he breathes. Far enough that I don't feel crowded.

I notice that.

I notice it more than I notice his body, which is impressive because his body is being extremely noticeable.

"You called me Dorothea," I say.

"It's your name."

"Most people call me Dottie."

"I'm not most people."

"That was not reassuring."

"No."

The candles nearest him flare, then settle.

I wrap my arms around myself, suddenly aware of the low neckline of the gown. "There's only one other person who calls me Dorothea."

"I know."

The answer is too quick.

My mouth goes dry.

"You know about Lorenzo?"

Lucian's gaze sharpens at the name.

Not jealousy. Not surprise.

Recognition.

"This realm knows what you brought with you."

"I did not bring Lorenzo."

"No? You carried him across the threshold like a hot coal under your tongue."

I glare at him.

"That is an insane thing to say to someone you just met."

"Yes."

"And rude."

"Also yes."

"I'm not thinking about him."

Lucian's gaze drops briefly to my mouth.

I press my lips together. The problem with Lucian's voice is that it sounds nothing like Lorenzo's and still somehow scrapes the same nerves.

Lucian says Dorothea like a title. Like something ancient. Like I'm a woman in a painting or a queen in a dark tower, desired from a respectful distance until I choose otherwise.

Lorenzo says Dorothea like a challenge.

Like he knows I'm hiding behind the counter, the apron, the rent, the list, the fake relationship, and he is one bad decision away from reaching over all of it.

Lucian is reverent and theatrical.

Lorenzo is real, irritating, dangerous.

I don't want to think about that.

So naturally, I think about it with impressive focus.

Lucian watches my face.

"You see the difference," he says.

"Between what?"

"Fantasy and hunger."

I swallow.

"Fantasy waits in the shape you prefer. Hunger arrives inconveniently and tracks flour into your life."

That hits too close.

"You don't know him."

"No."

"You know what I know."

"Yes."

"Then don't act wise. You're just reading my diary with better cheekbones."

He laughs.

The sound is low, pleased, and much too attractive.

I hate that too.

"Is that what I'm?" he asks.

"What?"

"A diary with cheekbones."

41

"I'm still deciding."

"Then allow me to clarify." He steps aside and gestures toward the mirrors. "The Arcane Room does not create desire. It gives desire form."

The mirrors brighten.

One shows me Lorenzo's hand on mine at the business association meeting.

I turn away so fast my neck protests.

Lucian continues, his voice gentle now. "It does not plant hunger where none exists. It does not force want into your body. It does not make you choose what you would otherwise refuse. It reveals what is already yours."

"That sounds like something people say before selling an expensive retreat."

"It would be an excellent retreat."

"I would leave a bad review."

"You would leave a detailed review."

"Obviously."

His smile flickers again.

I'm starting to understand the danger of him. It's not only that he is beautiful or that my body keeps having thoughts I did not approve in committee. It's that he listens like every word matters, even the ridiculous ones. He does not make me feel silly for being afraid.

He makes me feel seen.

I glance at the door behind him.

"Can I leave this room?"

"Yes."

"Can I leave the fantasy?"

"Yes."

"If I say return me."

"Yes."

"And you won't stop me?"

"No."

"What if I say stop?"

"Then I stop."

"What if I say no?"

"Then no becomes the law."

The certainty in his voice goes through me like warmth.

I hate that such a basic thing can feel like a gift.

"That should not be sexy," I say.

Lucian's gaze darkens a fraction. "Safety often is, when you have gone without it."

I open my mouth.

Close it.

Damn.

He sees too much.

I move toward the fireplace because standing still feels like losing. The hearth is black marble, wide enough to sit on. Flames burn inside it, but not orange. Red, blue, violet. No logs. Just fire rising from a bed of black stones. Above the mantle hangs another mirror, smaller than the others, framed in gold.

This one does not reflect the room.

It reflects a bakery.

Knead the Dough at closing.

Me behind the counter.

Lorenzo on the other side.

His folder between us.

I turn away.

"Stop doing that," I say.

"The mirror?"

"The realm."

"I'm not controlling the mirror."

"Convenient."

"True."

I look at him. "What are you controlling?"

"Myself."

"That's it?"

"That is not a small thing."

No, I think.

No, it's not.

He walks toward the fireplace, again stopping with careful distance between us. The chain at his belt glints. His cloak brushes the floor.

"This place will offer you doors," he says. "Rooms. Scenes. Touches. Temptations. Each one is connected to the card you chose."

"The Devil."

"Yes."

"Sex demon with a curriculum."

His mouth twitches. "If you like."

"I'm not sure I like any of this yet."

"You don't have to like it."

"That's a terrible sales pitch."

"I'm not here to sell you anything."

"Then what are you here for?"

His eyes hold mine.

"To tempt you."

Heat moves low in my belly.

Lucian takes in my reaction. "But not to choose for you," he adds.

I breathe again.

He steps closer by one measured pace. "I can offer anything you want," he says. "I can show you the shape of hunger without punishment. I can open doors. I can interpret what the realm gives us. I can touch you if you ask, stop if you ask, guide if you permit it."

His voice lowers.

"I can tempt you, Dorothea. I cannot want for you."

The words settle between us.

A limit.

Not his weakness.

His boundary.

That changes the room.

The iron rings on the walls look less like threats and more like questions. The chains embroidered into the velvet lose some of their menace. Loose chains, I remind myself. Loose enough to lift.

My throat feels tight.

"What if I don't know what I want?"

"Then we begin there."

"What if what I want scares me?"

"Then we name the fear before we follow the want."

"And if I'm embarrassed?"

"Then you will blush beautifully."

"Lucian."

"And survive it," he says, softer.

I let out a breath.

"I was told this was an experience."

"It is."

"No one said it came with emotional labor."

"You pulled The Devil."

"Fair."

The room warms again, though the fire has not changed.

My body is starting to understand what my mind keeps arguing with. I'm safe. I'm not trapped. I'm not being watched. I can leave. I can say no. I can ask.

Ask.

The word feels like a piece of candy placed on my tongue.

Sweet. Dangerous. Likely to stick to my teeth.

I glance at Lucian's mouth.

His gaze follows mine.

The control in him is not cold. It's alive, breathing, waiting. He wants, or at least the realm has made him capable of wanting, but he does not take. He holds still and lets me feel the space between us.

My fantasy, apparently, includes being driven insane by restraint.

Rude.

"Is this like a spa?" I ask, desperate for my own voice to sound normal. "Everything à la carte?"

Lucian tilts his head.

"A spa."

"Yes. Massage, facial, emotional breakdown, sexual awakening. Different packages."

"A useful metaphor."

"I'm a business owner. I like clear menus."

"Then here is the menu." He holds up one hand. "You may ask for touch. You may ask for distance. You may ask questions. You may explore the room. You may walk through the door. You may say return me. You may do nothing at all."

"Doing nothing sounds like a waste."

"Does it?"

I narrow my eyes.

He is doing it again.

Picking at the seam of something.

"Yes," I say.

"Because rest must be earned?"

I don't answer.

"Because pleasure must be justified?"

Still nothing.

"Because if you are not productive, you fear you will discover what you actually feel?"

"I liked the spa menu better."

"I know."

I look toward the bed.

The bed looks back with velvet confidence.

"Whatever I desire?" I ask.

"Whatever you choose to desire honestly."

"That qualifier seems important."

"It is."

"What if I ask for something because I think I should want it?"

"Then the room will sour."

I blink. "Sour?"

"Like cream left too long in heat."

"That is a very specific threat."

"You would notice it."

"I would."

His mouth curves.

"The realm speaks in your language too."

I glance around.

Velvet. Heat. Burnt sugar. Locked rooms. Mirrors.

"My language is dramatic."

"Your language is hunger disciplined into usefulness."

That makes my chest ache.

I look away.

He lets me.

Outside the windows, thunder rolls across the dark mountains. No lightning follows. The sound moves through the room like a giant shifting in sleep.

I cross to a small table near the bed. A silver tray rests on it, holding a decanter of dark red wine, two glasses, and a plate of fruit. Pomegranate seeds. Black grapes. Figs split open to show their red centers. Strawberries glossy as lacquer.

Temptation arranged as a snack board.

I pick up a grape.

"Is this safe?"

"Yes."

"Will it do anything strange?"

"It's a grape."

"In a magic Devil castle."

"Then perhaps it's a committed grape."

I laugh before I can stop myself.

Lucian smiles.

I eat the grape.

It bursts sweet and cold on my tongue.

Real.

Too real.

I close my eyes for a second.

The flavor is sharper than anything I have tasted all day. Maybe because I'm not eating over a sink. Maybe because I'm not shoving food into my mouth between customers. Maybe because magic grapes have better branding.

When I open my eyes, Lucian is watching me.

Not like a man watching someone eat.

Like a man watching someone receive.

That is more intimate than I expected.

I swallow.

"You're staring," I say.

"Yes."

"Why?"

"Because you allowed yourself to taste something without immediately turning it into work."

My cheeks heat.

"It was one grape."

"Yes."

"You are making a lot out of a grape."

"Desire often begins smaller than people expect."

I put down the stem with extreme dignity.

"Do all guides sound like this?"

"No."

"Do you have coworkers?"

"Not in the way you mean."

"Do they also wear dramatic cloaks?"

He glances down at himself. "Would you prefer a cardigan?"

"No."

The answer comes too fast.

His smile turns wicked.

"Good to know."

"I mean, the cloak is thematically appropriate."

"And the shirt is open because apparently my subconscious lacks subtlety."

"Your subconscious has taste."

"That seems debatable."

His gaze drops to the gown, then returns to my face. He does not linger on my body in a way that makes me feel consumed. He notices. There's no pretending otherwise. But the noticing feels like heat near my skin, not hands on it.

That is new.

Usually, the fear starts with being looked at.

Not because I think I'm ugly. I do not. Not always. But being looked at by someone who wants something can feel like becoming an object in a room full of hands. Jammie looked at me gently. Owen looked at me playfully. Lorenzo looks at me like he is trying to decide whether to ask permission or burn the whole room down.

Lucian looks at me like a door.

Closed, but not locked.

Waiting for my hand on the knob.

I don't know what to do with that.

So I ask the practical question.

"How many others can watch us?"

Lucian's eyebrows lift.

I immediately regret phrasing.

"I don't mean watch us. I mean, I'm assuming this is magic, yes, but there's still a shop. A room. Ms. Vesper. Maybe some IT guy if this is secretly virtual reality with incense. Not that I think Ms. Vesper has an IT guy. She seems more like she has a familiar that handles billing. But you know what I mean."

Lucian's face does something dangerous.

It softens.

"Dorothea."

"No. Don't say my name like I'm being endearing. I'm asking a very reasonable privacy question."

"You are."

"Good."

"No one can watch us."

"Not Ms. Vesper?"

"No."

"Not Park if he comes back for romance magic?"

"No."

"Not some magical server administrator?"

"No."

"Not you after I leave?"

He pauses.

I appreciate that he pauses.

"No," he says. "When you leave, I remain only as the experience shaped me. I don't follow. I don't spy. I don't remember in the way mortals mean memory unless you return with the same thread."

That answer should be confusing.

It is.

It also feels honest.

"The Arcane Room is discreet," Lucian says. "But more than that, the magic is private. It does not project your fantasy. It does not store it for entertainment. It does not feed on your shame."

"What does it feed on?"

"Choice."

I rub my arms.

The word settles over me like a cloak.

"Choice," I repeat.

"The card opens the realm. Your choices give it shape."

"So if I imagine something…"

"It may appear."

"If I want something…"

"It may be offered."

"If I fear something…"

His gaze flicks toward the mirrors.

"It may ask why."

I don't like that.

I also do.

I think of Lorenzo again, which is becoming less of a thought and more of a haunting.

Lucian's eyes sharpen.

"There he is."

49

"Stop."

"I did not summon him."

"Neither did I."

"Liar."

"Rude."

"Yes."

I turn toward the windows, needing something that is not Lucian's face. Outside, the stars pulse faintly. The landscape below is too dark to understand, but I can see the line of a road winding away from the castle, silver under the night.

"Why him?" Lucian asks.

The question is so direct I almost answer.

Then my defenses catch up.

"Why who?"

It's much too close to Lea's look, but with worse consequences for my nervous system.

"Lorenzo is not relevant."

"The realm disagrees."

"The realm is nosy."

"Yes."

"I don't trust him."

Lucian says nothing.

"He flirts with everyone."

Still nothing.

"He has a reputation."

Silence.

"He suggested the fake relationship because it helps with the festival and the lease situation, not because he actually wants me."

"Did he say that?"

"He did not have to."

"Ah."

"Don't ah me."

"I would never."

"You just did."

"Yes."

I turn around to glare at him properly.

He stands near the bed, one hand resting loosely at his side, the other brushing the chain at his belt. He looks infuriatingly patient.

"Lorenzo is real," I say.

"Yes."

"That is the problem." The useful answer, dragged out of me against my will.

Lucian's expression shifts.

My shoulders drop. "I can want you here," I say slowly, the admission strange in my mouth. "I can look at you and think things because you are fantasy. You cannot humiliate me in town. You cannot come into my bakery next week and order coffee like nothing happened. You cannot decide I'm too inexperienced, too guarded, too much work, and then tell everyone with your stupid beautiful mouth."

Lucian's gaze remains steady.

"You are not afraid Lorenzo will want you," he says.

My throat tightens.

"You are afraid he will want you and still leave."

The room goes still.

The candles stop flickering.

Even the fire seems to hold its breath.

I look away first.

"Again," I say. "Rude."

"Yes."

"Useful?"

"Possibly."

I laugh, but it comes out too thin.

Lucian steps closer.

This time, he does not stop quite so far away.

He leaves only a few feet between us.

Enough for choice.

Not enough for avoidance to feel comfortable.

"I'm not here to replace the real," he says.

"No?"

"No."

"What are you here for, then?"

"To show you where you have confused fear with wisdom."

My stomach twists.

"And if I don't want to be shown?"

"Then say return me."

I hate that the option is still there.

It makes staying my fault.

My choice.

The Devil card, wherever it is, seems to warm beneath my skin.

Loose chains.

I look at Lucian's hands.

Large. Strong. Still.

"What happens now?" I ask.

"What do you want to happen?"

"Menus," I remind him. "I like menus."

His smile returns, slow and wicked.

"All right. Option one. We remain here. You ask questions until your fear gets bored."

"My fear has excellent stamina."

"I assumed."

"Option two?"

"We explore the chamber. The mirrors. The wardrobe. The door."

"The mirrors can go to hell."

"We are near enough."

"Not funny."

"A little funny."

I refuse to smile.

Mostly.

"Option three?" I ask.

Lucian's eyes darken.

"I touch you."

My breath catches.

"Where?"

"Where you ask."

"And if I don't ask?"

"Then I don't touch you."

The simplicity is unbearable.

I think of Jammie's hand sliding inside my panties. The awkward discomfort. His immediate concern. My inability to speak. My shame afterward, so hot and sticky I vanished from his life rather than explain myself. He had not hurt me. That was the worst part. There had been no villain to blame. Only my own silence and the terrible fear that wanting something in theory meant I owed performance in practice.

I think of Lorenzo's thumb brushing my hand.

How quickly my body believed.

How violently my mind retreated.

I think of Lea saying I needed to remember I had a body.

Well.

My body is remembered now.

It stands inside a Devil castle in a black-red gown, looking at a man who may or may not be real, trying not to combust from eye contact.

"What if I ask wrong?" I say.

Lucian frowns slightly. "Wrong?"

"What if I say something stupid?"

"Then you will have spoken."

"What if I ask for something and change my mind?"

"Then your mind changes. I stop."

"What if I don't know the correct words?"

"This is not a recipe, Dorothea."

"Everything is a recipe if you are anxious enough."

His mouth softens.

"Then start with one ingredient."

I let out a breath.

The room waits.

Lucian waits.

No pressure. No reach. No command disguised as patience.

I look down at my hands.

They are clenched.

I open them.

One ingredient.

"I want…" I begin.

The word shakes.

I stop.

Lucian does not help.

I hate him for it and understand, at the same time, why he waits. If he gives me the word, I can hide behind his knowing. If I say it, it belongs to me.

"I want you to come closer," I say.

The room exhales.

Maybe I imagine that.

Lucian steps closer.

Only one step.

"More?" he asks.

My pulse jumps.

"Yes."

Another step.

Now he is close enough that I can smell him.

Smoke. Clove. Leather. Warm skin. A hint of the same burnt sugar scent from the tea, but darker on him.

The licking thought returns.

I ignore it with dignity.

"More?"

I look up at him.

He is very tall.

That should annoy me. It kind of does. My body has decided to file the annoyance under arousal, which is poor organization.

"Yes," I say.

This time, he steps close enough that the hem of his cloak brushes my gown.

No part of his body touches mine.

Still, my skin feels awake everywhere.

"Good," he says.

The word slides through me.

I swallow.

"Praise kink," I mutter.

His eyes flash with amusement. "Noted."

"I did not mean to say that out loud."

"Yes, you did."

"No, I didn't."

"The realm heard you."

"The realm is a gossip."

"Yes."

I press my lips together, but I'm smiling now.

A real smile.

That scares me more than the mirrors.

Lucian lowers his head slightly, bringing his face closer to mine.

"May I touch your hand?"

My heart does something stupid.

"Yes."

He reaches slowly.

I watch his fingers close around mine.

Warm.

That is the first shock.

His hand is warm and callused, not ghostly, not dream-like. His palm covers the back of my hand. His thumb rests lightly over my knuckles. The touch is simple. Almost formal.

My body reacts like he has put his mouth on me.

I go still.

Lucian notices.

"Too much?"

"No."

"You froze."

"I noticed."

"Dorothea."

"It is not too much." I breathe in. "I'm just… cataloguing. I like data."

"What does the data say?"

The answer comes before I can make it sound less naked.

"That I want more."

His thumb moves once over my knuckles.

I inhale sharply.

"More what?"

I glare.

He looks entirely unbothered.

"You are annoying."

"I'm precise."

"You know what I mean."

"Yes."

"Then why ask?"

"Because you need to hear yourself say it."

"I want you to touch my face," I say.

A pause.

Then his other hand rises.

He touches my cheek with the backs of his fingers.

Not my mouth. Not my throat. My cheek.

Gentle.

The kind of touch that should be nothing.

It's not nothing.

His skin brushes mine, and the room blurs at the edges. Not because of magic. Because I'm unused to tenderness that has nowhere to rush. His fingers trace along my cheekbone, then still.

"You are shaking," he says.

"I know."

"Fear?"

"Yes."

"And?"

I close my eyes.

The shame arrives first, loyal and unwanted.

Then heat.

Then curiosity.

"And I like it."

His breath changes.

Slightly.

Enough.

"Good."

That word again.

It moves through me like a warm knife through butter.

I open my eyes.

Lucian's face is close. Too close. Not close enough.

I want to know what his mouth feels like.

The thought arrives and stays.

"Ask," he says softly.

"No."

"That is allowed."

"I mean, no, I don't want to ask."

"Also allowed."

"But I do want…"

"Yes?"

I lick my lips.

His gaze drops.

The room warms another degree.

"I want to kiss you," I say, barely audible.

Lucian's hand stills against my cheek.

The fire in the hearth flares blue.

"And do you want me to kiss you," he asks, "or do you want to kiss me?"

The distinction hits like a small bell.

Do I want to be taken, so I can blame surrender on someone else?

Or do I want to choose?

Damn him.

Damn this room.

Damn Lea and her life-changing witch shop.

"I want to kiss you," I say.

Lucian's smile is slow, but not mocking.

"Then do."

My stomach flips.

He does not lean in.

I rise onto my toes because he is unfairly tall. My free hand lifts, hesitates, then settles against his chest. His shirt is warm beneath my palm. I feel muscle, breath, heartbeat.

Heartbeat.

I don't have time to think about that.

I press my mouth to his.

The kiss is soft because I make it soft.

Brief because I make it brief.

I pull back almost immediately, heart hammering.

Lucian's eyes are darker now.

He says nothing.

I stare at him.

"That's it?" I ask, flustered.

His eyebrows lift. "Was there more you wanted?"

"You are infuriating."

"Yes."

"You're supposed to… I don't know."

"Read your mind and do what you are too afraid to ask for?"

"Yes. No. Maybe."

"There are realms for that," he says. "This is not one of them."

I step back.

His hand falls from my face at once.

The loss of warmth irritates me.

"That seems inefficient."

"It's liberating."

"It's labor."

"Yes."

I cross my arms. "The fantasy realm is making me do work."

"The fantasy realm is helping you notice the work you have been avoiding."

"Again, terrible marketing."

"Effective magic."

I want to argue.

I also want to kiss him again.

Both facts sit in me, side by side, rude as customers who come in five minutes before closing.

Lucian takes one step back. "You did well," he says.

I scoff. "It was one kiss."

"It was a chosen kiss."

My face warms.

"That is different?" I ask.

"Yes."

The mirrors around the room shimmer.

Not all of them.

Just one.

I turn before I can stop myself.

The mirror shows me at the business association meeting. Lorenzo's hand over mine. His smile easy for the room. My smile fixed and brittle. Then the reflection shifts to show the second after, when no one is looking. His thumb brushes my knuckles. My face changes before I can hide it.

Want.

Fear.

A lock clicking shut.

The mirror darkens.

I breathe out slowly.

Lucian stands beside me now, not touching.

"You see?" he asks.

"No."

"Liar."

"Yes."

We stand in silence.

The chamber no longer feels only like a cage.

It feels like a room waiting for me to notice where the door is.

"What happens if I choose a door?" I ask.

"The realm opens."

"To what?"

"To the places you refused."

My stomach tightens.

"I don't like that."

"I know."

"Are they all sexual?"

"No."

"That was too quick."

"Sex is rarely only sex in this place."

"Great. Symbolic nudity."

He smiles. "Among other things."

I look toward the chamber door.

Black wood. Iron bands. A corridor beyond it, though from here I see only shadow.

"Do I have to go now?"

"No."

"What if I want to stay here?"

"Then we stay."

"What if I want the spa menu?"

"Then we begin with touch, comfort, and questions."

"What if I want you to tell me what to do?"

Lucian's gaze sharpens.

Ah.

That one means something.

"To obey can be a desire," he says carefully. "It can also be a hiding place."

I swallow.

"How do you tell the difference?"

"We ask who benefits from your silence."

The words land low in my chest.

I look away.

The Devil card. Loose chains. Desire. Fear. Surrender. Control.

This is not what I expected.

I expected, maybe, a sexy dream. A strange little magical escape where I could experience what I had been too afraid to try in real life, then wake refreshed, tip generously, and avoid eye contact with Lea for three to five business days.

I did not expect to be standing in a castle chamber, arguing with a demon guide about consent philosophy while my body quietly tried to climb out of my skin.

Lucian watches me think.

"You said you can give me anything I want," I say.

"I said I can offer."

"Right. Offer."

"Yes."

"What if I want something easy?"

His face softens.

"Then I will ask whether easy is truly what you want. You pulled The Devil, Dorothea. Not The Nap."

I laugh.

Loudly.

The sound startles me.

Lucian smiles like that was the point.

I press a hand to my chest. "That was stupid."

"It was funny."

"Debatable."

"No."

The laughter loosens me.

Just enough.

I look back at the bed.

Then the mirrors.

Then the door.

The room is beautiful. Dangerous. Mine. A gorgeous cage, yes, but cages have exits if the chain is loose enough and the prisoner is willing to admit she has hands.

I turn back to Lucian.

"I don't want to go through the door yet."

"Then we don't."

"I don't want the mirrors."

"Then we avoid them."

"I do want…" I stop.

He waits.

I take a breath.

Knead, rise, rest, heat.

My language, apparently.

"I want to learn how to receive without feeling like I owe something immediately."

Lucian's expression changes in a way that makes my throat tighten.

Approval, yes.

But more than that.

Recognition.

"That," he says, "is an honest beginning."

My pulse steadies.

A little.

"I thought you'd make that sound dirtier," I say.

"It will become dirty if you choose."

"There he is."

"There I'm."

I smile.

He offers his hand.

Not taking mine.

Offering.

"Would you like me to help you relax?"

"A massage?" I ask.

"If you want."

"Very spa menu."

"Very."

"With emotional danger?"

"Naturally."

I stare at his hand.

Warm. Strong. Waiting.

"Fine," I say. His mouth curves.

"Fine?"

"Yes. But if the bed starts reflecting my childhood wounds or something, I'm leaving."

"Reasonable."

"And no mirrors."

"No mirrors."

"And you stop if I say stop."

"Yes."

"And if I say return me…"

"You return."

I place my hand in his.

The chamber seems to deepen around us.

Not darker.

More present.

Lucian leads me toward the bed, but slowly, giving me room to change my mind with every step. The velvet curtains sway though no wind enters. The candles burn steady. The iron chains embroidered above the pillows gleam gold in the firelight.

My heart pounds.

Not only with fear now.

With anticipation.

At the edge of the bed, Lucian stops.

"Dorothea."

"Yes?"

"This realm will tempt you many times."

"I gathered."

"Not every temptation will look like me."

The words settle into the warm air.

I think of Lorenzo again.

His folder. His hands. His mouth. The real world waiting somewhere beyond this castle.

"No," I say.

Lucian's gaze holds mine.

"No," he agrees. "The most dangerous ones rarely do."

I sit on the edge of the bed.

The velvet gives beneath me.

Lucian kneels in front of me, still holding my hand. The sight of him there sends a rush of heat through me so intense I almost pull away.

He does not smirk.

That helps.

Maybe.

"Before anything else," he says, "tell me one boundary."

"One?"

"One to begin."

"My clothes stay on."

"As you wish."

The phrase should sound cheesy.

It does not.

It sounds like a vow.

"And one desire," he says.

I look at him.

My mouth goes dry again.

"One desire?"

"Yes."

I search for an easy one. A safe one. A silly one.

The realm waits.

Lucian waits.

The truth rises, inconvenient and warm.

"I want you to touch me like I'm not fragile."

His eyes darken.

Then I add, because the truth has apparently found momentum, "But stop if I'm."

Lucian's hand tightens gently around mine.

"Good," he says.

The word moves through me again.

Less like praise now.

More like permission.

He stands.

I lie back because I choose to.

The velvet is cool beneath me. The canopy rises above, all red darkness and golden chains. I should feel trapped.

Instead, for the first time in longer than I want to admit, I feel the shape of my own wanting.

Not mastered.

Not solved.

Not safe enough to be simple.

But mine.

Lucian sits beside me on the edge of the bed.

He places one hand on my shoulder, over the fabric of the gown, and waits.

"May I?" he asks.

I close my eyes.

My body answers before fear can.

"Yes."

His hand begins to move.

Slow. Firm. Warm.

Not taking.

Not demanding.

Kneading tension from muscle the way I knead air into dough, patient pressure, release, pressure again. My breath catches, then deepens. The room smells of jasmine, smoke, and burnt sugar. Beneath it, I catch something else.

Bread.
Warm bread.
Home.
Not the bakery.
Not Coral Cove.
Not Lorenzo.
Me.
The realization is so soft it nearly passes unnoticed.
Then Lucian speaks, voice low beside me.
"There you are."
My eyes burn.
I don't open them.
I'm not ready to see myself yet.
But for once, I don't run.

.

THREE

Lucian's hand begins at my shoulder.

Not my throat. Not my breast. Not my waist.

My shoulder.

It should be an easy place to be touched.

Functional, even. People touch shoulders all the time. Friends, coworkers, strangers trying to squeeze through crowded rooms. It's one of the least scandalous locations on the human body, practically public property if you work retail long enough.

Still, when his palm settles there over the fabric of my gown, my entire body forgets how to behave.

I go still.

Not relaxed still. Not peaceful still. The other kind. The kind where every muscle pretends to be stone while the mind sprints naked through traffic.

Lucian does not move.

He waits.

That might be the most dangerous thing about him.

He does not fill the silence with reassurance. He does not purr some dramatic line about surrender. He does not assume that because I said yes once, I have given him the rest of me by default.

He waits, one warm hand resting on my shoulder, until I breathe again.

"Name it," he says.

I open my eyes.

Above me, the canopy hangs in dark red folds embroidered with little gold chains. Candlelight moves across them in slow, molten waves. The room smells like jasmine, smoke, and warm bread, which is frankly manipulative. Somewhere beyond the castle windows, thunder rolls low through the mountains, but the chamber itself stays quiet.

"Name what?" I ask.

"What you feel."

"Suspicious."

His mouth curves. "That is not a sensation."

"It is if you're committed."

"Try again."

I stare up at the canopy.

The problem is, I do feel things.

Too many.

His hand is warm through the gown. Heavy, but not pressing. Steady. My shoulder has a dull ache from years of kneading dough and hauling trays, a tightness I usually ignore because acknowledging pain tends to make it invoice you. Beneath that ache, there's relief. Beneath the relief, fear. Beneath the fear, a pulse of want so direct I want to put a mixing bowl over my own head and hide.

"Warm," I say.

"Good."

The word sinks into me and feels like a praise.

"Heavy," I add.

"Too heavy?"

"No."

"Good."

"Stop saying good like that."

"Like what?"

"Like you know I like it."

His hand stays exactly where it is. "Do you?"

My face heats.

The candle flames lean toward us.

"Annoying," I say.

"That is also not a sensation."

"It's in my body."

"I believe you."

I huff a breath, but the tension in my shoulder eases a fraction.

Lucian's thumb moves.

Just once.

A slow circle over the tight muscle near the base of my neck.

My eyes close before I decide to let them.

"Oh," I say.

A tiny sound. Barely a word.

Lucian hears it anyway.

"There."

His voice is softer now.

My first instinct is to apologize.

For the sound. For the reaction. For wanting. For being too much and not enough and inexperienced and nearly thirty years old on a magical bed having a religious experience over a shoulder rub.

I almost say sorry.

Lucian's thumb stills.

"No apologies," he says.

I open one eye. "Are you reading my mind again?"

"No."

"Then that was a disturbing guess."

"You were about to make yourself smaller."

I shut my eye again.

Rude.

Accurate.

"I wasn't."

"You were."

"Maybe I was going to apologize for your benefit. Maybe I'm very polite."

"Are you?"

"No."

His laugh is low and quiet.

The sound moves through the room like smoke.

He begins again. His hand kneads slowly along my shoulder, then down toward my upper arm, still over the fabric of the gown. The pressure is firm enough to matter, gentle enough not to demand anything. It reminds me of working dough when it has finally stopped fighting.

Press, release, fold, rest. Pressure given with attention, not force.

That thought makes something inside me loosen.

"You are thinking of bread," he says.

My eyes open.

"Stop that."

"Stop what?"

"Being correct."

"Difficult."

"That was private."

His smile flickers. "The room speaks in your language. I only listen."

"I regret having a language."

"No, you don't."

I look up at him.

He sits beside me on the bed, one knee bent, cloak falling around him in a pool of dark red. His face is half shadow, half candlelight. Unfair. That is the word for him. Unfair in every possible direction.

He should look ridiculous.

No man should be able to sit on a velvet bed in a castle chamber wearing a dramatic cloak and still look like he knows how to change a tire.

Actually, Lorenzo would know how to change a tire.

Lorenzo probably changes tires in fitted black shirts and makes women in a five-mile radius reconsider roadside assistance.

The thought arrives without permission.

Lucian's hand pauses. "You brought him."

"I did not bring him. He followed because he has boundary issues."

"Does he?"

"Yes."

Lucian studies me. "Does Lorenzo cross your boundaries," he asks, "or does he stand at them and make you angry because you want to open the gate?"

The room goes very still.

I stare at him.

"I would like to return to the shoulder massage."

His mouth curves.

"As you wish."

"That phrase is getting less comforting."

"Good." His hand resumes.

This time, he moves to both shoulders, one hand on either side, his thumbs working along the knots near my neck. My body wants to melt. My mind wants to manage the melting, which defeats the purpose and is also very on brand for me.

I lie on the velvet bed with my gown still on and try to receive.

Try.

That is the correct word.

Receiving is much harder than people make it sound. People talk about pleasure like it is falling into water. Open your hands. Let go. Enjoy yourself.

Those people have never owned a bakery.

Those people have never opened alone at six in the morning because the assistant who promised to be reliable has a new boyfriend and a sudden allergy to punctuality. They have never watched a landlord's email arrive with the subject line Lease Renewal Terms and felt their entire digestive system become a fist. They have never stood in front of a customer who says, "I could make this at home," and resisted the urge to hand them a whisk and say, Wonderful, begin.

My life runs on doing.

Mix. Knead. Proof. Bake. Frost. Clean. Count. Schedule. Smile. Fix. Repeat.

Receiving requires stillness.

Stillness gives thoughts room.

Thoughts are untrustworthy little bastards.

Lucian's fingers find another knot, and I inhale sharply.

"Too much?" he asks.

"No."

"Name it."

I grit my teeth. "Tight."

"Where?"

"My neck. Shoulder. Everywhere."

"Everywhere is not specific."

"Now you sound like my bookkeeping software."

He presses a little deeper.

I groan.

The sound embarrasses me less this time.

Progress, unfortunately.

"Good," he says. "Again. Specific."

I let out a breath through my nose. "My right shoulder. The muscle near my neck. It feels like a rock."

"It has been holding more than trays."

I keep my eyes closed.

"No emotional commentary during bodywork."

"That was observation."

"Your observations are rude."

"Yes."

The pressure continues. Slow. Patient. Exact.

Warm.

Heavy.

Good.

I don't say the last one.

Lucian does not make me.

After a while, the room shifts around us.

Not physically. The black stone walls remain. The mirrors wait in their smoky silence. The candles burn in their iron sconces. The chains embroidered into the canopy glimmer gold overhead.

But my awareness changes.

The room narrows to his hands and my breathing.

His thumbs move along the back of my neck. His palms press gently down the slopes of my shoulders. He eases tension from muscles I did not know could unclench. My body, traitorous and exhausted, begins to believe him.

Safe.

The word arrives softly.

I don't know if it belongs to me or the room.

Lucian's hands slow.

"May I help you out of the gown?"

The question drops into me like a stone into water.

Ripples everywhere.

I knew this was coming. The gown has ties up the back. The bed exists for a reason. Lucian looks like the sort of man a fantasy invents when a woman pulls The Devil and has spent too many years pretending she is not curious about mouths, hands, weight, heat.

Still, my body locks.

Lucian removes his hands at once.

The absence is startling.

"I didn't say no," I say quickly.

"No."

"I just froze."

I push myself up on my elbows, then sit. The gown pools around my hips in dark folds. My hair falls forward over one shoulder. Across the room, one mirror catches my reflection and shows me not as I'm, but as I feel.

A woman with a chain around her throat, holding it in place with both hands.

I look away.

"Will it always do that?" I ask.

"The mirrors?"

"Yes."

"When you refuse to look directly, sometimes."

"I hate this castle."

"You made it."

"I have notes."

Lucian's expression is almost tender.

I look down at my hands.

"I'm not sure how much of this is real," I say.

The words come slowly because I have to pull them from behind my teeth.

"It feels real. I want it to feel real. But I also don't know what to do with that."

"That is honest."

"I'm not finished."

He inclines his head.

I swallow.

"I've never been intimate with anyone."

The room does not react.

No thunder. No candle flare. No judgmental gargoyle dropping from the ceiling.

Just the words, sitting there between us.

I force myself to keep going before I can shove them back inside.

"With anyone," I say again. "Not a man. Not a woman. Not beyond some awkward almosts and my own hands. I know I probably should have said that earlier, before the castle bed and the cloak and the whole Devil card situation."

Lucian says nothing.

My nerves rush to fill the silence.

"It's not religious," I add. "Not exactly. It's not purity. I don't think my body is some sacred cupcake that loses value if someone touches the frosting."

His mouth twitches.

I point at him. "Don't laugh."

"I would never."

"You absolutely would."

"Only at sacred cupcake."

"It was a bad metaphor."

"It was vivid."

I take a breath.

The joke helps for half a second.

Then the truth waits again.

"I'm not saving myself. I'm not proud of it. I'm not ashamed of it. Except I'm, sometimes. I don't know. It feels like something I should have figured out by now. Like taxes or how to buy jeans without wanting to set a store on fire."

Lucian's face remains calm.

Not blank.

Calm.

That helps.

"I thought if I waited until I trusted someone, it would be simple. But trust didn't make it simple. Want didn't make it simple. Being lonely didn't make it simple. Nothing made it simple."

My throat tightens.

"I thought you should know before..." I gesture vaguely at the bed, the gown, him, my body, the entire embarrassing existence of desire. "Before this becomes whatever this becomes."

Lucian studies me for a long moment.

Not hungrily.

Not pitying.

Thank God.

Then he says, "Thank you for telling me."

That is it.

No gasp. No reverent speech. No predatory delight. No "I will teach you, innocent one," which would have forced me to smother him with a velvet pillow.

Just thank you.

My eyes sting. My body has apparently decided today is a festival of inconvenient reactions.

"You're not surprised?" I ask.

"No."

"Because the realm told you?"

"Because your fear did."

That could sound cruel.

It does not.

Lucian shifts closer, but only slightly.

"Dorothea, your inexperience is information. It's not a flaw."

My breath shakes.

"It feels like a flaw."

"I know."

"I'm twenty-nine."

"Yes."

"That's old for this."

"No."

"You don't even know what this means where I come from."

"I know enough. I know people measure themselves against imagined clocks and call the bruises failure."

I stare at him.

He continues, voice low.

"Sex is not bread. It does not spoil because it was not served by a certain hour."

A laugh bursts out of me.

It turns wet halfway through. I wipe my face quickly.

He pretends not to notice, which is a kindness.

"I don't want you to perform experience you don't have," he says. "I don't want you to pretend boldness because you believe fantasy demands it. I don't want your silence in exchange for my pleasure."

The words settle over me one by one.

My chest hurts.

"In this room," he says, "you don't owe me arousal. You

73

don't owe me progress. You don't owe me courage. You may desire something and still slow down. You may ask and then change your mind. You may enjoy touch without permitting more. You may be nervous and still be wanted."

My breath catches on the last word.

Wanted.

"You say that like it's easy," I whisper.

"No. I say it like it is true."

I look at him.

The Devil guide. The fantasy man. The not-quite-real creature built from my desire and fear and whatever magic Ms. Vesper poured into that tea.

He is beautiful.

But that is not what undoes me.

What undoes me is his patience.

It's so erotic.

Safety makes my thighs press together.

Some part of me, the part that has been trying to survive on crumbs and customer compliments and accidental hand brushes from Lorenzo, is starving so loudly now that even magic can hear it.

Lucian's gaze drops.

Not to my body.

To my hands.

They are clenched in the velvet blanket.

"Name what you feel," he says again.

I close my eyes.

My instinct is to make it funny.

Overwhelmed. Dramatic. One bad decision away from licking a stranger in a haunted castle.

All true.

Not enough.

"Scared," I say.

"Yes."

"Embarrassed."

"Yes."

"Curious."

His voice softens. "Yes."

"Hungry."

That word changes the air.

74

Only slightly.

But enough.

Lucian inhales.

Not dramatically. Not like a man losing control. But he hears me. Feels the word land.

Good.

I want him to.

I want someone to know without making me apologize for it.

"Hungry for what?" he asks.

I open my eyes.

"That feels like a trick question."

"It's not."

"It feels like one because the answer is obvious."

"Is it?"

I want to say touch.

Pleasure.

Sex.

Him.

But underneath all that, something else rises. It sounds pathetic before I even say it.

"To not have to earn it," I whisper.

Lucian goes still.

I stare at the velvet in my hands.

"I'm hungry to be touched without proving I deserve it. To rest without a timer running in my head. To be looked at without immediately wondering what will be expected of me. To want something and not have it become debt."

The room is painfully quiet.

Then Lucian says, "There's the first chain."

I look up.

"What?"

He gestures lightly toward the mirrors.

In the nearest mirror, I see myself behind the counter at Knead the Dough. The reflection shifts, showing a younger version of me at twenty-one, working two jobs, falling asleep on a bus with a backpack in her lap. Then twenty-five, signing the first lease with a smile fixed on her face and terror under her ribs. Then now, alone in the kitchen after closing, eating dinner standing over the sink because sitting down feels like wasting time.

Around each version of my wrist is a chain made of little brass keys.

Keys to apartments.

Keys to the bakery.

Keys to the office.

Keys to doors I can lock behind me.

Keys to proof I survived.

Lucian's voice comes from beside me.

"You learned to make usefulness your offering."

The mirror shows me smiling at customers.

Carrying too much.

Refusing help.

Paying bills.

Avoiding sleep.

"Then you wondered why receiving felt like theft."

I cannot speak.

The mirror darkens.

The room returns.

I let out a breath I did not know I held. "If I take off the gown," I say, "I'm not promising anything else."

His face remains steady.

"I know."

"I mean it."

"I believe you."

"I may change my mind."

"Yes."

"I may panic."

"Then we stop."

"I may make a weird joke."

His mouth curves. "Almost certainly."

I laugh, and the knot in my chest loosens.

A little.

"Okay," I say.

Lucian rises from the bed and steps behind me.

I feel him there before he touches me. Heat at my back. The faint scent of clove and smoke. My own body's aware-ness spreading like butter in a warm pan, which is possibly the least dignified image available, but accurate.

"May I?" he asks.

His fingers hover near the laces.

I nod, then remember he cannot see my face.

"Yes."

"Thank you."

He begins slowly.

The gown loosens one tie at a time.

Not rushed. Not ceremonial. Practical, almost, which helps. His fingers work the lacing with careful competence, and I try very hard not to think about what else those fingers might do.

That strategy fails immediately.

My breathing changes.

Lucian notices.

"Name it."

"Anticipation."

"Good."

"Nerves."

"Good."

"Please stop saying good."

"No."

I laugh despite myself.

The gown loosens further. Cool air slips beneath the fabric, touching the line of my spine. Goosebumps rise across my skin.

"Cold?" he asks.

"A little."

"Do you want me to stop?"

"No."

The last lace comes free.

The bodice slackens against my chest.

I hold it in place with one hand, my heart hammering.

Lucian steps away.

I turn, surprised.

He is not behind me anymore. He stands beside the bed, facing away.

I stare at his back.

"What are you doing?"

"Giving you the choice to remove it."

"Oh."

That little word contains far too much.

I look down.

The gown has become something else now. Not a costume. Not a fantasy's dramatic flourish. A decision.

I could keep it on.

I could ask him to turn around.

I could say return me and wake up in the white room, refreshed or humiliated or both.

Instead, I stand.

The gown slips an inch.

My heart tries to escape.

"You can look," I say.

Lucian turns.

His gaze meets mine first.

Not my chest.

Not the gown.

My face.

Damn him.

I let the fabric fall.

It whispers down my body, pooling at my feet in black and red.

I stand in front of him in black lace panties and nothing else.

The chamber air is cool on my bare skin. The candles are warm. The mirrors wait. My arms twitch with the urge to cover my breasts, and for a moment, I almost do.

Lucian sees the movement.

"Do you want to cover yourself?" he asks.

"Yes."

"Do you want to?"

The second question lands differently.

Do I want to cover myself, or do I want to obey the fear that says being seen is dangerous?

My hands hover uselessly at my sides.

"I don't know."

"Then wait."

"Wait?"

"Yes. Do nothing for ten breaths. Then decide."

"That sounds awful."

"It may be."

"You're supposed to be tempting me."

"I'm."

"Standing still is not a temptation."

"You are standing uncovered before someone who wants you and has asked nothing from you. That is a temptation you have avoided for years."

My mouth opens.

Closes.

I stand there.

One breath.

My body screams at me to cover. To adjust. To laugh. To make some joke about lighting or nipples or how this is exactly why women invented robes.

Two breaths.

Lucian's eyes remain on mine.

Three.

The urge to cover becomes sharper, then duller.

Four.

I notice the cool air on my skin. The warmth rising under it. The weight of my breasts, the texture of the lace at my hips, the marble floor beneath my feet.

Five.

My body is not a crisis.

Six.

Lucian's wanting is present. I can feel it in the room, in his stillness, in the way his breathing has changed. But it is not grabbing at me.

Seven.

I'm embarrassed.

Eight.

I'm proud.

Nine.

I'm aroused.

Ten.

I lower my hands completely.

Lucian's expression shifts.

Not hunger first, though hunger is there. Reverence.

He looks at me as if I'm not a problem to solve, a body to evaluate, or a prize at the end of patience. He looks as if I'm an answer to a question he has been careful not to ask too soon.

My throat tightens.

"Name it," he says.

My voice is rough. "Seen."

"Does seen feel safe?"

I think about that.

"No."

His expression remains steady.

"But safer than I thought," I add.

"Good."

This time, I don't tell him to stop saying it.

He offers his hand.

I take it.

He leads me back to the bed and helps me lie on my stomach. The velvet is cool against my bare breasts and stomach. I expect to feel ridiculous. Exposed. Instead, with my face turned to the side and my arms folded beneath my head, I feel oddly protected. The bed holds me. The room is warm. Lucian drapes a sheet over my lower body, leaving my back bare.

He does not ask if I'm decent.

He asks, "Comfortable?"

"Yes."

"Truthfully?"

"Yes."

He sits beside me.

A glass bottle appears in his hand.

I lift my head. "Where did that come from?"

"The table."

"There wasn't a bottle on the table."

"There is now." He uncorks the bottle.

The scent rises at once. Lilac, almond, and something earthy. Not dirt. Not mud. Soil after rain. The smell of things growing where they cannot yet be seen.

"Oil," he says.

"I gathered."

"May I use it?"

"Yes."

He pours a small amount into his palm and warms it between his hands.

I hear the soft slide of skin against skin.

My eyes close.

My body has decided that sound is a category of pornography.

Lucian's hands touch my back.

Bare skin.

No fabric this time.

I stop breathing.

He stops moving.

"Breathe, Dorothea."

"I'm aware of the concept."

"Practice."

I pull air in.

It shudders.

His palms glide from my shoulder blades down the length of my back, slow and warm, oil leaving a slick trail over my skin. The first stroke is almost too much. Not because he presses hard. Because my skin has been waiting longer than I knew.

He reaches my lower back and starts again.

Up. Down. Slow.

The oil warms under his hands. My muscles, traitors that they are, begin to yield. His thumbs press along either side of my spine, careful and firm. He finds the tight places, works them without cruelty, waits when my breath catches, continues when I soften.

This is not sex.

Not exactly.

But it is intimate in a way I did not expect. There's nowhere to perform. No task to complete. No customer to satisfy. No order to fill. I can do nothing well here except receive, and I'm terrible at receiving.

Lucian knows. "Name it," he says.

I exhale. "Warm."

"Yes."

"Good."

"Yes."

"Too good."

His hands pause.

"That is not a warning," I say quickly.

"No?"

"No. Just alarming."

"Pleasure often is, when you expect a bill."

I laugh into my folded arms.

Then his hands move again, and the laugh becomes a sigh.

He works my shoulders first. Then the long muscles along my spine. Then lower, over the small of my back, where tension gathers from hours of standing. His pressure is perfect, which is unfair because a fantasy man should not have the technique of a licensed massage therapist and the face of a gothic sin.

"Did I create this level of skill?" I mumble.

"Yes."

"Good for me."

"Very good."

I smile into my arms.

The room grows softer around the edges.

I don't fall asleep, but I drift. There is a difference. Sleep takes you away from the body. This brings me deeper into it. The weight of my limbs. The slick warmth of oil. The velvet under my cheek. The candlelight against my closed eyelids. The steady rhythm of Lucian's hands.

Press.

Release.

Rest.

I think of dough again.

Of how too much force tears it. Too little does nothing. The right pressure develops structure. The right rest makes it rise.

My throat tightens unexpectedly.

"Why am I sad?" I whisper.

Lucian's hands slow, but don't stop. "Because you are receiving something you needed before today."

That is so unfairly accurate I almost tell him to shut up.

Instead, I breathe.

The sadness sits in me.

So does the pleasure.

Both at once.

Apparently bodies are ovens with multiple racks.

Lucian moves to my arms. He massages from shoulder to wrist, then my hands, one at a time. That nearly destroys me. My hands are the most used part of me. Burned, washed, nicked, dried out, strong, tired. He turns one over and presses his thumb into my palm.

A moan slips out of me.

I freeze.

He continues.

Not making a production of it.

Not praising the sound.

Just letting it be.

That almost makes me cry.

"You may make noise," he says after a moment.

"I know."

"Do you?"

"No."

His thumb presses into the base of my thumb, and my whole arm tingles.

"Noise is not debt," he says.

"You are very committed to this theme."

"You are very committed to needing it."

I huff.

Then moan again when he finds another tight place.

He is right.

Tragically.

After my hands, he draws the sheet slightly lower, asking with a pause before he does. I nod. He massages my hips through the edge of the sheet, then my thighs over the fabric.

I expect my body to tense again.

It does.

But differently now.

Not only fear.

Awareness.

Heat.

My thighs part a fraction before I can think better of it.

Lucian's hands move down my legs, over the sheet, slow and firm. Calves. Ankles. Feet. When he lifts one foot into his lap and presses his thumbs into the arch, I make a sound so indecent I would normally have to leave town.

Lucian pauses.

I lift my head. "If you make fun of me, I'll kick you."

His mouth curves. "I would not dare."

"You look delighted."

"I'm delighted."

"That is different."

"I'm delighted by your pleasure, not your embarrassment."

"Oh."

He returns to my foot.

The next press makes sparks shoot up my leg.

I drop my forehead to my arms.

"Good?" he asks.

"Fishing for compliments now?"

"Collecting data."

"Thief."

"Answer."

"Yes," I say. "Good. Very good. Annoyingly good."

"Better."

By the time he finishes both feet, I feel melted.

Not sexy melted. Not yet.

Well, maybe partly.

Mostly I feel like butter left near the oven. Softened beyond usefulness. Too relaxed to be productive. It's horrifying.

Lucian drapes the sheet more fully over me and sits beside me.

"You are fighting sleep," he says.

"I paid nothing for only twenty minutes. I'm not wasting it unconscious."

"You are not paying."

"I may tip."

"That does not change the principle?"

"Exactly."

He laughs.

I open my eyes.

He is watching me with an expression I cannot read.

"What?"

"You are learning to stay."

"On a bed?"

"In your body."

I look away.

The room does not shift.

The mirrors don't flash some humiliating image.

Maybe because I already know this one is true.

I have spent years living slightly above myself. In lists. In tasks. In future disasters I can maybe prevent if I think hard enough. In the bakery's margins, bills, schedules, proofing times. In other people's expectations. In the space between Lorenzo's hand touching mine and my own fear shutting the door.

My body has always been where I lived last.

Lucian touches the edge of the sheet near my shoulder.

Not me.

The sheet.

"Do you want more massage?"

I think about it.

That should not feel revolutionary.

It does.

I'm allowed to think about what I want.

"No," I say.

"Good."

"I want to turn over."

"Then turn over."

My face heats.

"I'm naked."

"You are covered."

"Partially."

"Yes."

"You'll see me."

"Yes."

"That is the point, I suppose."

"Only if you choose it."

I groan. "You and your choices."

"They matter."

"I know."

I roll onto my back before I lose my nerve, holding the sheet to my chest as I move. My hair spills over the pillow. The canopy hangs above me, dark and red and full of little gold chains. Lucian sits beside me, one hand resting on his knee, patient as sin.

The sheet covers me from chest to thighs.

Bare shoulders. Bare arms. The upper curve of my breasts hidden by my own white-knuckled grip.

I look at him.

He looks at my face.

Again.

I laugh once, breathless. "Do you ever get tired of being respectful?"

His eyes darken. "Respect is not restraint from desire, Dorothea. It's how desire proves itself worthy of being trusted."

That sentence should be illegal.

I stare at him.

"Do you practice these?"

"No."

"Terrible news."

"Why?"

"Because I like it."

His smile is slow. "There," he says softly.

I'm not sure which part of me he sees. Maybe the part that finally admitted it.

I lie there with the sheet clutched to my chest and my skin warm from his hands, and for the first time, I understand that wanting does not have to arrive fully formed. It can arrive in pieces. A shoulder touched. A hand massaged. A name said without flinching. A grape tasted slowly. A boundary held. A joke survived.

Not a plunge.

A recipe.

One ingredient at a time.

Lucian brushes a loose strand of hair from my cheek.

"May I ask you something?" he says.

"You've been asking me things for what feels like a suspiciously long therapy session."

"This one matters."

"Fine."

"What happened the first time someone touched you and you wanted to disappear?"

My body goes cold.

So much for being melted butter.

Lucian sees it immediately.

"We don't have to go there."

No.

That is the trap, isn't it?

Not his trap.

Mine.

I could avoid it. Make a joke. Say Jammie was not worth discussing. Say the past is past, which is what people say when the past is chewing on their ankle.

But this room was built from my chains.

If I pretend the chain is decorative, I will leave wearing it.

"Jammie," I say.

Lucian's expression does not change.

I appreciate that too.

"Who was he?"

"A man I dated for several months."

"And?"

"And he had a crushed velvet couch."

Lucian's eyebrow lifts.

"That is the detail?"

"It was a very memorable couch."

"Tell me about the couch, then."

I let out a breath.

The room around us dims at the edges.

Not gone. Just softer.

The velvet beneath me changes texture.

I know before I look.

The bed is no longer a bed.

I'm sitting on a couch.

Crushed velvet. Dark green. Too low to the ground, with one cushion that sagged more than the others. The castle chamber remains around the edges, but in front of me appears the memory like a stage set. Jammie's apartment. The leaning bookshelf. The record player. A lamp with a shade he insisted was vintage and I privately thought was ugly. A coffee table stacked with coasters no one used.

I sit up, clutching the sheet.

But I'm not on the couch.

I'm still on the bed.

The memory plays in front of us.

Younger me sits beside Jammie on the green velvet couch. Twenty-six, maybe. Hair shorter. Body tense. Wearing a sweater I remember because I donated it after that night as if fabric could testify.

Jammie is handsome in a gentle, forgettable way. Sandy hair. Kind eyes. Nice hands. He was romantic, patient, always asking for permission before anything moved further.

He was not a villain.

That was the worst part.

If he had been cruel, I could have given the fear a face.

Lucian sits beside me on the bed as we watch the memory.

"He was kind," I say.

"I believe you."

"We had nothing in common."

"That does not erase kindness."

"No."

In the memory, Jammie kisses me.

I remember this.

The awkward angle. The scratch of his jaw. The nervous sweetness. The way I tried to want the moment enough to become someone who knew what to do with it.

His hand slides along my waist.

I stiffen.

The memory-me stiffens too.

"I had been rehearsing," I say quietly.

Lucian looks at me.

"In my head. What I would say if things went further. I was going to tell him I was inexperienced. Not a big speech. Just enough. I thought maybe if I said it calmly, it would become a normal fact. Like an allergy."

"Did you?"

"No."

In the memory, Jammie's hand moves carefully, slowly, into the waistband of my pants.

He is not rough.

He is not careless.

That almost makes it worse.

"He asked," I say. "Earlier. Not in that exact second, but before. He asked if it was okay. I said yes."

"Did you want to say yes?"

"I wanted to want yes."

Lucian's gaze stays on the memory.

"That is different."

"Yes."

Jammie's hand slips beneath the fabric.

Memory-me's face changes.

It's small, but I see it now. The flinch. The sharp discomfort. The immediate shame at discomfort.

"It was supposed to feel good," I whisper.

Lucian says nothing.

"It felt like being poked. Like my body had locked a door and he was jiggling the handle. Not because he was doing something wrong. Maybe he was. I don't know. I didn't know enough to know. But it felt wrong. Not dangerous. Just wrong."

In the memory, Jammie notices.

He pulls away immediately.

His mouth moves.

Are you okay?

I remember those words.

I remember nodding.

Lying.

I remember sitting up too fast. My sweater twisted. My hair stuck to my mouth. I remember trying to speak.

"I was going to tell him," I say.

My throat burns.

"I tried. I had the words lined up. I've never done this. I need to go slow. I don't know what I'm doing. I'm embarrassed. Can we just stop for a second?"

The memory-me says none of it.

She smiles.

A terrible smile.

A smile made of panic and apology.

Then she stands.

"I ran," I say.

The memory shows it. Me fumbling for my shoes, my keys, my bag. Jammie standing, confused and concerned, giving me space because he thought that was kind. It was kind. It also gave me room to escape.

"I practically ran out of his apartment."

The memory darkens.

"I never answered his calls."

Lucian looks at me now.

"He called?"

"Yes. Texted. A lot at first. Then less. Then not at all."

"Was he angry?"

"I don't know. Probably hurt. Confused. Maybe both."

"Did you want to talk to him?"

"Yes."

"Why didn't you?"

The memory fades, leaving only the castle chamber.

The velvet bed. The candles. The mirrors.

I sit with the sheet around me and feel younger than I want to.

"Because I thought he would look at me differently."

"How?"

"Like I was childish. Broken. Too much work. Not sexy. Like my body was a problem that came with instructions he hadn't signed up for."

Lucian is quiet.

The words keep coming now.

"I thought if I told him I was a virgin, he would become careful in a way that made me feel worse. Or excited in a way that made me want to crawl out of my skin. I thought he'd ask why. I thought I'd have to explain something I didn't understand myself."

My fingers twist in the sheet.

"And part of me was angry at him."

"For touching you?"

"For needing me to know what I wanted."

The truth lands hard.

I look at Lucian.

"That sounds unfair."

"It sounds honest."

"He wasn't responsible for my silence."

"No."

"But I blamed him anyway because blaming him was

easier than admitting I had no idea how to ask for what I needed."

Lucian nods once.

"The second chain," he says.

The mirrors flicker.

This time, I don't look away.

A reflection shows me on Jammie's couch with a chain around my mouth.

Not tight.

Loose.

So loose I could lift it away.

But I don't.

The reflection fades.

I press my hand over my lips.

Lucian does not reach for me.

Again, patience.

Again, safety.

Again, the infuriating thing I apparently crave.

"What would you say now?" he asks.

"To Jammie?"

"To yourself."

I look down.

The younger woman from the memory has vanished, but I can see her anyway. Scared. Sweater twisted. Keys in hand. Already deciding to disappear.

"I'd tell her to stop running."

Lucian waits.

"No," I say. "That's not right. That's what I wish she had done, but it's not what she needed."

"What did she need?"

I breathe in.

The answer is softer.

"I'd tell her she wasn't bad at wanting. She was afraid. There's a difference."

Lucian's eyes warm.

"And?"

"I'd tell her that yes is allowed to become wait."

"And?"

"I'd tell her that uncomfortable is enough of a reason to stop, even if no one has done anything wrong."

The room seems to loosen around us.

The candles burn steadier.

The mirror that showed the chain over my mouth clears into ordinary glass.

Lucian's expression is not triumphant.

Good.

I don't feel fixed.

I feel opened, which is messier.

"May I touch you again?" he asks.

The question roots me back in the present.

My skin, still warm from the oil.

The sheet against my chest.

The bed beneath me.

Lucian beside me.

"Yes," I say.

"Where?"

The word makes my pulse jump.

No one has asked me that so plainly before.

At least, no one in a context where I understood the answer mattered.

I look at his hands.

"Shoulders," I say first.

He nods.

His hands return to my shoulders, warm over bare skin this time.

I inhale.

Not freezing.

Not melting.

Receiving.

"Name it," he says.

"Warm."

"Yes."

"Safe."

His hands still for the smallest moment.

Then continue.

"Good."

I close my eyes.

"Sad."

"Yes."

"Good."

"Yes."

"Aroused."

The word barely makes it out.

Lucian's hands don't change.

That is the lesson, I think.

My arousal does not make his control vanish.

It does not turn the room into a debt collector.

It does not force the next thing.

It's only information.

Warm.

Safe.

Sad.

Aroused.

Mine.

"Good," he says again.

This time, I let the praise settle.

His hands move down my arms, then back up. Over my collarbones, careful. He does not touch my breasts. The absence of touch becomes a kind of touch. My body notices what he avoids, and that notice becomes heat.

I open my eyes.

Lucian's face is close enough now that I can see the tiny gold flecks in his dark eyes.

"Do you want to be kissed?" he asks.

I know what he is asking.

Not do I want to kiss him, like before.

Do I want to receive.

To allow him to come to me.

"Yes," I say.

"How?"

I almost laugh.

"Must we make everything an essay?"

"Not everything. This, yes."

I think. My instinct is to say however you want.

The phrase rises, easy, eager, dangerous. I stop it.

Who benefits from your silence?

"I want you to kiss me slowly," I say. "Not like you're trying to convince me. Like we have time."

Lucian's expression changes.

There's heat in it now. Openly.

"Good."

He leans in.

Slowly.

The first brush of his mouth is softer than I expect. A question, but not a timid one. A question asked by someone confident enough to wait for the answer.

I answer.

My lips part.

He deepens the kiss by degrees, not taking more than I give, but making it very difficult not to give. His hand cups the side of my face. The other stays at my shoulder. My fingers curl into the sheet instead of his shirt because I need something to hold that is not him.

The kiss builds.

Slow becomes warm.

Warm becomes hungry.

Hungry becomes a pressure low in my belly that makes me ache.

I make a sound against his mouth.

He pulls back a fraction.

"No," I say, too quickly.

He stills.

I feel my face burn.

"I mean, don't stop."

His thumb brushes my cheek.

"Say it cleanly."

I groan. "You are the worst."

"Say it."

"I want you to keep kissing me."

His eyes darken.

"There."

Then he does.

This time, when I make a sound, I don't swallow it.

Lucian kisses like he listens. That is a ridiculous thought, but there it is. He feels the way my mouth opens, the moment I need air, the tiny hesitation before I dare to touch him back. He does not rush the kiss toward proof. He lets it exist as its own thing.

I finally lift one hand to his chest.

Then to his collar.

Then the side of his neck.

His skin is hot beneath my fingers.

Real.

Fantasy.

Both.

I want to lick him again.

The thought returns with such clarity that I laugh against his mouth.

Lucian draws back, eyes bright. "What?"

"Nothing."

"Liar."

"It's undignified."

"Excellent."

"No."

"Dorothea."

"I wanted to lick your neck earlier."

His smile turns devastating.

"And now?"

"I still do."

"Then do."

My whole body flushes.

"You can't just say things like that."

"You can want things like that."

"That is not the same."

"It can be."

The room waits again.

Always waiting.

I stare at his throat.

The open collar of his shirt shows warm skin, the line of tendon, the place where his pulse beats. He is offering. Not pushing. Not teasing cruelly. Offering.

I lean in before courage burns off.

My mouth touches his neck.

First a kiss.

Then, because apparently this magical realm is determined to make me honest, I lick him.

A slow touch of tongue against hot skin.

He inhales sharply.

That sound nearly ruins me.

Power moves through me, sudden and bright. Not power

over him. Not exactly. Power in myself. I wanted. I chose. He reacted.

I did that.

He lets me do it again.

This time, his hand tightens at my shoulder.

Not stopping me.

Holding on.

"Dorothea," he says.

My name in his mouth sounds rough now.

Not theatrical.

Not guide-like.

Wanting.

I sit back, breathless.

"I liked that," I say, because apparently we are naming things.

His smile is dark. "I noticed."

"Did you like it?"

"Yes."

The blunt answer hits me harder than flattery would have.

Yes.

No performance. No overpraise.

Just yes.

I look down, suddenly overwhelmed.

Lucian lifts my chin with one finger. "Too much?"

"No."

"Name it."

I breathe. "Powerful."

His eyes warm. "Good."

"Scared of that."

"Also good."

"Hungry again."

His thumb pauses beneath my chin.

The air between us thickens.

"Hungry for what?"

The answer comes more easily now, but still not easily. "To know more."

His gaze drops to my mouth. "Of me?"

"Yes."

"Of yourself?"

The question catches me.

I think of Jammie's couch. The chain over my mouth. The way I ran from not knowing.

"Yes," I whisper.

Lucian smiles.

Not wicked this time.

Pleased.

"Then we continue carefully."

"Carefully sounds boring."

"Careful is not timid. Careful is devotion with attention."

I stare.

"You are going to be a problem for me."

"I already am."

"Yes."

He kisses my forehead.

The gesture is so tender it makes my chest ache.

Then he stands.

I sit up quickly, clutching the sheet. "Where are you going?"

"Nowhere."

He moves to the foot of the bed and takes one of my ankles in his hand.

My breath catches.

He pauses.

"Yes," I say before he can ask.

His mouth curves.

He begins massaging my calf again, this time with my body turned toward him, the sheet still covering me. The position feels different. More exposed. I can see him touching me. He can see me react.

His hands move over my shin, my calf, the arch of my foot. I try to stay composed.

I fail.

The second moan is less embarrassing than the first.

The third is almost satisfying.

Lucian's eyes stay on me.

"Does receiving still feel like debt?" he asks.

I laugh weakly. "You ask that while holding my foot?"

"Yes."

I close my eyes. "No," I say. "Not as much."

"What does it feel like?"

"Like rest."

"Yes."

"Like being cared for."

"Yes."

"Like I might cry if I think about it too hard."

His hands slow. "Then don't think too hard."

"That is against my religion."

"Your religion is overthinking?"

"And pastries."

"Then let the pastry rest."

I open my eyes. "That was terrible."

"It was."

"I loved it."

"I know."

The laugh that comes from me is easier this time.

Lucian's hands move to my other leg.

After a while, the warmth returns. The heaviness. The good. My body becomes less of a locked room and more of a place I'm standing inside.

Then Lucian asks, "What's your deepest desire?"

I freeze.

The question from the original doorway, returned now that I'm too softened to deflect cleanly.

"My deepest desire?" I repeat.

"Yes."

"That's a lot of pressure."

"It is."

"What if I get it wrong?"

"You cannot get it wrong if you answer honestly."

"Honesty is a high bar."

"Yes."

I stare at the canopy.

Respectable answers arrive first.

I want rest.

True.

I want a partner.

True.

I want trust.

True.

I want someone safe.

Very true.

I want the bakery to survive. I want the lease situation resolved. I want Lorenzo to stop looking at me like he sees all the hunger I keep hiding in the back office next to the mop bucket. I want Lea to stop being right. I want Park to stop smirking about romance magic. I want to sleep eight hours. I want a body that does not feel like a machine for producing other people's comfort.

All true.

None deep enough.

Lucian waits.

The room waits.

The mirrors are quiet.

My body is not.

I look at him.

"Can I say something ugly?"

His expression sharpens. "Yes."

"Not ugly. Maybe crude."

"Yes."

"Not respectable."

"Yes."

"Stop saying yes like it's easy."

"It's easy for me."

"Show-off."

His smile flickers.

I sit up more fully, holding the sheet around me. My heart pounds, but the fear is different now. Less like a lock. More like standing at the edge of a very high place and realizing the view is worth the vertigo.

"I want…" I stop.

Lucian does not help.

The words are hot in my mouth.

I have thought versions of them before, alone, where no one could hear. In the shower. In bed. While folding laundry. Once during a town council livestream, which was disturbing and not my finest hour. Thinking is not the same as saying. Saying gives desire a body.

"I want you to make love to me," I say.

Lucian's eyes darken.

My pulse roars.

"And I want you to fuck me."

Lucian stilled.

The candles flare hot.

I keep going before shame can break my jaw shut. "I want to know the difference. I want to know what tenderness feels like when it becomes heat, and what heat feels like when it stops asking to be polite. I want to know what carnal pleasure is. I want to feel wanted without wondering if I'm doing it right."

My voice shakes.

I don't stop.

"I want to feel someone inside me when I come. I want to feel alive. I want to do the things I've always been too afraid to do. I want to ask without apologizing. I want to stop running from the parts of me that aren't useful."

Lucian's presence seems to fill the room.

Not physically.

Magically, maybe.

Or maybe this is what happens when a woman tells the truth and the world has to make space for it.

I breathe hard.

The silence after is enormous.

My face is burning. My whole body is burning. I want to hide under the sheet, then set the sheet on fire, then open a bakery on another continent under an assumed name.

Lucian does not laugh.

He does not pounce.

He does not reward my confession by immediately turning it into action.

He kneels at the side of the bed until his eyes are level with mine.

"Dorothea," he says.

My name is rough in his mouth.

"Yes?"

"That was not crude."

I swallow.

"That was prayer."

My breath leaves me and my eyes fill again.

This is becoming absurd.

"I'm not religious," I whisper.

"Desire does not require doctrine."

"That sounds like a bumper sticker for a very intense cult."

His smile is small.

"Perhaps."

Then he reaches for my hand.

I give it to him.

He turns my palm up and kisses the center.

A shiver moves through me.

"If that is your desire," he says, "I will help you find the freedom you seek."

Heat rushes through me.

But beneath it, fear.

Lucian sees both.

"You said if it was my desire…"

His thumb moves across my palm.

"You asked for the destination. We are still learning how you travel."

I stare at him.

That should frustrate me, and it does. But it also makes me want him more.

Possibly because my fantasy guide has just refused to let my own dramatic declaration become another form of running.

"Are you denying me in my own fantasy?" I ask.

"I'm guiding you in your own fantasy."

"That sounds like yes."

"It is."

"You are very inconvenient."

"Yes."

I look away, but my mouth is twitching.

Lucian stands and moves to the wardrobe on the far wall. I had not noticed it before. Black wood. Iron handles. A serpent carved along the top.

He opens it and removes a robe.

Soft black silk, lined in red.

He brings it to me.

"For now," he says.

I take it, frowning. "A robe?"

"You are cold."

"I'm aroused."

"You are both."

I glare at him.

He smiles.

Both can be true, apparently. Annoying.

I slip into the robe. It feels indecently good against my oiled skin. Lucian turns away while I tie it, which is gentlemanly in a way that makes no sense after everything he has seen and heard, and yet, I like it.

When I'm covered, he offers his hand.

"Come," he says.

"Where?"

"To the door."

I look toward the chamber door.

The black wood waits.

My stomach tightens.

"I thought I said not yet."

"You did. Now I'm asking again."

"You said I choose."

"You do."

"I could say no."

"Yes."

I look at him.

"Will we come back here?"

"If you choose."

"Will the room change?"

"Yes."

"Do I have to be brave?"

"No."

"Good, because I'm wearing a silk robe and emotionally compromised."

"A powerful combination."

I laugh.

Then I take his hand.

The moment my fingers close around his, the castle chamber shifts.

The mirrors darken. The candles lower. The door ahead glows faintly at the edges, red light leaking around the frame.

Lucian does not pull.

I walk with him because I choose to.

At the door, he stops.

"This was the first room," he says.

"The gorgeous cage."

"Yes."

"What was the chain?"

He looks at me.

"Receiving."

My throat tightens.

I look back at the bed. The fallen gown. The oil bottle. The velvet. The canopy embroidered with loose golden chains.

Receiving.

Not sex.

Not yet.

Receiving without owing.

Being seen without vanishing.

Speaking without running.

A smaller chain than I expected.

A stronger one.

Lucian touches the door handle but does not turn it.

"When you are ready," he says.

I look down at our joined hands.

"What's on the other side?"

"More truth."

"Terrible."

"Yes."

"And more temptation?"

"Always."

I take a breath.

My body feels different now.

Not transformed. Not solved. Not suddenly bold enough to march back to Coral Cove and ask Lorenzo to do something obscene with his stupid beautiful mouth.

But different.

Looser.

The chain around my mouth is not gone.

But I know it is there.

I know it is loose.

That has to count for something.

I look at Lucian.

"Open it."

His smile is not triumphant.

It's warm.

He turns the handle.

The door opens onto darkness, and somewhere deep inside it, I hear the faint metallic sound of chains slipping against stone.

I should be terrified.

I'm.

But underneath the fear, there's something else.

Hunger.

This time, I don't apologize for it.

FOUR

The darkness beyond the door is not empty.

I know that immediately.

It has weight. Heat. A pulse.

Lucian stands beside me, one hand on the open door, his other still wrapped around mine. The chamber behind us glows with candlelight, velvet, black stone, and all the things I have already survived tonight, which is a ridiculous sentence considering I have been inside this fantasy for what feels like an hour at most.

Maybe less.

Maybe more.

Time has already proved itself unreliable.

Ahead of us, the dark waits.

Not hallway dark. Not closet dark. Not the bakery at four in the morning before I hit the lights and remind the ovens that we are all suffering together. This is deeper. Thicker. It smells like smoke, rose, wine, and hot metal.

"Absolutely not," I say.

Lucian turns his head. "No?"

"I didn't say no."

"You said absolutely not."

"That is an emotional observation, not a decision."

His mouth curves.

"Yes."

His thumb moves once over the back of my hand.

The touch does not calm me exactly. Calm is a large ask while standing in a magical Devil castle wearing a silk robe with a man who looks like sin decided to learn manners. But it steadies me.

Behind us, the first chamber breathes softly. The bed. The mirrors. The gown pooled like spilled wine on the floor. The bottle of lilac oil. The place where I said things out loud that I had never said to another person. I should feel embarrassed.

I do feel embarrassed.

But the embarrassment has changed texture.

Before, it was sticky. Heavy. Shame that clung to my ribs and made me want to sprint back to Coral Cove, lock myself inside the bakery, and communicate only through muffin labels for the rest of my life.

Now it feels more like heat.

Still uncomfortable.

Still mine.

But not poisonous.

That is alarming.

Lucian watches me think because apparently that is his hobby.

"What?" I ask.

"You are deciding whether the last room changed you."

"I'm deciding whether I should invoice The Arcane Room for emotional labor."

"Both may be true."

"Don't start."

His smile deepens. "The room changed you because you chose to let it."

"That sounds like a motivational poster in a dungeon."

"This is not a dungeon."

I glance into the dark beyond the door. "That is still under review."

Lucian looks ahead. "This room won't harm you."

"That's vague."

"It will tempt you."

"Again, vague."

"It will ask whether being desired can feel safe."

My throat tightens. The next chain.

I should have known.

The first room was receiving. Letting myself be touched without immediately turning it into a debt. Letting Lucian massage tension from my body without asking what he needed in return. Saying hunger without apologizing for having an appetite.

Apparently, the Devil is organized.

Awful.

Efficient.

Very branded.

I peer into the dark. "What if I don't like the answer?"

"Then we learn that too."

"That is not comforting."

"Truth often fails at comfort first."

"Lucian."

"Yes?"

"Are all the rooms going to be this rude?"

"No."

I relax a fraction.

"Some will be ruder." He offers the door with a small tilt of his head. Not pushing. Not leading. Offering.

Always offering.

That might be worse than if he dragged me, because choice keeps putting things in my hands.

I take one breath.

Then another.

The silk robe brushes my skin. Beneath it, my body still feels warm from his hands, soft from oil, alive in a way that makes me want to both thank him and file a complaint.

I step into the darkness.

The room lights itself slowly.

A line of candles flares along the floor, one after another, red flame catching in black glass holders. Then wall sconces. Then chandeliers overhead, though they are not normal chandeliers. They are iron circles suspended by chains, each one holding dozens of candles that burn without dripping. The light rises in layers until the room reveals itself.

"Oh," I say.

It's not a dungeon.

Not exactly.

It's a bedchamber, but the word feels insufficient. The

space is circular, built from black marble veined with gold. The ceiling arches high above us, lost in shadow. Red curtains hang along the walls, floor to ceiling, thick as theater drapes and embroidered with flames, keys, and little open locks. The floor is polished enough to reflect candlelight, but not clearly enough to show my face.

Thank God.

I have had enough mirrors for one emotional era.

At the center of the room is another bed.

This one is lower than the four-poster, wider, covered in black sheets and a red velvet coverlet folded neatly at the foot. No canopy. No curtains. No hiding. Just an open expanse of fabric lit by candlelight, waiting with the smug confidence of furniture that knows exactly what it is for.

Around the bed, iron chains hang from the ceiling.

Decorative, I think at first.

Then I see that each chain ends in nothing. No cuffs. No hooks. No tools. Just loose links, suspended in the air, swaying slightly though there's no breeze.

Loose chains.

The Devil is getting less subtle.

"This room is very on theme," I say.

Lucian steps in behind me. The door closes without a sound.

I don't turn.

"Do you feel trapped?" he asks.

I take inventory.

Door behind us. Lucian to my left, not blocking anything. Bed ahead. Chains above. Candles everywhere. My own pulse being loud and obnoxious.

"No."

"Good."

"I feel judged by interior design."

"Also useful."

"I disagree."

The room is beautiful in a way I don't trust. Everything looks expensive, dramatic, and slightly threatening. Like a restaurant where the menu has no prices and the waiter describes the foam with spiritual intensity. The air is warmer here, brushing the skin exposed at my throat. The robe suddenly feels thin.

Lucian releases my hand.

The loss of contact moves through me.

I wish it did not.

He walks a few steps away and turns to face me. The red cloak hangs from his shoulders, dark as blood in the candle-light. His white shirt is open at the throat. The chain at his belt glints.

"You said you wanted to know the difference," he says.

My mouth goes dry.

Between making love and fucking.

Between tenderness and heat.

Between being cherished and being taken apart.

I said that.

Out loud.

Like some kind of woman who had not built an entire life around swallowing sentences until they became acid.

"I did say that," I manage.

"You also said you wanted to feel alive."

"I may have been emotionally compromised."

"You were honest."

"Same thing, sometimes."

Lucian smiles, but it fades quickly.

"This room is not for all of that."

I blink. "No?"

"No."

"Oh."

The disappointment arrives first.

Then the embarrassment about the disappointment.

Then irritation, because apparently my desire has developed a personality and it is impatient.

Lucian sees each piece cross my face.

I know he does.

"That bothers you," he says.

"No."

"Dorothea."

"Fine. Yes."

"Why?"

"Because I finally said the embarrassing thing, and now the fantasy realm is putting me on a payment plan."

His laugh is sudden and warm.

I point at him. "Don't laugh."

"I'm deeply fond of that metaphor."

"It was not for you."

"Most of your best lines are not."

I cross my arms over the robe. "Explain."

"This room is about being wanted and staying present for it."

"That sounds less fun."

His gaze drops to my crossed arms, then returns to my face. "Is that true?"

No.

Obviously no.

My body is already too aware of him. Too awake. The room's heat is sliding beneath the robe, warming the oil still on my skin. My pulse has found a new rhythm, low and insistent. Lucian stands ten feet away and somehow the space between us feels crowded.

"No," I say, because lying is becoming less efficient in here.

He inclines his head once.

Not smug.

Approving.

That is somehow worse for my nervous system.

"I'm not denying you," he says. "I'm slowing the part of you that wants to rush past fear and call that freedom."

Because yes.

Part of me wants to rush. Not because I'm suddenly brave, though I would enjoy that misunderstanding. I want to leap to the dramatic part. The part where the body overwhelms the mind and I don't have to think anymore. The part where Lucian becomes responsible for what happens because I'm swept away.

That is the fantasy, maybe.

Or one of them.

To be wanted so intensely I'm spared the burden of asking.

Lucian studies me in the candlelight.

"There," he says.

"What?"

"You found it."

"I found nothing."

"You found the hiding place inside the desire."

I stare at him.

"Again, I would like to remind you that this experience was advertised as sensual, not as a subpoena."

"And yet."

I sigh.

He is unbearable.

He is also right.

The room hums around us. The chains above the bed sway. Tiny sounds move through the air, metal against metal, soft as breath.

Lucian reaches for the clasp of his cloak.

My thoughts stop.

Not slow. Stop.

His fingers unfasten the heavy red fabric. It slips from his shoulders and falls to the floor in a dark pool. Underneath, the white shirt looks almost too simple for him. Old-fashioned. Loose through the sleeves, open enough at the throat to show the hollow there, the line of his collarbone, the warm skin I licked in the last room because apparently I'm a person who does that now.

My mouth remembers.

That is alarming.

Lucian watches me watching him.

"You may look," he says.

My eyes snap to his face.

"I wasn't…"

He waits.

I press my lips together.

"Yes, I was."

"You may."

"That feels like a trap."

"It's an invitation."

"They often look similar."

"Yes. That is why consent matters."

The words settle in the space between us.

I look at him.

Not by accident. Not in quick guilty flicks. I let myself look.

His shirt is soft linen, the sleeves gathered at the wrists, the fabric loose enough that it shifts when he breathes. It should look outdated. It does. It also looks devastating. The black trousers are full through the legs and tucked into tall boots. Not modern. Not practical. Very fantasy. Very yes.

"Your outfit is ridiculous," I say.

"I know."

"It's working for you."

"I know that too."

"Arrogant."

"Accurate."

A laugh escapes me.

The laugh helps.

Lucian's hands move to the hem of his shirt.

He pauses.

"Do you want me to remove it?"

I swallow.

The question should not matter. He is a fantasy guide in a Devil-card sex castle. He clearly intends to remove it. The scene practically has lighting cues. But he still asks.

And that asking makes the wanting mine.

"Yes," I say.

He pulls the shirt over his head.

My brain does something unhelpful.

I have seen attractive shirtless men before. Beaches exist. So do social media algorithms, unfortunately. I have watched enough romance adaptations with Lea to under-stand the cultural function of the male torso. I should be prepared.

I'm not prepared.

Lucian is all controlled strength and warm bronze skin, lit by candlelight until every ridge and hollow looks carved. His shoulders are broad, his chest defined, his abdomen so unfairly sculpted that my first thought is, That is more abs than I have fingers to count on.

My second thought is, Lick.

Again.

Apparently my inner monologue has become one of those dogs that knows only three commands.

My mouth goes dry.

Lucian sees that too.

He does not smirk.

That is helpful.

He only stands there and lets himself be seen.

The realization hits slowly.

He is letting me look.

Not performing. Not posing. Not turning my gaze into a transaction. He is standing in the room with me, half undressed, allowing desire to move both ways.

I look at his chest.

His stomach.

The narrow line of hair disappearing beneath the waist-band of his trousers.

Then back to his face.

His eyes are darker now.

Not because of magic.

Want.

His want is present, disciplined, and unmistakable.

My skin prickles.

In the mirrorless floor, candlelight trembles under my feet.

"Name it," he says.

I laugh weakly. "We are still doing that?"

"Especially now."

"Unfair."

"Yes."

I press my fingers to the knot of the robe at my waist. "Overwhelmed."

"Yes."

"Curious."

"Yes."

"Embarrassed."

"Yes."

"Turned on."

The last words come out barely above a whisper.

The chains above the bed stir.

Lucian's expression sharpens with heat, but he does not move toward me.

"Good."

I close my eyes for one second.

Good.

The word is dangerous now. It curls low in my belly, warm as caramel.

When I open my eyes, Lucian is still waiting. No one has ever made waiting look so indecent.

"What now?" I ask.

"What do you want now?"

"Menus."

His mouth curves. "Very well."

I exhale in relief.

"You may keep the robe on. I may touch you over the silk. You may remove the robe yourself. You may ask me to remove it. You may come to the bed. You may stay where you are. You may ask me to come to you. You may ask me to put my shirt back on."

"No."

The word comes out fast.

His smile turns wicked.

I lift one hand. "I mean, unnecessary." I look toward the bed.

The black sheets. The red coverlet. The hanging chains, loose and swaying.

"What does the bed mean?"

Lucian glances at it. "A place to stay while being desired."

"That sounds like a very expensive therapy pillow."

"It can be that too."

"What does that mean?"

"It means you may lie down and do nothing."

I stiffen.

"That bothers you more than undressing," he says.

"No, it does not."

I look at the bed again.

Lie down and do nothing.

Let him look.

Let him touch.

Let him desire.

Let myself want.

The urge to make a joke is so strong it almost becomes

physical. But the room waits. Lucian waits. The chains sway above the bed, loose enough to lift, decorative enough to deny.

I'm tired of denial.

At least in this room.

I walk to the bed.

My bare feet move over warm marble. I don't remember the floor becoming warm. Magic or metaphor, take your pick. The robe brushes against my thighs. I feel Lucian behind me, though he does not follow until I sit on the edge of the mattress and turn back toward him.

"Do you want me closer?" he asks.

"Yes."

He comes to me.

Slowly.

The room seems to narrow with every step. His bare chest catches the candlelight. The chain at his belt whispers. He stops at the edge of the bed, standing between my knees but not touching them.

I could reach out and put my hands on him.

Lucian looks down at me, and for one second the power difference should scare me. He is tall. Strong. Half dressed. I'm sitting on a bed in a silk robe, heart pounding, trying to remember that I have a return phrase and a body that belongs to me.

But his hands stay at his sides.

He waits.

I'm the one who reaches.

My palms touch his waist first, bare skin hot under my hands. His abdomen tightens. That reaction hits me like a spark landing in dry sugar.

I did that.

I look up.

His jaw is set.

"Is this all right?" I ask.

"Yes."

The word is rough.

Power moves through me again. Not control over him. Not triumph. More like discovering a door opens when I push.

I slide my hands up his sides, slowly, learning the shape of him. The muscle beneath skin. The warmth. The way his breath changes when my thumbs brush the lower edge of his ribs.

He remains still.

Too still.

"You can touch me," I say.

His eyes darken.

"Where?"

The question lands in my lap.

Where?

Everywhere is the first answer. Useless and cowardly because it sounds bold while offering no instruction.

I look down at myself.

The robe is still tied. My breasts are covered by black silk. My thighs are parted around him, which I try not to think about too hard because thinking too hard has never improved a sexual awakening.

"My face," I say first.

His hand rises.

Slow.

Always slow until I ask otherwise.

He cups my cheek.

Warm palm. Callused fingers. Thumb near my mouth.

I lean into it before I can stop myself.

"Where else?" he asks.

My breath catches.

"My throat."

His gaze sharpens.

Not alarm.

Attention.

"Hand or mouth?"

My entire body lights.

I did not know a question could do that.

"Hand," I say.

His hand slides from my cheek to my throat.

Not squeezing. Not claiming. Resting. His thumb along one side, fingers on the other, the pressure so light I could pull away without effort.

I swallow beneath his palm.

His eyes flare.

Good God.

This is how people ruin their lives, isn't it? Not with grand declarations. With one hand at the throat and enough restraint to make the lack of pressure feel like a promise.

"Color?" he asks.

I blink. "What?"

"Green, yellow, or red."

"Oh."

I know the system. I have read books. I'm not new to concepts, only implementation, which feels deeply unfair.

"Green," I say.

Then, because I'm me, "Mortified green, but green."

His laugh is quiet.

"Good."

His hand remains at my throat.

I feel my pulse beat against his palm.

"Where else?"

This is what the room is doing.

Not seduction as escape.

Seduction as language class.

"Shoulders," I say.

His other hand touches my shoulder.

"Back."

His fingers move along the line of my collarbone, then around to the back of my neck.

"Waist."

His hand leaves my throat and moves down to my waist, over the silk robe.

I breathe through the disappointment.

He notices.

"You wanted my hand to stay?"

I look away.

"Dorothea."

"Yes."

"Then say that."

I glare at his chest because his face is too much. "I wanted your hand to stay."

"Good."

He returns it to my throat.

The pleasure that moves through me is embarrassing.

No, not embarrassing.

Mine.

"I also want your other hand on my waist," I say.

His mouth curves.

He gives me that too.

I sit there with his hand at my throat and his other hand at my waist, and for the first time in my life, I understand that asking is not always begging for scraps. Sometimes it is placing an order in a kitchen you trust to feed you well.

A bakery metaphor. My brain is nothing if not brand consistent.

Lucian's thumb strokes once over the pulse in my neck.

"Being desired," he says softly, "is not the same as being inspected."

The words go through me.

I close my eyes.

There's the real lesson.

Not him shirtless. Not the bed. Not the robe. Not even the heat building low in my body.

This.

"You don't know that," I whisper.

"I do."

"Because you are a fantasy."

"Because I'm paying attention."

My eyes open.

He looks at me.

Not through me. Not over me. Not at my body as separate from the rest. At me.

"The gaze that consumes asks, what can I take?" he says. "The gaze that cherishes asks, what are you willing to share?"

I stop breathing.

Lucian's hand leaves my throat and moves to my chin.

"Breathe."

I do.

Badly.

But I do.

"Do you want to share more?" he asks.

I know what he means.

The robe.

The knot at my waist.

My hands go to it.

Then stop.

"Wait," I say.

He stills at once.

The whole room seems to still with him.

"Good," he says.

I laugh, startled.

"What?"

"You stopped."

"You told me to."

"That shouldn't feel revolutionary."

"No."

"It does."

"I know."

I look down at the knot.

"I'm scared I'll hate how I look."

Lucian says nothing.

"I'm scared you'll look at me and I'll feel like a tray of pastries in a case. Like someone deciding if I'm worth buying."

His face changes.

Not pity.

Anger, maybe.

Not at me.

Good.

"I'm not here to purchase you," he says.

"I know."

"Do you?"

"Not yet."

"Then we wait."

The bluntness knocks the breath from me.

He lets go.

He takes one step back.

My body protests so fast I almost laugh.

"What are you doing?" I ask.

"Waiting."

"I didn't tell you to leave."

"No. You said you were scared. I'm giving the fear room to speak before desire answers over it."

I sit on the bed, hands on the knot of my robe, and wait.

Fear is never shy when given a microphone.

It says I'm too inexperienced. It says my body will be awkward. It says I won't know what to do with my hands. It says Lucian will see every place I'm soft, every place I'm tense, every place I have not been loved into confidence. It says Lorenzo would be worse because Lorenzo is real, and if a real man looks and finds me wanting, I will still have to see him at the bakery.

Fear says, Keep the robe on.

Desire says, Let him see.

Neither voice is quiet.

Lucian waits.

The room waits.

The chains sway.

I think of the mirror in the last chamber. The chain around my throat. The chain over my mouth. Loose. Always loose.

I take one breath.

Then I untie the robe.

Not fast.

Not dramatically.

A simple pull.

The knot gives.

The silk parts slightly.

Lucian does not move.

I slip the robe from one shoulder.

Then the other.

It falls around my waist.

My breasts are bare.

For one second, instinct wins. My arms start to lift.

I stop them halfway.

Not because I'm suddenly fearless.

Because I want to know what happens if I don't obey fear immediately.

Lucian's eyes move.

Slowly.

With permission because I gave it, because he waited, because I chose.

He looks at my shoulders first. My collarbones. My breasts. My stomach. My face again.

His expression does not become clinical.

It does not become greedy.

It becomes reverent in the same way a person might look at the first loaf of bread after a famine, which is a strange thing to think about my own breasts, but there we are.

Heat rushes through me.

Not shame.

Heat.

"You are magnificent," he says.

I make a sound that is almost a laugh. "That is a lot of word."

"It's the correct amount."

"I don't know what to do with it."

"Let it exist."

"Like a sourdough starter?"

His mouth twitches. "If that helps."

"It does, unfortunately."

He steps closer again, but slowly.

"May I touch you?"

"Where?"

His eyes warm.

"You are learning."

"Don't sound so pleased."

"I'm pleased."

That warms me too.

"My shoulders," I say.

His hands settle there.

"My back."

He draws his fingers down my spine, making me shiver.

"My waist."

His hands come to my waist.

I breathe.

"Good?"

"Yes."

"Color?"

"Green." The word feels steadier now. I lift my gaze to his. "My breasts."

Lucian goes very still.

The room heats.

"Hands or mouth?" he asks.

My thighs press together.

He notices, but does not smile.

That feels like mercy.

"Hands first," I say.

He lowers his hands slowly.

When his palms cover me, I nearly come out of my skin. No one has ever touched me there before with permission, patience, and want all in the same breath.

My body does not know what to do with that much information.

His thumbs brush lightly.

Pleasure sparks through me, bright and sharp.

My eyes close.

"Name it," he says.

"Warm."

"Yes."

"Too much."

His hands still immediately.

"No," I say quickly. "Not stop. Just, too much like... a lot. A lot much. Not bad much."

"Yellow or green?"

I breathe.

"Green. But slow."

He resumes slower.

Perfect.

Awful.

Perfect.

He learns me by degrees. The weight I like. The pressure I don't. The places that make me inhale. The places that make my hips shift before I know they are going to. Every time my body answers, he listens as if the answer matters.

Because it does.

That is the point.

It matters.

His mouth lowers to my neck.

"May I?"

"Yes."

His lips touch the side of my throat.

Soft at first.

Then warmer. Open. A slow kiss that grows hungry by careful degrees.

I feel it behind my knees.

That is new.

Absurd, but real.

My head tips back.

The hand at my breast tightens slightly, then eases. His mouth moves along my neck, tasting, learning. Not taking. Not rushing. My body floods with sensation so fast I grip his shoulders.

Bare skin.

Hard muscle.

Heat.

He groans softly against my throat.

The sound moves through me like fire.

"I like that," I say, breathless.

His mouth pauses. "What?"

"When you make noise."

He lifts his head. His eyes are dark. "You like knowing I want you."

The words should embarrass me.

They do.

They also thrill me.

"Yes."

His thumb brushes over me again, and I gasp.

"Good," he says.

The praise lands differently now.

Less like approval.

More like a hand at my back, guiding me deeper into myself.

Lucian leans forward, and I let him guide me down onto the bed. My robe slips loose around my hips. He crawls over me, but he keeps his weight braced on his forearms, careful not to pin me beneath him.

I notice.

I love that I notice.

He kisses my mouth first, then my jaw, then my neck again. The bed is soft beneath me, the sheets cool against my back, his body warm above me without trapping me. My hands move over him with growing confidence, shoulders, back, the flex of muscle under skin.

I have no idea what I'm doing.

That thought comes and goes without ruining anything.

Maybe because he does not seem to need me to know.

Maybe because I'm allowed to learn.

His mouth trails to my collarbone.

I stiffen when he moves lower.

He stops.

Instantly.

His head lifts.

"Color?"

I stare at him, breathless and half furious at myself.

"Green," I say.

He waits.

"Green, but I panicked because I knew where you were going."

"Do you want me not to go there?"

I swallow.

"No."

"Do you want me to ask again?"

"Yes."

His face softens.

"May I kiss your breasts, Dorothea?"

The directness makes my whole body pulse.

"Yes."

His mouth lowers.

The first kiss is gentle, almost sweet, placed high on my chest. Then another, lower. Another along the curve of my breast. By the time his tongue brushes over me, pleasure snaps through me so sharply I cry out.

He stops.

My hands fly to his hair.

"No," I gasp. "Don't stop."

He stills anyway.

"Say it cleanly."

I let out a frustrated breath. "I want your mouth on me. Please."

The please changes the room.

I feel it.

Not humiliation.

Not weakness.

Permission.

A full ask.

A chain slipping one link looser.

Lucian's eyes burn.

"There," he says.

Then he gives me what I asked for.

The world narrows.

His mouth is heat and pressure, his hand at my waist, the other braced beside my head. I arch before I can stop myself. My body moves with no concern for dignity. The velvet sheets twist beneath me. My breath breaks into sounds I don't recognize, soft, sharp, needy sounds that would embarrass me if I had any spare attention.

I don't.

Lucian shifts to my other breast, and I laugh once, breathless, overwhelmed by the strange fairness of being touched symmetrically.

He lifts his head just enough to look at me.

"What?" he asks.

"Nothing."

"Liar."

"I just thought, well, at least he's thorough."

Lucian stares.

Then he laughs against my skin.

The vibration nearly kills me.

"That is what you think right now?"

"I'm anxious. My mind multitasks."

"You are extraordinary."

"I'm ridiculous."

"Yes," he says, kissing me again. "That too."

The laughter does something important.

It keeps me here.

Inside my body, not above it. Inside the room, not fleeing to a list, a worry, a future disaster I can rehearse until it becomes familiar enough to mistake for safety.

Lucian moves lower, kissing the center of my chest, then my ribs, then the soft place just above my stomach.

My whole body tightens.

He stops again.

I groan. "I'm ruining the pacing."

"This is the pacing."

"That sounds fake."

"It's not."

"I'm sorry."

"No."

His voice hardens slightly.

Not at me.

For me.

"No apologies for your body's honesty."

I blink.

He kisses the spot above my stomach again.

Softly.

This time, I breathe through the tension.

The tension does not vanish.

But it makes room.

He continues down, kissing over the silk robe where it has bunched around my hips. He does not untie it further. Does not move beneath it. Does not take the opportunity just because I'm breathless and wanting.

He stops at my hip.

His cheek rests there for a second.

The intimacy of that almost undoes me.

"You are doing beautifully," he says.

My throat tightens.

"I'm lying here."

"You are staying."

The words land hard.

I close my eyes.

I'm.

Staying.

Being seen.

Being wanted.

Being touched.

Not apologizing every four seconds, which is honestly heroic.

Then he lifts his head, and the heat in his expression changes.

Darkens.

"Now," he says. "We speak of begging."

My stomach drops.

The original line from the fantasy I knew was coming, somehow. Maybe from the card. Maybe from myself.

I push up on my elbows.

The robe is loose around me. My breasts are bare. My hair is probably a disaster. My mouth feels swollen. I should want to hide.

I don't.

Not entirely.

"What about begging?" I ask.

Lucian rises over me, then sits back on his heels between my legs. He is still in his trousers. I'm suddenly very aware of that. Very aware of him. Very aware of myself.

"Begging can be a game," he says. "It can be an erotic challenge. It can be surrender."

"It can also be pressure."

"Yes."

The immediate agreement steadies me.

He places one hand on the bed beside my hip.

"In this room, begging is not humiliation unless you ask for humiliation."

"I'm not asking for humiliation."

"Then begging is something else."

"What?"

"Permission to want with your whole mouth."

My breath catches.

Lucian's gaze holds mine.

"You have spent years wanting in silence," he says. "Wanting by implication. Wanting and hoping someone else would guess correctly, so you could receive without admitting you asked."

I look away.

"Dorothea."

He touches my knee, over the robe.

I glance back at him.

"If I tell you to beg, it won't be because I require you beneath me," he says. "It will be because some part of you still believes asking fully makes you weak."

My mouth goes dry.

"And if I don't beg?" I ask.

His answer is immediate.

"Then I don't give what requires that ask."

I stare at him.

He continues.

"No resentment. No punishment. No withdrawal of care. Your no remains no. Your silence remains not yet. Your hesitation is information, not failure."

The room seems to breathe around us.

"What if I want to beg but can't?"

"Then we practice smaller asks until your mouth believes it will survive."

My eyes burn.

Again.

Apparently my body has a direct pipeline from arousal to tears, which is inconvenient but efficient.

"I thought this would be different," I whisper.

"What did you think it would be?"

"I thought once I said I wanted sex, the fantasy would just… happen."

His mouth curves. "Magic is rarely improved by skipping the work."

"I disagree on principle."

"Noted."

I laugh weakly.

He moves his hand from my knee to the bed.

"Do you want me to touch you between your legs?"

My heart slams once.

Hard.

There's no euphemism to hide behind. No poetic smoke. No "explore my depths" nonsense, thank God. Just a direct question.

Do I want that?

Yes.

No.

Yes.

Panic.

Curiosity.

Memory.

Jammie's hand. The discomfort. The silence. Running.

Lucian's hand. The waiting. The asking.

Lorenzo's thumb brushing my knuckles. My body answering before fear shut the door.

I press one hand to my stomach.

"I don't know," I say.

"Good."

I look at him sharply. "That is not good."

"It's honest."

"I'm tired of honesty being exhausting."

"You are building a muscle."

"I prefer pastry."

"You also built those muscles."

"By accident."

"No."

He is right. I did not build the bakery by accident. I built it by showing up before I felt ready, burning things, learning, trying again, ruining batches, fixing recipes, asking for help late and badly, then earlier and better.

The thought is not sexy.

It helps anyway.

Lucian's hand rests on my knee again.

"Let us find the edge," he says.

"The edge of what?"

"What you can ask for without abandoning yourself."

I breathe in.

"All right."

"Color?"

"Green."

"Boundary?"

"No penetration."

"Good."

"No hand inside me."

"Good."

I hesitate.

He waits.

"Over the lace is okay," I say, barely audible.

Lucian's eyes darken.

"Say it again."

I close my eyes.

Not because I'm hiding.

Because I'm gathering.

"I want you to touch me over my panties," I say. "Slowly. And stop if I say stop."

When I open my eyes, Lucian is looking at me like I have done something holy.

"That," he says, "was a clean ask."

Pride moves through me.

Unexpected. Bright.

My cheeks are burning, yes. My pulse is reckless, yes. My body is so awake I can feel the air between my thighs.

But beneath all that, pride.

I asked.

I did not vanish.

Lucian bends and kisses my knee through the robe.

Then higher, over silk.

Not where I asked yet.

He is giving me time to change my mind.

I know it now.

I appreciate it so much it makes me want to scream.

His fingers slide under the edge of the robe at my thigh, stopping just before they reach bare skin. He looks up at me, eyes dark with hunger and patience.

"Yes," I whisper.

Instead of his hand, Lucian lowers his head. He presses a slow, open-mouthed kiss to the inside of my thigh, then higher, breathing warm against the black lace that covers me. When his mouth finally settles over my covered pussy, the heat of it makes me jolt.

I gasp sharply and grab fistfuls of the sheets.

He pulls back immediately. "Too much?"

"No—don't stop," I say, voice shaking. "Just… slow. Please."

Lucian makes a low sound of approval and dips his head again. This time he takes his time. He kisses me through the lace—soft at first, then deeper, hotter—pressing the soaked fabric against my swollen folds with his tongue. The sensation is maddening. Wet heat, gentle pressure, the rough texture of lace dragging over my clit with every slow stroke.

I whimper, hips twitching. My body has known pleasure from my own fingers, but never like this. Never this wet, never this warm, never while being watched so intently by someone who looks like he wants to devour me.

Lucian groans against me, the vibration rolling straight through my core. "You're soaking already," he murmurs, voice rough. "Such a sweet, needy little virgin cunt."

The filthy words make my face burn with embarrassment, but my hips lift toward his mouth anyway. For a moment he just looks—hungry, reverent—then leans in and licks a long, slow stripe up my bare pussy.

I cry out, back arching hard.

He takes his time devouring me. Long, luxurious licks through my dripping folds. Swirling circles around my swollen clit. Gentle suction that makes my toes curl and my thighs tremble. Every time I get close to begging, he pulls back just enough to kiss my inner thighs or blow cool air over my overheated flesh, keeping me right on the agonizing edge.

"Please…" I finally whimper.

Lucian glances up at me, lips glistening with my arousal, eyes burning. "Please what, Dorothea?"

My face flames. The words stick in my throat.

He waits, patient and merciless, pressing the softest kiss just above my clit. "Say it. I won't let you come until you do."

The restraint somehow makes it worse and better at the same time. I squeeze my eyes shut.

"I… I'm going to come," I choke out, mortified and aching. "Please make me come with your mouth."

"Good girl," he growls, the praise hitting me like lightning.

Then he truly devours me.

Lucian seals his mouth over my clit and sucks, tongue flicking fast and firm while two fingers slide just inside me— not deep, just enough to stretch and fill the aching emptiness. He curls them gently, stroking that sensitive spot inside while his tongue works my clit in perfect, relentless rhythm.

The pleasure builds like molten sugar—thick, sweet, and unstoppable. My thighs start shaking uncontrollably around his head. My breathing turns into desperate sobs. The chains above the bed rattle softly as I writhe.

"I'm— Lucian—I'm coming—oh god—"

He moans into my pussy like my pleasure is feeding him

and doubles down, sucking harder, fucking me deeper with his tongue The orgasm rips through me like nothing I've ever felt. White-hot. Devastating. My back bows violently off the bed as I scream, thighs clamping around his head while my virgin pussy spasms and gushes against his tongue. Wave after wave crashes through me, longer and stronger than I ever imagined possible. He keeps licking me through every pulse, every shudder, drawing it out until I'm shaking and whimpering, oversensitive and dizzy.

Only when I go limp does he ease back, pressing one last soft, reverent kiss to my twitching clit before resting his cheek against my thigh. His lips and chin are shiny with my release.

I lie there panting, face burning, stunned, and fighting the ridiculous urge to laugh and cry at the same time. I cover my face with both hands, mortified by how loud I was, how wet I'm, how completely I fell apart for him.

"Well," I manage weakly.

Lucian's low, warm laugh vibrates against my skin. "Name it," he says, teasing.

"No."

"Dorothea."

I lower my hands just enough to glare at him, cheeks still flaming. "I'm not naming the aftershock of my first magic castle orgasm like it's a tasting flight."

His mouth curves. "That was specific."

"I'm a specific woman."

"Yes."

I stare at the ceiling.

The hanging chains sway.

Loose.

Always loose.

"I feel…" I start.

He waits.

"Proud," I say.

The word surprises me.

Proud.

Not ashamed. Not ruined. Not foolish. Not too late. Not broken because another person's hand touched me and my body answered.

Proud because I asked.

Proud because I stopped when I needed to.

Proud because I said please and meant give me what I want, not please let me be worthy of wanting it.

Lucian's face softens.

"There," he says.

I laugh once, shaky.

"Also mortified."

"Yes."

"And smug."

His eyebrows lift.

I nod. "A little."

"Good."

"And hungry."

The word leaves me before I can stop it.

Lucian's gaze darkens.

The air changes.

My body, traitor that it is, stirs again, softer but unmistakable.

"Hunger can wait," he says.

I sit up on my elbows, incredulous. "Excuse me?"

He smiles.

Now he looks a little wicked.

Finally.

"I said hunger can wait."

"This is my fantasy."

"Yes."

"And you are denying me again."

"I'm teaching you appetite without panic."

"That is very inconvenient for my appetite."

"I know."

I glance down his body before I can stop myself.

He is still kneeling between my legs, shirtless, controlled, beautiful, and clearly not unaffected. The evidence of his wanting is there, held in check by will that should be annoying but is instead making every thought I have less holy.

"What about you?" I ask.

His eyes return to mine.

"What about me?"

I gesture vaguely. "You are very… present."

His smile sharpens.

"Present?"

"Don't make me say things while my bones are still liquid."

"Your bones seem intact."

"You don't know that."

His hand moves to my ankle, thumb brushing once over the delicate bone there. "I'm pleased by your pleasure."

"That cannot be enough."

"For this room, it is."

"But don't you want…"

"Yes."

The answer is immediate.

My breath catches.

Lucian leans closer, bracing one hand beside my hip.

"I want many things," he says. "But my wanting is not a debt you owe."

The words hit hard.

I look away.

"There it is again," he says softly.

"What?"

"The place where being desired begins to feel like pressure."

I close my eyes.

Yes.

Because if someone wants me, then I have to decide what to do with it. If they want me and I want them, then there are stakes. If they want me and I don't answer correctly, they can be hurt. If they want me and I cannot give enough, I become the problem. If they want me and leave anyway, then wanting was not protection at all.

Lucian's fingers touch my chin.

I open my eyes.

"Desire is not an invoice," he says.

My laugh comes out cracked. "You keep saying things like you're trying to put me out of business emotionally."

"Perhaps I'm."

"I dislike how effective it is."

"Good."

I push myself upright slowly.

The robe has slipped almost completely from my shoulders. I don't immediately pull it closed. That alone feels like a victory. Lucian's eyes move over me again, warm and open, but not demanding.

Being desired is not the same as being inspected.

I'm starting to believe him.

"What would happen," I ask, "if I begged now?"

Lucian stills.

Not frozen.

Focused.

"What would you be begging for?"

I swallow.

That is the question, isn't it?

Not what does the fantasy expect. Not what would be hottest. Not what should come next according to the invisible script I have absorbed from every book, movie, joke, and overheard conversation about sex.

What do I want?

The answer is not penetration.

Not yet.

I want him, yes. I want the idea of him inside me. I want the knowledge. The experience. The shattering threshold crossed.

But underneath that, right now, I want something else.

"I want to feel more of you inside of me."

His eyes darken so quickly my pulse jumps.

"Where?"

My face heats.

I almost look away.

"Between my legs," I say.

The room seems to flare around the words.

Lucian's breath changes.

I feel it like a hand.

Then he does the worst possible thing.

He waits.

He lets the words sit.

I don't die.

Interesting.

"Is that what you want now," he asks, "or what you are proud you can say?"

Damn him.

Damn him directly.

I glare. "Both."

His mouth curves.

"Honest."

"I'm beginning to resent honesty."

"No. You are beginning to trust it."

I consider the difference.

Awful man.

"Do you want that now?" he asks again.

I listen to my body.

Still warm. Sensitive. Open, but also trembling at the edges. Curious, yes. Hungry, yes. But there's a slight pull backward too. A small need to rest inside what just happened before opening another door.

"No," I say slowly.

Relief and frustration rise together.

"No," I repeat, stronger. "Not now."

Lucian nods once.

"Good."

"But I want to want it."

"You do want it."

"I mean I want to be ready."

"You are allowed to arrive at ready slowly."

"I hate slowly."

"You own a bakery."

"That is different."

"Is it?"

I think of proofing dough. Of rushing and ruining. Of the way heat only works if the structure is ready to hold. Of how patience is not the absence of progress, but the condition that makes progress edible.

I sigh.

"I hate when my own profession betrays me."

Lucian laughs.

I tie the robe closed again, not because I'm ashamed, but because I'm done being bare for the moment. That distinction matters. I feel it in my hands as I knot the silk.

Lucian stands and retrieves his shirt from the floor.

"Don't," I say.

He pauses.

I surprise myself as much as him.

"I mean, not yet."

His smile is slow.

I lift a finger. "Aesthetic choice."

He leaves the shirt where it is.

Then he offers me his hand.

I take it, and he helps me stand.

My legs are steady enough, though only because the room has the decency not to tilt. The candles burn lower now. The chains above the bed have stopped swaying. Something in the room feels finished, though not complete.

Like a batch pulled from the oven and set to cool.

Not ready to frost yet.

But transformed.

Lucian steps back, giving me space.

"What was the chain?" I ask.

His gaze stays on mine.

"Being seen."

I nod.

"And?"

"Asking."

My throat tightens.

"And?"

His voice softens. "Believing that another person's want does not erase your own."

That one lands deepest.

I look at the bed.

At the robe.

At Lucian's bare chest.

At the place on the sheets where I learned I could ask for pleasure and survive the sound of my own voice.

Then I look toward the far wall.

A door appears there.

Not the door we entered through. A new one. Tall, narrow, black wood banded with gold. A single loose chain hangs across it, not locked. Just draped over the handle.

Behind it, I hear faint sounds.

Wind.

Distant laughter.

Something that might be music.

Or memory.

Lucian follows my gaze.

"The next room?" I ask.

"The hallway."

I don't like the way he says it. "What hallway?"

"The one with the doors you did not open."

My stomach tightens.

Ah.

Regret.

Of course.

The Devil is nothing if not thorough.

"I don't suppose there's a hallway of snacks?"

"There may be snacks later."

I walk toward the new door, then stop.

Lucian waits beside me as I glance back at the bed one more time.

Part of me wants to stay. Not forever. Just longer. Long enough to repeat what I learned until it feels less like an accident and more like a skill. Long enough to ask for the next thing and the next. Long enough to never have to walk into a real bakery with real Lorenzo and real consequences.

Lucian sees that too.

"This room will remain," he says. "But it is not the point."

"I thought The Devil was the point."

"The Devil shows you the chain. He is not the chain."

"And you?"

He smiles faintly. "I'm not the prize."

That should not sting.

It does anyway.

Maybe because I like him. Maybe because he is safe and beautiful and impossible. Maybe because fantasy is cleaner than real life, and part of me wants to curl up inside it where asking works and no one has to come by tomorrow for an Americano and lease paperwork.

Lucian touches my cheek. "You are learning for yourself," he says. "Not for me."

"And if I'm learning for Lorenzo?"

His expression shifts.

"Then learn honestly."

I swallow.

The name sits between us.

Real. Irritating. Dangerous.

"I don't know if I can do this with someone real."

"You don't know. That is not the same as cannot."

I place my hand on the chain draped over the door handle.

It's warm.

Loose.

So loose.

I lift it away.

The metal slips from the handle and falls softly to the floor.

Not a crash.

A whisper.

Lucian smiles.

"Good," he says.

This time, the word does not make me blush.

It makes me proud.

I open the door.

Beyond it waits a long hallway lined with doors, each one different, each one dark, each one quietly, patiently closed.

My body still hums from Lucian's touch.

My voice still remembers asking.

My fear is still here.

So is my hunger.

For once, I don't make either one leave.

I step through.

FIVE

"Every part of you is beautiful," Lucian murmured against my skin. His touch was demanding and tender, a weird balance that left me humming for more.

"You're a tease," I said, digging my fingers into the blanket, willing him to touch more of me.

Lucian kissed the inside of my thighs, dangerously close to my fiery center. "Tell me what you want." Laying between my legs, he placed two kisses on my belly. "Surrender to the experience and your fears."

"Surrender…" I let the thought trail off. I thought of all the times that I said no. Every time in my life, I let fear get the better of me. "Okay."

Lucian maneuvered off the bed quickly, stood, and held a hand out for me. "Lady Dorothea."

"I thought…" I sighed as a wave of disappointment washed over me. I sat up and took his hand.

Lucian's eyes darkened with desire. It was pure, unadulterated lust. "Come to me," he said, his voice a command that left no room for hesitation.

I moved to him, my body responding to his call with a fluid grace. Lucian took me in his arms, his touch possessive and still somehow tender. The contradiction did not escape me.

Lucian led me to a wardrobe. He opened the door to an

array of dresses. "You may walk out wearing nothing but panties, or you may let me pick one of these out for you."

"You're going to pick my clothes out for me?" I asked with a raised brow.

"Your boyfriend never saw your fear. You refused to show him—to be vulnerable with him," Lucian said. "Vulnerability doesn't come easy for you."

I blinked. He was right.

"I'm going to show you something. Would you prefer panties or a gown of my choosing?"

I looked down at my nearly naked body. "A gown."

Lucian flipped through the items on the rack and stopped at a burgundy gown. If you could call it that. The flowing skirt was a thin cotton. I knew it would offer little warmth. The top was a low-cut leather corset. Lucian helped me into the clothes. He laced up the back of the corset, and I was suddenly self-conscious of my breasts bubbling out the seams.

He bent to a knee and took one foot at a time, slipping shoes onto my feet, tracing the lines of my ankles.

"Do you feel it?" Lucian asked, his voice a rough whisper. He stood, letting my ankle go.

Fire licked the skin where his hand was. "Feel what?" I asked, holding a hand to my chest, as if I could calm my racing heart.

Lucian smiled instead of answering my question. "This is just the beginning, Lady Dorothea. I'm going to show you what it means to live."

"This is the hallway of secrets," Lucian said as he opened the chamber door to a long stone hallway.

We stepped into the hall. The silence was only broken by our steps and the swishing of my skirt. Every few feet, there was another chamber door. The hallway went on forever, with no end in sight.

"Where do these doors lead?" I asked, tracing a finger along one as we passed.

"They are doorways to the places you regret not going," Lucian said. "Every part of this place is designed to enhance your experience. Each room not only shows something you missed out on, but it's a different facet of The Devil Card."

"Regret doors?" I shook my head with an uncomfortable chuckle. "That doesn't sound like one of my fantasies."

"Your fantasy was to face your fears. Here are all the moments you were afraid. Every desire you were too afraid to act on, instead passing them up out of fear of the unknown," Lucian gestured with a hand.

"There haven't been that many," I said in utter disbelief.

"Pick one and I will show you."

"Why would I do that?"

"Pick one, Dorothea," Lucian wasn't asking.

I narrowed my eyes and looked at the doors. They were each a little different. Details, color, even size. One of them almost reminded me of clouds. I pointed to that door. Clouds couldn't be that bad, right?

"That one."

"Ahh, yes, this is a good one to start with," Lucian said. He walked to the door and stood waiting for me to open it. His words were a promise, a tantalizing glimpse into the future. A surge of anticipation moved through me, my desire for him growing with every passing moment.

I nodded, wondering if whatever lies behind this door would let me feel Lucian again.

"Take me," I whispered, my voice a plea. "I want you to show me everything."

Lucian's smile was pure temptation. His eyes gleamed with a predatory hunger. "As you wish, Dorothea."

I slipped a hand on the cold doorknob and opened it.

Six

Blue swallows me.

For one terrible second, there's no floor beneath my feet.

Only sky.

I gasp and reach blindly for something solid, dignity leaving my body like it was never attached particularly well. My hand finds Lucian's arm. His other hand settles at my waist, steadying me before I can tumble backward into panic, or forward into whatever nonsense this door has decided to call personal growth.

"Breathe," he says.

"I'm busy regretting choices."

"Breathe while regretting them."

"Multitasking is how I got here."

Still, I breathe.

The world steadies.

My feet are on the ground.

Not stone. Grass.

Soft, damp grass presses beneath my shoes. Morning light spills over an open field that stretches in every direction, gold and green and misty at the edges. The air smells like wildflowers, dew, warm dirt, and a kind of freshness I usually only experience when opening a bakery window before sunrise, right before the day turns into work and invoices.

Behind us stands the door.

It's alone now, upright in the middle of the field, with no wall around it. On this side, it's made of iron, black and delicate as lace, its frame twisted into shapes of clouds and feathers. Through the open doorway, I see the Hallway of Secrets, red-flamed and dark, waiting like a bad decision I already know I will have to revisit.

Then the door swings shut.

I jerk forward.

Lucian catches my hand before I can reach it.

"It will be there when you are ready to leave this place," he says.

I stare at the iron door.

It stands in the grass, closed and still.

"Ready is doing a lot of work in that sentence."

"Yes."

"I don't like when doors decide things."

"They rarely decide. They reveal."

"That is exactly the kind of sentence a suspicious door would pay you to say."

Lucian laughs softly.

It helps.

Beyond the field, a low hill rises under the blue morning sky. Sunlight pours over the crest, turning the tall grass silver at the tips. A gravel path winds up the side of it, narrow and pale, disappearing around the bend. Wildflowers crowd both sides of the path, bluebells, poppies, little white stars on thin green stems. They nod in the breeze as if they know me and are being polite about it.

I don't trust polite flowers.

Lucian is still shirtless.

That is also a problem.

The burgundy corset holds me snugly, my breasts lifted enough that I remain aware of them with every breath. The skirt is thin and light, fluttering around my legs. The shoes are soft, at least. Magic may be emotionally invasive, but it has excellent footwear.

Lucian's hand remains around mine.

I look down at our joined fingers.

"Do I need to be holding your hand?"

"No."

I don't let go. "I'm gathering data," I say.

"About my hand?" a smile plays at his beautiful lips.

We begin walking.

The gravel crunches beneath our shoes. The path curves around the hill, rising just enough that my calves notice. The air is cool but not cold. Wind slides under the loose layers of my skirt, lifting the fabric around my knees. I hold the side of it down with my free hand because I have not yet decided how much exhibitionism I'm emotionally prepared for before breakfast, even imaginary breakfast.

The hill blocks whatever waits ahead.

That is clearly intentional.

The Devil realm enjoys suspense.

Poorly behaved place.

With every step, the sound becomes clearer.

At first, I think it's thunder.

Then a giant breath.

Then a roar.

A rush of flame, low and hungry.

My stomach drops before we round the hill.

"No," I say.

Lucian looks at me. "You have not seen it yet."

"I heard it."

"You heard a burner."

"I heard aviation malpractice."

His mouth twitches.

We come around the hill.

In the open field below, tied down by thick ropes and sandbags, a hot-air balloon waits.

It's enormous.

That is the first insult.

People say hot-air balloon as if the object is whimsical. Charming. A bright little bubble in the sky. They don't mention that up close, it's a towering beast of fabric and fire, a giant striped lung attached to a wicker basket by cables, ropes, and optimism.

The balloon itself is a deep blue streaked with white clouds and gold stars. Not painted stars. Stitched ones. Each star catches the sunlight and flashes like a tiny flame. The fabric billows and breathes as hot air fills it. The burner roars again, sending a blade of fire upward into the envelope.

Heat washes across the field.

I stop walking.

Lucian stops with me.

The basket sits on the grass, rectangular and sturdy-looking, though sturdy-looking is not the same as sturdy. Wicker. Wicker is what people use for picnic baskets, laundry hampers, and chairs that betray you on porches. It's not a material that should be asked to participate in the sky.

"No," I say again.

The balloon tugs gently at its ropes.

A man stands beside the basket.

For one second, I think it's Owen.

My chest tightens.

Then I realize it's not. Not exactly. He has Owen's easy posture and sun-browned forearms, but his face remains blurred, impressionistic, a memory not fully summoned. A guide or a ghost of the moment. He checks one of the ropes, then looks toward us and smiles.

That smile hurts.

Not because I loved him.

I did not.

Not properly.

But because I recognize who I was in the memory.

A woman already braced to disappoint the invitation.

Lucian watches my face.

"Do you remember when Owen rented a hot-air balloon for the two of you?" he asks.

"I had almost managed to pretend I did not."

"Owen."

"Yes."

The blurred Owen raises a hand.

Then fades.

Not vanishing all at once. Becoming less necessary. The ropes remain. The balloon remains. The field remains.

"He was adventurous," I say.

"Tell me."

"Do I have to?"

"No."

I glare at him.

"You know that makes it worse."

"Yes."

We stand at the top of the small hill, looking down at the balloon.

The morning wind moves over us.

"Owen was nice," I say.

Lucian says nothing.

"He was funny. Intelligent. One of those people who could make ordering coffee feel spontaneous, which is frankly excessive. He did things. Skydiving. Cliff jumping. Rock climbing. Racing cars on tracks, not public roads, because he was reckless but not technically criminal."

Lucian's mouth curves.

"He liked waking up early on his days off," I continue. "On purpose. To go experience things. We dated for two months. Maybe less. I was still pretending I had time for dating then."

"Did you?"

"No." I look at the balloon. "Or yes. I could have. If I had wanted to rearrange anything."

The burner roars again.

The balloon swells.

My pulse follows.

"Owen came into the bakery with two tickets tucked into a card," I say. "A sunrise ride. He had planned the whole thing. Coffee after. Breakfast somewhere with outdoor tables. He said I deserved a morning where I was not responsible for anything."

Lucian's hand tightens once around mine.

"I told him I had a catering order." The wind lifts my skirt. I grip the fabric harder. "A small one," I admit.

Lucian waits.

"I could have prepped it the night before."

He waits.

"I accepted it after he asked."

The words taste stale.

Like bread left unwrapped.

The balloon pulls against its tethers. The basket creaks faintly.

"I didn't want to die," I say quickly, because guilt has arrived and I would like to argue with it before it makes itself comfortable. "That was not irrational. People fall. Things catch fire. Fabric rips. I have seen news stories. The basket is wicker, Lucian. Wicker. It's barely suitable for muffins."

"True."

"And Owen, bless his adventure-loving heart, was not always good at measuring danger for other people. He thought being scared meant something was worth doing. I think fear is sometimes your body reading the warranty information."

"That is also true."

I look at him.

His eyes remain steady.

He is not making me wrong.

That makes it harder to hide inside being right.

"But?" I ask.

He turns toward the balloon. "But this was not only fear of death."

I swallow.

No. "It was risk," he says. "And trust. And pleasure that had no obvious use."

My stomach tightens.

The field below blurs for a second.

"Owen wanted to give you delight," Lucian says.

I look away.

"That is a dramatic way to describe a balloon ride."

"It's an honest one."

"I did not owe him delight."

"No."

"I did not owe him a yes."

"No."

"I did not owe him proof I was adventurous."

"No."

"Then what's the problem?"

Lucian looks at me fully.

"The problem is that you wanted to say yes and let fear answer for you."

The chain under the memory.

Not refusal.

Not caution.

The moment I stopped listening to the part of me that leaned toward the sky.

The balloon waits below.

I remember Owen holding the card out, hopeful but trying not to be too hopeful. I remember the little cartoon balloon on the front. I remember thinking, For one morning, I could be the kind of person who does this.

Then I remember crushing that thought flat before it could rise.

"No," I whisper. "I don't think I wanted to go."

Lucian says nothing.

The worst thing about his silence is that it lets me hear myself.

"I wanted to want to go," I say.

The blue sky seems wider.

"I wanted to be the sort of woman who could take one morning away from work and not spend the whole time imagining disaster. I wanted to be easy. Not easy like cheap. Easy like... open. Like a window."

My throat tightens.

"Owen saw a version of me that could laugh in a basket above the fields, and I hated him for it because I could see her too."

Lucian's hand warms around mine.

"The idea was terrifying," I say.

"Yes."

"Maybe more terrifying than the balloon."

"Yes."

I look down at the basket.

It rocks gently against the ropes.

"Am I supposed to climb into that thing now?"

"Only if you choose."

"I'm getting tired of choice."

"No," Lucian says softly. "You are getting tired of noticing it."

Rude.

Accurate.

The path leads down the hill.

I don't move.

"What if it rips?" I ask.

"It won't."

"What if the burner fails?"

"It won't."

"What if the basket tips?"

"It won't."

"What if I panic and do something stupid?"

"I will hold you."

The answer is too fast.

Too simple.

I look at him.

"That was one of my questions before," I say.

"Yes."

"Will you hold me if I get scared?"

"Yes."

"Will you keep me warm if this dress proves too cold?"

His gaze drops briefly, not to leer, but because the dress is thin and the wind is making a point.

"I will do many things to keep you warm," he says. "You have my word."

My body reacts to that sentence in an extremely unhelpful way.

Lucian sees.

The corner of his mouth lifts.

"Don't," I say.

"I said nothing."

"You were about to."

"I was appreciating your body's agreement."

"My body is not an authorized spokesperson."

"It has valuable testimony."

"It's biased."

"Toward?"

I look away.

His thumb brushes mine.

"Toward aliveness," he says.

The word travels through me.

Aliveness.

Not danger.

Not recklessness.

Not bad judgment with better lighting.

Aliveness.

I want that.

The admission is soft at first.

Then louder.

I want that.

Not necessarily Owen. Not the life he offered. Not a man who thought joy required adrenaline and a signed waiver.

But the part of me that might have climbed in.

The part that might have watched the ground fall away and discovered fear had exaggerated itself for years.

I start down the path.

Lucian walks beside me.

The balloon grows larger with every step.

By the time we reach the field, my palms are damp. The basket is bigger than it looked from the hill, chest-high, lined with dark leather around the rim. The wicker is thicker too, tightly woven and reinforced with polished wood and metal. Not a picnic hamper after all. More like a small boat that has made a questionable career change.

The burner flares.

Heat blasts downward.

I flinch.

Lucian's hand steadies at the small of my back.

"Color?" he asks.

"Green," I say.

Then, "An extremely annoyed green."

"Still green."

The balloon crewman, if that is what he is, has no face now. Only hands. Strong, capable hands moving over ropes and knots. He gestures to the little gate in the basket.

I stare at it.

It's open.

Waiting.

I grip the edge of the basket.

The wicker is rough beneath my fingers.

"What if it doesn't take off because of our weight?" I ask.

"It will."

"What if it does and then we get caught in a tree?"

"We won't."

"What if the fabric rips?"

"It won't."

"What if we fall?"

"We will not."

"You cannot guarantee that."

"In this realm, I can."

"But in life, no one can."

Lucian pauses.

The pause matters.

"No," he says. "In life, no one can."

I nod once, tight.

That is the difference.

This is why I can step in with him. Because he is magic, fantasy, a guide made from desire and smoke and whatever strange power Ms. Vesper keeps behind her counter. He can say I won't die today, and the realm obeys.

Lorenzo cannot guarantee anything.

Lorenzo can only stand in my bakery with real hands and real paperwork and a real mouth, and if I step toward him, I step into a world where the balloon might rip.

That is the problem.

Lucian's gaze sharpens.

He knows where my thoughts have gone. I grip the basket harder. "I trust this because it isn't real."

The words sting.

The field grows very quiet.

Lucian's expression softens, but he does not rescue me from the truth.

"And Lorenzo?" he asks.

I close my eyes.

My body knows his name now.

The room, the hallway, this whole cursed, beautiful realm knows it.

"Lorenzo is real," I say. "That is the problem."

Wind moves across the field.

The balloon tugs upward.

My throat tightens.

"I can climb into a magic basket with you because you were built to keep me safe. You have rules. Magic has boundaries. Consent forms. Return phrases. Even your danger is curated."

Lucian's mouth curves faintly at that.

"Lorenzo is not curated," I say.

"No."

"He is messy. He flirts too much. He wants things I don't understand. He might want me because it's convenient or because the town is watching or because men like him enjoy difficult women until we become actual labor."

Lucian waits.

"He could leave," I whisper.

"Yes."

The word hurts more because he does not soften it.

"He could want me and still leave," I say.

"Yes."

"I could climb into that basket and fall."

Lucian steps closer.

"Yes."

The burner roars above us.

Heat washes over my face.

My heart pounds.

"That is living," he says. "Not because the fall is noble. Not because danger makes desire purer. But because there are choices that cannot become safe enough to satisfy fear before they are worth making."

I look up at the balloon.

The fabric swells overhead, blue and white and gold.

"This is a terrible lesson."

Lucian smiles. "I know."

"And I'm still getting into the basket."

Lucian winks at me. "There she is."

I glare. "Don't sound proud. I'm mostly doing it out of spite."

"Spite is a sturdy first step."

I climb in.

It's not graceful.

I want the record to show that personal transformation often involves getting one's skirt caught on a wicker edge while a shirtless fantasy man politely pretends not to notice.

He does notice.

He also untangles the fabric without comment.

A gentleman.

A menace.

Both.

The basket floor shifts under my weight, and my stomach flips so hard I grab the side with both hands.

"Still on the ground," Lucian says.

"I know that."

"You made a face."

"I have many faces. Some are unrelated to aviation."

He steps in behind me.

The little gate clicks shut.

The sound is small.

Final.

Lucian stands at my back, his body warm behind mine but not pressing. The basket smells like wicker, leather, sun-warmed rope, and faint smoke. A set of sandbags lies outside the edge. Ropes stretch from the basket to iron stakes in the ground.

The faceless crewman begins untying them.

One rope falls.

Then another.

With each one, the balloon pulls harder.

The basket rocks.

I make a sound I refuse to categorize.

Lucian's hands settle on my waist.

"Color?"

"Green."

Another rope falls.

The basket lifts one inch.

I stop breathing.

Then another inch.

Grass slips away beneath us.

The final rope falls.

The basket rises.

"Oh," I say. It's not a scream.

I'm proud of that.

The ground drops slowly at first, then more quickly. The grass becomes a soft green carpet below us. The gravel path thins into a pale ribbon. The iron door stands alone in the field, smaller with every second. The hill becomes a curve. The wildflowers become color.

The burner roars.

Heat blasts over my face and shoulders, sudden and enormous.

The balloon rises higher.

My stomach flips again, but it's different now. Not the sharp, cold drop of terror. Something brighter. A lift inside me that matches the lift outside.

The basket creaks.

I grip the rim.

Lucian's body comes closer, not pinning me, just standing behind me. His arms slide around my middle. Firm. Warm. Real enough.

"I have you," he says.

"I know."

"Do you?"

I look down.

The field shrinks.

The iron door is a toy.

The world widens.

"Yes," I whisper.

The balloon climbs.

The air changes as we rise. Cooler first, a soft chill brushing along the tops of my breasts where the corset leaves me exposed. Then warm again as the burner fires. Cool. Warm. Cool. Warm. The rhythm becomes almost hypnotic. Fire, lift, breath. Fire, lift, breath.

Below us, the field gives way to rolling hills. A silver river cuts through the valley, catching sunlight in bright pieces. Forest stretches beyond it, dark and dense, then opens into patchwork farmland. Tiny fences. Tiny roads. A cluster of houses with red roofs. Smoke rising from chimneys no bigger than threads.

Everything looks delicate from up here.

Even danger.

I loosen my grip.

One finger at a time.

The basket remains steady.

The balloon does not rip.

The sky does not open and drop me.

The world does not punish my yes.

A laugh bursts out of me.

Lucian's arms tighten slightly.

"What?" he asks.

"I'm not afraid."

His breath warms my hair.

"No?"

"No." I laugh again, shocked by the truth of it. "I mean, I'm aware that we are in a wicker basket suspended under a bag of hot air, which remains structurally absurd. But I'm not afraid."

The balloon drifts higher.

The wind carries us over the field.

"The idea was worse," I say.

Lucian's cheek brushes my temple.

"Yes."

"The idea was so much worse."

"Yes."

I stare at the valley below us.

The view is impossible.

Not because it's fantasy, though it is. Because no description would have convinced me of the feeling. The ground falls away, and instead of becoming smaller, I become larger somehow. My body is still mine, corseted and trembling and alive, but my mind has room. The bakery is not here. The invoices are not here. The town is not here. No one is looking through the window to see if I'm working hard enough, smiling correctly enough, wanting quietly enough.

Up here, there's only wind, flame, sky, and the pulse beneath my skin.

"It's beautiful," I say.

"Tell me."

"The river looks like sugar pulled too thin."

Lucian laughs softly.

"The fields look like uncut pastry squares. The trees look like... I don't know. Like they're keeping a secret but from a distance it seems peaceful."

"Better."

"I'm bad at landscapes. I mostly know ingredients."

"You know transformation."

I look over my shoulder at him.

His face is close.

Too close.

The wind moves his hair back from his face. Candlelight made him look like sin. Sunlight makes him look almost human.

Almost.

"Transformation?" I ask.

"Flour to bread. Sugar to caramel. Fear to aliveness."

I roll my eyes because otherwise I might melt.

"That was nearly too poetic."

"Nearly?"

"Don't get comfortable."

His smile warms.

The basket creaks.

I don't flinch.

That feels important.

The burner roars again, and heat pours over us. My back presses slightly into Lucian's chest. Not because he pulls me. Because the warmth, the height, the sudden swell of fire make me lean back without thinking.

His arms are around me.

My hands rest on the rim of the basket.

The world is thousands of feet below.

No one can see me.

The realization arrives like a spark.

No one can see me.

Not Lea through the bookstore window. Not Park with his knowing grin. Not Lorenzo across the bakery counter. Not customers. Not town gossips. Not the version of myself who stands outside every feeling with a clipboard and a concern about liability.

No one can see.

No one can judge.

No one can make my desire into gossip, obligation, performance, debt.

My body responds to that freedom with such force I inhale sharply.

Lucian stills behind me.

"There," he says.

I close my eyes.

"Don't."

"You felt it."

"Yes."

"What?"

I keep my eyes closed because the sky is too wide and he is too close.

"Freedom."

His hand spreads gently over my stomach.

"And?"

"Heat."

His mouth brushes near my ear.

"And?"

"Arousal," I say, and the word does not scrape as badly as it once did.

"Because I hold you?"

"Yes."

"Because of the height?"

"Yes."

"Because no one can see?"

My breath catches.

"Yes."

The admission burns.

Not with shame.

With wanting.

Lucian's lips touch the side of my neck.

A soft kiss.

Then another.

My body answers immediately.

I tip my head without meaning to.

He does not take advantage of it. Not yet. He lets the offered space remain offered until I say something.

"I want that," I whisper.

"What?"

"Your mouth. On my neck."

He kisses me again, open-mouthed this time.

Pleasure ripples down my spine.

The basket creaks under the shift of our bodies.

For one second, fear spikes.

Lucian stops.

His arms hold me steady.

"Color?"

"Green," I say.

"You are sure?"

"Yes." I open my eyes and look down at the tiny world. "The basket creaked. I didn't like it. But I'm still green."

"Good."

He kisses my neck again.

The basket sways gently in the wind.

Not dangerous. Alive.

That distinction matters.

His hands remain over my corset at first. One at my waist. One across my stomach. Warm. Contained. The heat between my legs builds slowly, not frantic, not demanding, but undeniable. I grip the basket rim and let myself feel the contrast. Cool wind on my face. Hot mouth at my throat. Firm arms around me. Open sky all around.

The burner roars.

Fire above.

Fire beneath my skin.

I laugh once, breathless.

Lucian's mouth pauses. "What?"

"This is absurd."

"Yes."

"I'm in a magical hot-air balloon with a shirtless Devil guide, and I'm aroused because no one can see me."

His lips curve against my skin. "That seems reasonable."

"It does?"

"Your whole life, you have been watched through expectation. Up here, there's no witness except the one you chose."

The words move through me.

The witness I chose.

I turn in his arms.

The basket is not large, but it's wider than it seemed from the ground. It gives us enough room to face each other. Lucian keeps one hand on my waist and one on the basket rim behind me. The valley drifts below us. Clouds move near enough to touch.

I look at him.

No cloak. No shirt. Wind in his hair. Sun on his skin.

"May I touch you?" I ask.

His eyes darken.

"Yes."

My hands go to his chest.

His skin is warm from the sun and the burner. His heart beats under my palm, steady but not calm. That matters too. He is controlled, not untouched. Desire is there in him, held with care.

I slide my hands up over his shoulders.

Then down again, because I can.

Because he lets me.

Because I like the way his breath changes when my nails lightly scratch over his ribs.

"Name it," he says, voice rougher now.

"Power."

His eyes flare.

"Not over you," I add quickly.

"I know."

"Power in me."

"Yes."

"That sounds like something embroidered on a pillow."

"A very good pillow."

"I would not buy it."

"You would judge the font."

"Obviously."

His laugh dissolves when I lean in and kiss his throat.

He lets out a low sound.

There.

That sound.

The one that makes me feel like my wanting has hands.

I kiss him again, lower, where his collarbone would meet the shirt if he had one. My tongue touches warm skin. Salt, smoke, sun. He tastes real enough to be a problem.

Lucian's hand flexes at my waist.

"Dorothea."

I love the way my full name sounds when he wants.

That may be dangerous information.

I lift my head.

"What?"

"If we continue, we do it with your hand on the edge of the basket."

I blink.

"What?"

He taps the wicker rim. "One hand here. The whole time."

"Why?"

"To keep you present."

I glance down at the world below us.

Then back at him.

Oh.

Not for safety.

Not only.

For the lesson.

I want to get lost in sensation. I want that. I want pleasure to take me so completely that I don't have to think about the height, the risk, the choice, the real world waiting somewhere below.

Lucian won't let this become another escape route.

"You're annoying," I say.

"Yes."

"And correct."

"Also yes."

I place my right hand on the rim of the basket.

The wicker is rough.

Real.

My left hand stays on his chest.

Lucian watches me.

"What do you want?" he asks.

I look at his mouth.

Then his hands.

Then down at my own body, the corset lifting me, the skirt whipping around my legs, the thin fabric hiding and revealing in the wind.

I want everything.

Unhelpful.

I breathe.

One ingredient at a time.

"I want your hand on my throat again."

His gaze sharpens.

"Color?"

"Green."

"Pressure?"

"Light. Like before."

His hand rises.

He touches my throat gently, fingers resting along one side, thumb along the other. Not squeezing. Holding. Letting me feel the pulse beneath his palm.

I inhale.

The basket sways.

My hand tightens on the rim.

"Good," he murmurs.

"I want your mouth on mine."

He kisses me.

Slow at first.

Then less slow because I ask for it with my mouth, with the hand on his chest, with the way I press closer while still keeping my other hand on the basket. The kiss grows hot, open, deep. His hand stays at my throat, a controlled touch that makes my knees weaken and my spine straighten at the same time.

The world drifts.

The sky holds.

I don't fall.

When he pulls back, I'm breathing hard.

"What else?" he asks.

"Your hand on my breast."

"Over the corset?"

I look down.

The leather cups me tightly, pushing me up. There's enough exposed skin to make the question feel complicated.

"Inside," I say.

He waits.

I add, "Slowly."

His mouth curves.

"Good."

He reaches with his free hand and loosens the top edge of the corset just enough to slip his fingers inside. My breath catches as his knuckles brush bare skin. Then his palm covers me, warm and firm.

I grip the basket harder.

The wicker bites lightly into my palm.

Good.

Present.

Lucian's thumb moves over my nipple.

Pleasure snaps through me.

My eyes close.

"No," he says.

They open.

"What?"

"Look."

"At what?"

"The world."

Oh God.

I turn my head.

The valley stretches below. We are higher now, the river a silver thread, the houses tiny, the fields squares of gold and green. Clouds cast shadows over the hills. The world is vast and bright and indifferent to my terror.

Lucian's hand moves again.

A slow roll of fingers.

My knees tremble.

I keep looking.

The pleasure does not shrink because I see the world.

It expands.

My body in the sky.

My wanting over the valley.

My hand on the basket. My breath in the wind. My breast in Lucian's hand. My name still mine in my mouth.

"Tell me what you see," he says.

"You are very demanding."

"Yes."

"The river."

His fingers tighten slightly.

"The fields."

His mouth brushes my shoulder.

"The door down there. It's tiny now."

"Yes."

"The road."

"And?"

I swallow.

"Possibility," I say.

The word feels too large.

So does the sky.

Lucian kisses the back of my shoulder.

His mouth travels down until the corset stops him. Then he turns me fully toward him again.

I expect him to keep going.

He does not.

He lowers to his knees in the basket.

My heart slams.

The basket is sturdy, but my hand instinctively grabs the rim with both hands.

Lucian looks up from below me.

"Color?"

"Green," I say, voice thin.

"Fear?"

"Yes."

"Desire?"

"Yes."

"Good."

He kneels in front of me, not touching.

The wind moves between us.

The balloon drifts.

"Tell me what you want," he says.

I know the answer this time.

It has been waiting since the red room.

I have already asked once, then listened to my body and said not yet.

Now my body is not saying not yet.

It's saying yes with its whole foolish self.

"I want your mouth between my legs," I say.

The words leave me cleaner than before.

Lucian's eyes darken.

"Here?"

I look down at the basket.

Here's the rewritten scene, cranked all the way up to a filthy, breathless 10 while keeping every emotional beat, her nervousness, the traffic light system, and the balloon setting intact.

"At three thousand feet in a wicker basket?" I say. "Yes."

The question isn't logistical. It's about danger. Exposure. Trust. I'm soaked because no one can see us. Because the world is tiny below. Because I chose this man as my witness.

"Yes," I breathe.

"Boundary?" Lucian asks.

"No penetration with your cock. But... fingers are allowed if I say." My voice shakes. "Mouth and fingers only. Hands stay where I can see them unless I ask. I keep one hand on the basket at all times."

His gaze darkens with heat and pride. "Understood."

"And if I say stop?"

"I stop."

"Yellow?"

"We pause and check in."

"Red?" "Everything stops immediately."

I exhale. "Green."

Lucian's hands slide up my thighs, lifting the heavy burgundy skirt with agonizing slowness. Cool wind rushes over my skin, making me shiver. My black lace panties are drenched. I can feel it, warm and slick against my swollen folds. When his eyes drop to the evidence of my arousal, he lets out a low, hungry sound that goes straight to my core.

"Don't," I whisper, embarrassed. "Don't what?" "Make me feel how wet I am."

"I'm not making you feel anything you don't already feel, Dorothea. You're fucking dripping for me."

The blunt words make my face burn, but my hips twitch forward anyway.

He kisses the inside of my thigh, then higher, teasing. When he finally presses his mouth over my lace-covered pussy, I moan loudly. The sound flies out into the open sky and disappears. He groans at the taste of me through the fabric, then hooks his fingers into the waistband.

"May I?"

"Yes."

He peels my soaked panties down my legs and tucks them safely away. The wind kisses my bare, exposed cunt and I gasp, gripping the basket rim so hard the wicker bites into my palm. Lucian spreads my thighs wider, one strong hand anchoring my hip, and looks at me like I'm the most beautiful thing he's ever seen.

"Look down," he murmurs.

I do. The valley sprawls beneath us, impossibly far away.

Then his mouth is on me.

Hot. Wet. Insistent. His tongue drags slowly through my folds, lapping up my slickness before circling my swollen clit with devastating precision. I cry out, the sound raw and wild in the open air. He feasts on me like he's starving — long, filthy strokes, gentle suction, teasing flicks that make my knees buckle.

"Color?" he asks against my dripping pussy.

"Green— fuck— green."

He slides one thick finger inside me without warning. I moan sharply at the stretch, clenching hard around him. He curls it perfectly, stroking that sensitive spot inside while his tongue works my clit faster. The dual sensation is overwhelming. My thighs start to shake.

"More?" he growls.

"Yes— please—"

A second finger joins the first, stretching me open. He fucks me with them in slow, deep strokes while sucking on my clit like it's his favorite candy. The wet, obscene sounds of his fingers pumping into my soaked cunt mix with the roar of the burner and the wind. I'm dripping down his hand, down my thighs.

"Oh god— Lucian—"

Pleasure coils tight and vicious in my belly. I'm panting, whimpering, hips grinding shamelessly against his face and fingers. The height, the exposure, the way he's devouring me while the entire world sits unaware below — it's too much.

"I'm— I'm going to—"

"Say it," he commands, fingers thrusting harder, curling relentlessly.

"I'm going to come— fuck, I'm coming—"

He growls against my clit and sucks harder, fingers pumping fast and deep. The orgasm rips through me like lightning. I scream — loud, broken, unrestrained — as my pussy spasms violently around his fingers. Hot, pulsing waves crash over me again and again. My vision whites out. My legs shake so badly I would collapse if not for his strong hands holding me up and my death grip on the basket. I gush around his fingers, soaking his hand and chin as the climax tears me apart in the open sky.

Lucian works me through every shudder, every after-shock, until I'm whimpering and oversensitive. Only then does he gently withdraw his fingers and press a soft, reverent kiss to my twitching clit.

He rises slowly, wrapping his arms around me as my skirt falls back into place. I'm still bare underneath, slick and puls-ing, the secret thrill making me tremble. I bury my face in his chest, shaking, embarrassed by how loudly I screamed and how hard I came.

"You are smug," I mumble against him.

"I'm honored," he replies, voice warm. He kisses the top of my head. "Name it."

I laugh weakly into his chest. "You have terrible timing."

"Name it, Dorothea."

I close my eyes, still catching my breath. "Alive. Exposed. Not ashamed. Powerful... and still hungry."

His arms tighten around me, and I feel his cock, hard and insistent, press against my stomach. He doesn't push. He just holds me while the balloon drifts into a bank of clouds, the mist cool against my flushed skin.

The basket creaks. The burner roars. The air smells damp and clean. Lucian stands beside me, one hand resting lightly at my back. We are inside whiteness, suspended, unseen.

A cloud is not empty, I realize.

It only looks that way from far away.

Up close, it's cold droplets, shifting air, wet light. Not solid. Not nothing. Something in between.

Like fear.

From a distance, it looked like a wall.

Inside it, it moves.

The balloon breaks through.

Sunlight explodes around us.

I gasp.

Above the cloud, the sky is bluer than anything I have ever seen. The tops of clouds stretch out beneath us like a white sea, bright and soft and endless. The balloon casts a faint shadow across them, a tiny moving shape.

For a moment, I forget Lucian. I forget the doors, Lorenzo, I even forget myself as problem, invoice, body, fear.

I look.

That is all.

Just look.

Lucian stands quiet beside me.

Good guide.

Good temptation.

Bad influence, probably.

But good guide.

"I should have gone," I say.

Not because Owen was owed it.

Not because every risk must be taken.

Because I wanted to.

Lucian nods.

"Yes."

"I'm sorry to her."

"Who?"

"The woman who almost went."

The words make my throat ache.

"She was trying," I say. "I thought she was weak for being afraid. But she was looking up, wasn't she?"

Lucian's face softens.

"Yes."

"I kept calling myself cautious."

"Yes."

"Sometimes I was."

"Yes."

"And sometimes I was chained."

"Yes."

The balloon drifts.

The clouds glow.

I think of the blue door behind us. Owen's laugh. The tickets. The morning I refused. The versions of myself I have left standing at doors, waiting for permission from a future me who never returned.

"What do I do with regret?" I ask.

Lucian rests his forearms on the basket rim, looking out over the clouds.

"You stop asking it to be a prison."

"What does that mean?"

"Regret can be a teacher."

I smile despite myself.

Lucian continues. "Regret says, look here. This mattered. This was where fear spoke louder than truth. This is the shape of a choice you may meet again."

I look at him.

"And if I don't get the same choice again?"

"You rarely do."

"Then that's depressing."

"No. You get a different door."

I look out over the clouds.

A different door.

Not Owen.

Not that morning.

Not that field.

Maybe Lorenzo in the bakery after closing. Maybe a conversation without the apron as armor. Maybe saying yes to something small before my fear has time to draft a report.

"You are thinking of him," Lucian says.

"Yes."

No defense this time.

No joke.

Just yes.

Lucian looks at me.

The sunlight makes his eyes warmer. Less black. Brown with gold at the edges.

"What's the door with Lorenzo?" he asks.

I laugh softly. "I thought we established it was black and smug."

"What choice waits behind it?"

The question opens slowly.

Not sex.

Not only sex.

Not even love.

Truth.

That is what waits behind Lorenzo's door.

The possibility of letting someone real see me wanting and scared at the same time. The possibility of saying, I don't know how to do this. The possibility of asking whether he wants me or only the usefulness of a story the town already believes. The possibility of hearing an answer I cannot control.

"I don't know," I say.

Lucian's eyes hold mine. "Liar."

"Truth," I say. The word is small. The sky is huge around it.

Lucian nods. "Yes."

"I may not open it."

"That's okay."

"Don't reverse psychology me."

"I'm not."

"You are standing there being accepting in a way that makes me want to prove something."

His smile appears.

"That is not reverse psychology. That is you being stubborn."

"Stubbornness has built civilizations."

"And bakeries."

"Exactly."

He reaches for my hand and places it over the basket rim again, beside his.

"Feel that?"

"Wicker?"

"The ground is far below."

"I had noticed."

"The basket moves."

"Yes."

"The wind changes."

"Yes."

"The burner is fire above your head."

"Yes, thank you for the safety overview."

"And still, you are here."

I look at our hands on the basket.

Mine smaller. His larger. Both steady.

"Yes."

"Danger is not always the same as harm," he says. "Fear is not always the same as wisdom. Pleasure is not always a trap."

I swallow.

He touches my chin, turning my face toward his.

"And being alive will never feel as controlled as being closed."

The words settle into me with the same terrifying gentleness as the balloon rising from the field.

Being closed had felt safe.

It had also been airless.

Up here, I understand the difference.

The balloon begins to descend.

I notice it slowly at first. The clouds rise around us. The burner fires less often. The air warms as we drop beneath the white sea, and the valley returns below us. Field. River. Hill. The iron door.

I'm disappointed.

That surprises me.

Lucian sees.

"Would you stay up here longer?" he asks.

"Yes."

"Why?"

I think of the sky, the freedom, the distance from judgment.

"Because no one can reach me."

Lucian nods.

"The Devil's temptation," he says.

I stiffen.

"What?"

"To mistake distance for freedom."

The balloon lowers.

The field grows.

The iron door waits below.

"No," I say. "That's not what I meant."

"Isn't it?"

I look down at the landscape.

Up here, no one can judge me.

Also, no one can know me.

No one can ask anything of me.

No one can touch me unless I choose them.

No one can hurt me.

No one real, anyway.

The freedom of altitude has an edge.

Stay high enough and everything becomes miniature.

Even life.

My throat tightens.

"I don't want to live in a basket," I say.

Lucian smiles faintly.

"No."

"But I needed to know the sky was real."

"Yes."

The basket approaches the field.

The faceless crewman waits below, hands on the ropes.

The landing is not smooth.

Not violent either.

The basket bumps the ground once, skids through the grass, then settles with a jolt that makes me grab Lucian's arm. He laughs as he steadies me, and I laugh too, breathless and a little wild.

Ground.

We are on the ground.

I expected relief.

I feel grief.

Not enormous. Not tragic. Just a small ache, like leaving a window open behind me.

The crewman secures the basket. The balloon sags slightly overhead, still beautiful, but less impossible now. Fabric and rope and heat. A thing that carried me and won't carry me forever.

Lucian opens the gate.

He steps out first, then offers his hand.

I take it.

When my feet touch the grass, the ground feels different.

Not safer.

More immediate.

I look back at the balloon.

The blue fabric ripples.

Owen's blurred figure appears for one second beside it.

He smiles.

Not sad. Not accusing.

Just kind.

Then he fades into morning light.

"I'm sorry," I whisper.

Lucian stands beside me. "To him?"

I think about it.

"No. To me."

The balloon dissolves.

Not all at once. The ropes go first, slipping into light. Then the basket. Then the envelope, blue and white fabric becoming sky until only the field remains. The iron door stands ahead, black and delicate, waiting to return us to the hallway.

In the grass where the basket rested lies one object.

A little paper ticket.

I pick it up.

Sunrise Flight for Two.

The ink shifts.

Not Owen's name.

Not Lucian's.

Mine.

Then the words change again.

One door opened.

The ticket warms in my hand and vanishes.

I exhale.

Lucian watches me.

"What was the chain?" I ask.

His gaze moves from the sky to me.

"Confusing safety with stillness."

The answer hurts.

"Yes," I say.

"And?"

He waits because he knows I know.

I look up.

The sky is wide.

"Believing the imagined disaster more than the actual moment."

His smile is gentle.

"Yes."

I touch the place where the ticket disappeared from my palm.

"And thinking fear means stop."

"Does it?"

"Sometimes."

"Yes."

"But not always."

"No."

The iron door opens.

Beyond it waits the Hallway of Secrets.

Red flames. Dark stone. Doors.

So many doors.

The black door with the brass handle is somewhere in there.

The Lorenzo door.

I'm not ready.

But for the first time, not ready does not feel exactly like no.

Lucian steps toward the doorway.

I don't follow immediately.

He turns.

I stand in the field, looking back at the empty sky.

"Dorothea?"

"I want one more second."

He nods.

No rush.

No push.

No taking the moment away because the lesson has been named.

I stand there and let the wind touch me.

I let myself feel the strange combination of pride, arousal, sadness, and longing. I let myself want to go back up. I let myself know I cannot stay in the sky. I let both things be true, which is becoming an irritating theme in my magical education.

Then I turn.

Lucian offers his hand.

I take it.

The moment we step through the iron door, the field vanishes behind us.

The hallway receives us with red flame and stone.

The blue cloud door stands closed now.

Across its surface, the clouds have stilled.

A loose chain lies at its base, not broken, simply lifted away and left behind.

I stare at it.

"Good," Lucian says softly.

I look down the hall.

The other doors wait.

Some whisper.

Some glow.

Some remain silent because they know silence works better.

Farther down, the black door with the brass handle sits in shadow.

Espresso.

Leather.

Bakery sugar.

Lorenzo.

I feel the pull of it now more clearly than before.

Not because I'm ready to open it.

Because I know what it is.

A real door.

A different kind of sky.

I turn away before I can think too hard.

Lucian notices.

"Not yet," I say.

"No."

"But maybe."

His smile is small.

"Yes."

The hallway stretches ahead.

The next door is not black.

It's green and gold, covered in vines and flowers, with light spilling from beneath it like late afternoon in a garden.

Warmth drifts from the seams. Not danger this time, but tenderness.

I sigh.

Lucian's mouth curves. "Ready?"

"No."

He offers his arm.

I take it anyway.

Together, we walk toward the light.

SEVEN

The green door is worse than the blue one.

    Not immediately.

    Immediately, it's lovely.

That is how it gets you.

The hot-air balloon door had the decency to announce itself as a problem. Wind. Height. Fire. A wicker basket held together by optimism and dark magic. A person could stand in front of that and say, quite reasonably, absolutely not, because the danger had dressed for the occasion.

The green door is gentler.

It stands in the hallway with flowers carved around its frame, vines curling over the lintel, little leaves etched into the brass handle. Warm light glows from beneath it, golden and soft. The air leaking through the edges smells like cedar, roses, ripe peaches, and sun-warmed earth.

Nothing about it says danger.

That is how I know it's lying.

Lucian stands beside me, his arm still offered, his expression patient in the way that has become both comforting and deeply irritating. He is still shirtless, because apparently I made one aesthetic request and the realm decided to honor it with religious commitment. The red light of the Hallway of Secrets warms his skin. His hair is wind-tangled from the balloon, and every time I look at him, I remember the sky, his mouth, and the way my own voice disappeared into open air.

I look back at the green door.

"Absolutely not," I say.

Lucian's mouth curves.

"You said that about the balloon."

"And I was correct then too."

"You opened it."

"That was before I understood how emotionally aggressive this hallway is."

"The hallway has been very clear."

"Yes. Aggressively."

The green door glows brighter, which feels smug.

I narrow my eyes at it.

"Is there a possibility this one contains a nap?"

"No."

"Snacks?"

"Yes."

I pause.

"That was quick."

"You respond well to food."

"I'm a bakery owner. Food is one of my foundational languages."

"Yes."

"But if the snacks are metaphorical, I'm leaving."

Lucian's smile deepens. "Some will be literal."

"Some?"

"This door is not about fear of risk."

"No?"

"No."

I look at the vines carved into the wood. They seem to shift when I don't stare directly at them, leaves unfurling and curling back into place. The flowers carved along the edges are not all the same. Roses. Lilies. Peonies. Poppies. Something that looks like honeysuckle. In the center, near the handle, a single open blossom has been carved with petals like flames.

"What's it about?" I ask.

Lucian looks at the door, then at me.

"Being cherished."

My stomach drops.

No.

No, no, absolutely not.

A hot-air balloon is one thing. Letting a fantasy guide kneel in a basket and teach me that fear does not always get to speak first, fine. Alarming, but manageable. Or at least survivable.

Being cherished is worse.

Being cherished means receiving with nowhere to hide. It means tenderness. It means patience. It means someone looking at the soft, private parts of you and not wanting to consume them, fix them, mock them, or use them against you.

I don't have a clean argument against it.

That is the problem.

"I don't think I have a chain about that," I say.

Lucian says nothing.

I sigh. "Could you at least pretend to believe me for morale?"

"No."

"Rude."

"Yes."

The green door waits.

Warmth spills over my shoes.

Beyond it, something chimes softly. Not a bell. Something smaller. Glass in wind, maybe. Or a spoon stirring sugar into tea.

The scent of peaches grows stronger.

My stomach answers.

Traitor.

Lucian notices.

"We can open the door and eat nothing," he says.

"That is an insane suggestion."

"It was a test."

"I failed?"

"Beautifully."

"Good."

The word slips out before I realize what I have done.

Lucian's eyes warm.

I point at him. "Don't make that face."

"What face?"

"The one that knows exactly how pleased I'm with myself for learning."

"I'm pleased too."

"I said don't."

"I'm not good at obedience."

"That is objectively false. You have followed every boundary I've named."

His expression shifts.

Not a smile this time.

Something softer.

"That is not obedience," he says. "That is respect."

The words move through me.

Small.

Steady.

Annoying in their ability to matter.

I look away first, because tenderness is already trying to get in and we are not even through the door.

"This is going to be terrible," I say.

"Yes."

"You agree too often."

"You are often correct in incomplete ways."

The green door's brass handle warms under my palm before I touch it.

I still touch it.

The metal feels alive.

Not breathing, exactly. More like holding sunlight.

"What if I'm not ready?"

"Then we don't enter."

"What if I enter and want to leave?"

"Then we leave."

"What if I enter and like it too much?"

Lucian's gaze sharpens.

There.

The real question.

The hallway goes quiet around us.

Doors behind and ahead stop whispering. Even Lorenzo's black door, farther back in the red-lit shadow, seems to hold its breath.

Lucian steps closer.

"Then we learn why liking it frightens you."

I swallow.

This is the problem with the Devil. He is not here to shame

me for wanting the wrong things. He is here to make me notice how afraid I'm of the right ones.

I turn the handle.

The door opens.

Gold light spills over us.

The scent hits first.

Flowers, yes. Too many to name. Roses and jasmine and lavender and lilacs, sweet but not cloying. Beneath that, cedar warmed by sun, ripe fruit, damp soil, and the faint clean smell of water moving over stone. The air is thick and soft, almost visible. It settles on my skin like a hand.

I step through.

The hallway vanishes behind us.

We stand at the edge of a garden.

Not a tidy garden. Not the sort with labeled beds and benches donated in memory of people named Agnes. This garden is lush, overgrown, and impossibly alive. Flowers crowd every inch of the ground, bursting in layers of color so vivid they look painted from the inside. Deep red roses climb iron arches. White lilies bend over pools of clear water. Blue irises cluster beside stone paths that don't seem to have decided where they want to go yet. Vines loop from tree to tree, heavy with purple blossoms and tiny gold lanterns.

Butterflies move through the air.

No, not butterflies.

Some are butterflies. Others are little sparks with wings. One lands on a flower near my hand, opens translucent blue wings, and vanishes into light.

"Normal," I say.

Lucian looks amused. "You expected normal?"

"No. I expected symbolic. This is symbolic with a budget."

A path forms beneath my feet.

It's not there until I take a step.

The flowers bend away without breaking, making room for a narrow strip of moss and pale stone. I look back. Behind me, the flowers rise again, untouched, pristine, as if I had not walked there at all.

I stare.

"We didn't crush them."

"No."

"How?"

"The path appears where you choose to walk."

I look ahead. No path.

I shift one foot to the left.

Moss and stone form there.

I pull back.

The path closes.

Lucian holds out an hand. "You hate evidence that choice matters." The garden seems to brighten at the sound.

We walk and the garden decides to be accommodating about it. Lucian stays beside me, no longer holding my hand. I notice the absence, then decide not to immediately reach for him.

This is about being cherished.

Not managed.

Not guided every second.

Cherished.

The word sits in me like something warm I don't yet know how to digest.

A branch dips low over the path, heavy with peaches. They are perfectly ripe, pink-gold and fuzzy, their scent so lush it nearly makes my knees weak.

Lucian reaches up and plucks one.

"Hungry?"

"Always, apparently."

He offers it to me.

I take it carefully. "Will this do something strange?"

"Yes."

I freeze.

He smiles.

"What kind of strange?"

"The kind fruit often does in enchanted gardens."

"That is deeply unhelpful."

"It will taste like a memory."

I stare at the peach.

It looks innocent.

Fruit should not have narrative ambition.

"What memory?"

"I don't know."

"That seems dangerous."

"It may be."

"Emotionally?"

"Most things here are."

I look at the peach again.

The skin is warm from the sun. A drop of juice beads where Lucian's thumb bruised it slightly when he plucked it. The scent is unbearable. Sweet, bright, summery, almost floral.

"Do I have to?"

"No."

That helps.

I take a bite.

Juice floods my mouth.

For one second, it's only peach. Soft flesh, sweetness, sun, the faint tart edge near the skin.

Then the memory opens.

I'm twelve years old, standing in my grandmother's kitchen. The window above the sink is open, and outside, bees move through the lavender. My grandmother stands beside me in a blue housecoat, flour on her cheek, teaching me how to roll pie dough without pressing all the life out of it.

Gentle hands, Dottie. You are not punishing it.

I feel the rolling pin beneath my small hands.

The counter dusted white.

Her laugh when I wrinkle my nose because the peaches are too slippery.

I taste sugar, butter, summer, and a kind of safety that existed before I knew safety could be lost.

Then the garden returns.

I stand with a peach in my hand and tears in my eyes.

"Rude fruit," I whisper.

Lucian's face softens. "What did you taste?"

"My foster mother, the good one."

He waits.

"Peach pie. Summer. Being small enough that someone else handled the rent."

A smile curves his mouth, but it's gentle.

"She taught me pastry," I say. "Not professionally, obviously. She made everything by feel and insulted measuring cups. But she taught me dough. She used to say you could feel when it was ready if you stopped trying to bully it."

Lucian's eyes warm. "I see."

I look down at the peach.

The bitten edge glistens.

"She died before I opened the bakery," I say.

"I'm sorry."

"She would have hated my croissants."

Lucian blinks.

"Not the taste," I add. "She would have said they were fussy. She distrusted laminated dough on principle."

I take another bite.

This time, it only tastes like peach. I'm thankful.

I'm not sure I could survive another ambush.

We keep walking. The garden path winds beneath cedar trees and through beds of flowers that release different scents as we pass. Some smell like real flowers. Others smell like memories I cannot quite catch. Rain on sidewalks. Vanilla batter. A clean towel warm from the dryer. Lorenzo's coffee.

I stop.

Lucian stops with me.

The scent is gone.

I look ahead, pretending nothing happened.

Lucian does not call me on it.

That is suspicious.

We pass a cluster of candles growing from the ground like white flowers. Flames burn at their tips. When I lean closer, the flames bend toward me.

"Are those candles or plants?"

"Yes."

"Wonderful."

A small flame flares bright as I pass it.

I freeze.

Lucian looks at it.

"What?"

"You thought something true."

"I think true things constantly."

"No."

I give him a look.

He nods toward the candle. "The garden hears truth. It does not punish lies, but it does not bloom for them either."

I stare at the candle.

It has returned to a steady flame.

"What did I think?"

Lucian waits.

I rewind my own mind, which is not a task I recommend.

Lorenzo's coffee.

The scent in the garden.

I thought, I want him here.

The candle flares again.

Heat rushes up my throat.

"Oh, come on."

Lucian's mouth curves, but his eyes are too sharp.

"You wanted Lorenzo here?"

"No."

The candle gutters.

Not out.

But lower.

I sigh. "Fine. Yes. For half a second."

The flame rises again.

"This garden is invasive."

"It rewards honesty." Lucian offers his arm.

I take it, mostly because the garden has become too interested in my thoughts and I require moral support.

The path curves around a pond.

Water lilies float on the surface, white and gold. In the center, a fountain spills from a stone figure. Not an angel. Not a cherub. A woman holding two bowls, one tilted toward the water, one toward the flowers at her feet.

"Wrong card," I say.

Lucian follows my gaze.

"The Star is never fully absent from a place of healing."

"I pulled The Devil."

"Yes."

"Is this a crossover episode?"

He laughs.

The fountain water catches the light. For one moment, the surface reflects not my face, but the black door from the hallway. Lorenzo's door.

Then the water ripples, and my reflection returns.

I decide not to comment.

Mostly because the candle flowers nearby look eager.

At the far end of the garden, a gazebo waits.

It's built from cedar, intricately carved, warm honey-brown under the late-afternoon light. Vines climb the posts, heavy with white flowers that look like stars. The roof is open in the center, letting sunlight spill down onto a blanket spread across the floor. Pillows in deep jewel colors are scattered around. A low tray holds food.

Actual food.

Praise be.

Fruit. Chocolate. Little honey cakes. Cheese. Bread. A silver pot of something steaming. Two glasses of dark red wine. Candles of every size surround the blanket, their flames steady in the golden air.

It's beautiful.

Not dangerous-beautiful like the castle chamber.

Not exposed-beautiful like the balloon.

This is sanctuary-beautiful.

That is harder.

The gazebo reminds me of one back home, a little.

Not in Coral Cove. At the botanical garden two towns over, where I went once alone on a Monday because the bakery was closed and I could not stand the apartment. I sat in a cedar gazebo for forty minutes watching a couple take engagement photos near the roses. I remember feeling foolishly sad, then angry at myself for being sad, then buying a terrible scone from the cafe out of spite.

This gazebo smells like cedar too.

I inhale.

Despite myself, I smile.

Lucian sees it.

"What else brings a smile to your lips?" he asks.

The question is gentle.

The candles flicker.

Truth garden, I remember.

I could say peaches. The cedar. The ridiculous butterfly sparks. Food that appears without menu costing.

Instead, the answer arrives before I can protect myself from it.

"The thought of you," I say.

The candles flare.

Lucian stills.

Heat rises to my face.

"I mean, as a general feature of this experience," I add.

Several candle flames shrink.

"Stop doing that," I tell them.

Lucian laughs.

I glare at him.

"You enjoy this."

"I enjoy your honesty fighting for its life."

"That is very unkindly phrased."

"But accurate."

We climb the gazebo steps.

The wood is warm under my feet. The blanket is soft when I lower myself onto it. Lucian sits beside me, not too close, which is the problem and the relief. My body wants closeness. My mind wants the room to breathe. Lucian keeps offering both.

A sanctuary, he had called it.

Or maybe the notes did.

No, this place called itself that without words.

"This place is special," Lucian says.

"Everything here is special. Even the grapes were over-achievers."

"This place is a sanctuary."

I look around.

The flowers lean in at the edges of the gazebo. Not watching, exactly. Listening. The candles wait. The food smells impossible. The garden hums with birdsong and distant water.

"A sanctuary from what?"

"Performance."

My chest tightens.

Lucian reaches for a fig from the tray and splits it open with his thumbs. The inside is dark red and glossy.

"Do you want one?"

"Will it taste like another emotionally loaded memory?"

"No."

I take half.

It tastes like fig. Sweet, seedy, soft.

Good.

I eat the whole half quickly enough that Lucian looks amused.

"What?"

"You were hungry."

"I had magical sky sex-adjacent activities and no lunch."

"Sex-adjacent?"

"You know what I mean."

"I do."

"Don't make me define the categories."

"I would enjoy that."

"I know. That's why I won't."

He hands me a honey cake.

I take it.

The cake is small, golden, sticky with honey and scattered with pistachios. I bite into it, and this one does not taste like a memory either. It tastes like butter, almond, orange blossom, and a level of tenderness I resent from a pastry I did not bake.

"It's good," I say.

"Good? You are difficult to impress."

"I'm a professional."

"You are smiling."

"I smile at competent crumb structure."

"You are flushed."

"It's warm."

"It's not."

I take another bite to avoid answering.

Lucian reaches for the pot and pours tea into two small cups. Steam rises, scented with mint and something floral.

I eye it.

"No magical transportation tea?"

"No."

"Trauma tea?"

"No."

"Truth serum?"

"The garden handles truth without assistance."

"Unsettling."

I take the cup anyway.

The tea is light and sweet, cooling on the tongue in a way that makes my body slowly realize how tired it is.

Not exhausted.

Open.

There's a difference.

The hot-air balloon left something in me humming. The red room before that left something awake. Now, sitting in this golden garden, eating honey cake beside a half-naked Devil guide who is somehow less alarming when surrounded by flowers, I feel all the things I have been avoiding stack themselves gently in my chest.

Desire.

Fear.

Gratitude.

Lorenzo.

There he is again.

Lucian says nothing.

I sigh. "You can ask."

His eyes meet mine.

"Can I?"

"You were going to."

"I was waiting."

"Politely invasive."

"Yes."

I set down my tea.

"This is where I think about Lorenzo, isn't it?"

The candles flare.

"Apparently," I mutter.

Lucian leans back on one hand, watching me.

"Tell me why."

"Because this place is safe."

"Yes."

"And because that makes me think of unsafe things."

"Unsafe?"

"Real things."

He waits.

A bird sings somewhere beyond the flowers, bright and careless.

"I want him in my bed," I say.

The candles flare so dramatically I jump.

"Oh, for God's sake."

Lucian's eyes darken, but he stays quiet.

The truth is out now.

No point trying to stuff it back in like overproofed dough.

"I do," I continue. "I want him in my bed. I want his hands on me. I want to know what he looks like when he stops being charming and starts being honest. I want to know if he says my name like that when he's losing control."

The gazebo grows warmer.

My voice shakes, but I keep going because the garden rewards truth and because I'm tired of every room in my life being built from unfinished sentences.

"And I don't trust him."

The flames steady.

Lucian's expression is unreadable.

"Why?"

"Because historically, Lorenzo is untrustworthy."

"How?"

"He flirts with everyone."

"That is behavior, not proof of harm."

"He has a reputation."

"Does he?"

"Yes."

"With whom?"

I open my mouth.

Close it.

People talk.

Coral Cove is made of salt air, artisan signage, and gossip. Lorenzo De Luca's name has moved through the town attached to women, rumors, late nights, smiles, and more than one story told with laughter over wine. But when I try to pin down a specific cruelty, it slips away.

"He doesn't do real," I say.

"Does he say that?"

"No."

"Did he tell you he cannot be trusted?"

"No."

"Did he treat you carelessly?"

I think of his hand over mine at the business meeting. His

voice when he noticed I had not eaten. His folder of lease paperwork. The way he kept showing up to discuss things I avoided.

"No," I say, irritated.

Lucian nods.

"Then what are you afraid of?"

"He could," I snap. "He could be careless. He could want the chase and not me. He could enjoy the fake relationship because it's convenient. He could make me feel like I'm special while the town watches, then walk away when it becomes real."

The candles flare, but this time they tremble.

Not because of the truth.

Because I do.

Lucian's voice is quiet.

"You are not afraid Lorenzo will want you."

I glance at him.

He holds my gaze. "You are afraid he will want you and still leave."

The garden goes still.

No birdsong. No wind. No water. Even the candles seem to freeze with their flames raised in perfect points.

The words enter me like a blade warmed over fire.

Precise.

Cruel only because they are true.

I look away.

A vine near the gazebo curls around one post and blooms, white flowers opening one by one.

"That's not fair," I say.

"No."

"You don't know him."

"No."

"You don't know me with him."

"I know you with the thought of him."

I laugh once, sharp. "And?"

"And you are more afraid of the real man than of any fantasy because he can choose differently than you want."

My throat tightens.

Yes.

There.

That is the part fantasy cannot replicate.

Lucian may tease, delay, deny, challenge, and strip me down to every last hidden fear, but he won't leave unless the realm requires it. He won't wake up tomorrow and decide I'm too complicated. He won't walk into Knead the Dough and order an Americano like his hands have never touched me. He won't make me risk seeing him in town with someone else after I have let him see me hungry.

Lorenzo can.

Any real person can.

"That is the real chain," I whisper.

Lucian does not answer for me.

"I thought the chain was sex," I say.

"Sex is one door."

"And this?"

"Being cherished."

I look around the gazebo.

The pillows. The food. The cedar. The candles that flare at truth. The flowers that make a path where I choose to walk.

"A person can cherish you and still leave," Lucian says.

I flinch.

His face softens, but he keeps going.

"They can love you and still fail you. Want you and still choose badly. Stay and still hurt you. Leave and still have meant every word."

"That is a terrible sanctuary speech."

"Yes."

"I preferred the honey cake."

"So did you want a sanctuary," he asks, "or another beautiful cage?"

I stare at him.

A sanctuary that promises no one can hurt me is not sanctuary.

It's fantasy.

A real sanctuary is a place where I can tell the truth, hear the truth, feel the fear, and remain.

"You're teaching me tenderness by making me think about heartbreak."

"Tenderness without risk is decoration."

"Lucian?"

"Yes?"

"Could you please say one less devastating thing?"

He considers.

"The figs are excellent."

I laugh.

The sound breaks the stillness.

Birdsong returns. The water resumes. The candles flicker as if relieved.

I wipe beneath one eye with the back of my hand.

"If I can't trust that someone will stay, how am I supposed to let anyone in?"

Lucian leans closer.

"By learning to trust yourself to survive the answer."

I close my eyes.

That might be the worst one yet.

Not trust him.

Not trust the relationship.

Not trust the outcome.

Trust myself.

To ask.

To hear no.

To hear yes.

To be wanted.

To be left.

To say stop.

To say more.

To say this hurts.

To say I need you to be clear with me.

To say, I don't know how to do this, but I want to try.

The chain is not around Lorenzo's throat.

It's around my own hands.

I look down.

No visible chain.

But I feel it.

A small tightening when I imagine texting him. When I imagine letting the fake relationship conversation become a real one. When I imagine saying, Tell me what this is to you, because I cannot keep pretending I don't care.

"I don't know how," I say.

Lucian's gaze softens.

"Then we practice."

My body hears that word in the context of him and the blanket and the candles and immediately becomes less philosophical.

Lucian notices.

His mouth curves.

"Communication," he clarifies.

"I knew that."

"Did you?"

"Eventually."

He shifts closer on the blanket.

Not touching yet.

Good.

I need the moment before touch now. I need the ask. I need the space where I can decide.

"In this sanctuary," he says, "you will ask for what you want and need clearly. Small things first."

My heartbeat changes.

"Small things," I repeat.

"Yes."

"What if I ask wrong?"

"You revise."

"What if I don't know?"

"You say that."

"What if I ask for something and it's too much?"

"I say so."

That startles me.

"You can say no too."

"Yes."

"I know that."

"Do you?"

I look at him.

Lucian smiles faintly.

"I'm a guide, Dorothea. Not a vessel for every desire you are brave enough to name. My no matters too."

That lands somewhere important.

Consent is not a one-way offering made to protect me. It's the structure of the whole room. The whole realm. The whole experience. My desire does not become righteous simply because I finally said it out loud.

Good.

That means desire can be honest without becoming hunger with a crown.

I nod.

"All right."

Lucian sits fully facing me.

"Ask me for one touch."

My mouth goes dry.

After everything, after his hands, his mouth, the balloon, the orgasm I sent into the sky, this should be easy.

It is not.

That proves the point.

"One touch," I say.

"One."

I think.

The obvious answer is kiss me.

The deeper answer is hold me.

The dangerous answer is both.

"Kiss me," I say.

"How?"

I close my eyes for half a second.

Specific.

"Softly."

His expression warms.

"Where?"

I blink. "My mouth?"

"Is that a question?"

"No." I breathe. "Kiss me softly on the mouth."

He leans in.

The kiss is exactly what I asked for.

Soft.

Not teasing. Not hungry. Not asking for more than I offered. His lips brush mine like a promise to keep the shape I gave him. Warm, gentle, brief.

He pulls back.

I'm shocked by how much the brevity affects me.

He did exactly what I asked.

Nothing more.

Something inside me steadies.

"Again?" he asks.

I swallow.

"Yes."

"How?"

"Softer."

His eyebrows lift slightly.

"Yes," I say, firmer. "Softer. Slower. And touch my face."

Lucian's hand comes to my cheek. His mouth returns.

This kiss melts.

Slow, soft, his thumb near my jaw, his breath mingling with mine. I feel my body lean toward more, but he keeps the kiss inside my words.

When it ends, I'm breathing harder.

"Good?" he asks.

"Yes."

"What did you learn?"

"That I like being obeyed."

His laugh is low.

The candles flare.

I laugh too, embarrassed but not ashamed.

"Good," he says. "Again. Ask."

I consider.

"Tell me I'm safe."

Lucian's face changes.

The garden grows quieter.

"I'm safe," I add quickly. "I know that. I mean, I want to hear it."

He nods.

Then he reaches for both my hands, giving me time to pull away.

I don't.

He holds them between us.

"You are safe with me," he says.

My throat tightens.

The candles brighten.

"You are safe to want. Safe to stop. Safe to change. Safe to ask for more and safe to ask for less. You are safe to be embarrassed and still be desired. You are safe to be uncertain and still be here."

My eyes fill.

"That was more than I asked for."

"Yes."

"Did I need it?"

"Yes."

"Annoying."

"I know."

I grip his hands.

"Again," I whisper.

He says it again.

Shorter this time.

"You are safe with me."

I breathe.

The words don't erase all fear.

They give it a chair in the corner and tell it to sit down.

"My turn?" Lucian asks.

"You ask me for something?"

"Yes."

That makes me more nervous than I expect.

"All right."

"Let me see you."

Heat flushes through me.

"You have seen me."

"Parts. Moments. Defenses. I'm asking now."

"What does that mean?"

"Take down your hair."

My hand flies to my hair instinctively.

It's already loose from the balloon wind, half tangled, half pinned by some magic that has given up on updos. But I understand the ask. Not nudity. Not sex. Something smaller and weirdly more intimate.

My hair in the bakery is always up. Bun. Clip. Braid. Practical. Contained. Out of the dough.

Lorenzo once watched me pull a pencil from it during a meeting, and the whole mess fell around my shoulders. He stopped speaking mid-sentence. I made a joke and twisted it back up so fast I nearly hurt myself.

"Why?"

Lucian's gaze stays steady.

"Because you hide when you are soft."

The candles flare.

Rude flowers. Rude candles. Rude garden.

I reach up.

One pin.

Then another.

My hair falls around my shoulders, messy from wind and heat and his hands. I don't smooth it.

Lucian looks at me.

Not my breasts. Not the corset. Not my mouth.

Me.

"Beautiful," he says.

The word is simple.

It does not feel like a performance.

I swallow.

"Thank you."

The candles flare bright enough that I laugh.

"Apparently I meant that."

"You did."

I touch my hair, then lower my hand.

"Ask again," he says.

I look at him.

This is becoming easier.

Not easy.

Easier.

"I want you closer."

"How close?"

I glance at the pillows.

"Sit behind me."

His eyes warm.

He moves, settling behind me with his legs on either side of mine, his chest near my back but not touching yet.

"Like this?"

"Closer."

His chest touches the back of my corset.

I inhale.

His arms come around me loosely, waiting.

"Arms around me," I say.

He does.

Warm.

Solid.

Not demanding.

I lean back.

"Good?" he asks.

"Yes."

"What else?"

"Don't tease me yet."

His body stills behind mine.

Then he laughs softly against my hair.

"That was excellent."

"It was necessary."

"Did you expect me to tease?"

"Yes."

"Did you want me to?"

"Eventually."

"But not yet."

"Not yet."

"Good."

I close my eyes.

We sit like that for a while.

No escalation. No lesson announced. No door opening under my feet. Just Lucian behind me in a cedar gazebo, flowers around us, candles flickering, the fountain whispering somewhere beyond the trees. His hands rest over my stomach. Mine settle over his. The corset keeps me upright, but his body lets me rest.

Cherished.

The word arrives again.

This time, I don't push it away so hard.

"This is harder," I say.

"Than the balloon?"

"Yes."

"Than pleasure?"

"Yes."

"Why?"

"Because pleasure can be explained away as chemistry. Heat. Touch. Nerves. A body doing what bodies do."

"And this?"

"This asks something of me after."

Lucian's thumb moves lightly over my hand.

"What?"

"To believe I deserve it."

The candles flare.

I laugh once, shaky. "Yes, yes. Very truthful. Calm down."

Lucian kisses the top of my head.

I did not ask for that.

I also don't mind.

But the lesson is communication.

So I say, "That was okay."

His arms tighten once.

"Thank you for telling me."

I smile.

Small.

Proud.

The garden path beyond the gazebo shifts, opening toward a bed of dark red flowers.

Somewhere far away, a door whispers.

Lorenzo.

This time, I don't pretend I did not hear.

"I don't know what to do about him," I say.

Lucian rests his chin near my hair. "No?"

"No. I know what to do with fake. Fake is easy. We have terms. Public affection as needed. Festival optics. Business overlap. Smile at town events. Hold hands when his ex is watching. I can do fake because fake has rules."

"Yes."

"Real has too many variables."

"Yes."

"I don't know what he wants."

"Ask."

I make a disgusted sound.

Lucian laughs.

"I know."

"You make it sound so simple."

"It's simple. It's not easy."

"What if he says it was all strategy?"

"Then you will know."

"What if he laughs?"

"Has he been cruel to you?"

"No."

"Then why choose that fear?"

I sigh.

Because fear is cheap and always in stock.

Because if I imagine the worst first, I can pretend I'm prepared.

Because wanting him without knowing if he wants me back feels like standing in a balloon basket, watching the ground fall away.

Because if he does want me, the risk does not disappear.

It gets bigger.

"What if he says yes?" I ask.

Lucian's arms still.

There.

The real terror.

"What if he says yes," I continue, "and I have to become someone who can accept it? What if he looks at me the way you do, and I can't turn it into fantasy because he's standing in my bakery with coffee and lease paperwork? What if I want him and he wants me, and then I have to be a person with needs in front of someone who can remember them tomorrow?"

The garden goes quiet.

Lucian's voice is low.

"Then you practice."

"With him?"

"With yourself first. Then with him, if he earns the room."

I turn slightly to look at him.

"If he earns it."

"Yes."

"That matters."

"Very much."

He shifts, allowing me to turn fully in his arms. Now we face each other, knees touching, the tray of food beside us, candles around us like tiny witnesses.

"Lorenzo is real," Lucian says. "That means he can disappoint you. It also means he can answer you in ways I cannot."

I blink.

That hurts.

"Because you're fantasy."

"Yes."

"Mercy with abs."

His mouth curves. "Among other things."

"But he might choose me."

"Yes."

The truth settles.

Lucian does not feel less real because of it.

But he feels different.

A guide.

Not the prize.

I have known that in theory. He said it in the hallway. But here, in the sanctuary, with honey on my tongue and his warmth around me, I understand the temptation more clearly.

Staying with Lucian would be easy.

I look at Lucian. "I want to practice more."

His eyes darken gently.

"Then ask."

I take a breath.

"Kiss me again."

"How?"

"Slow first. Then deeper if I touch your neck."

"And if you don't?"

"Keep it slow."

His smile is small and proud.

"Yes."

He kisses me. Slow. I let it stay there for several breaths. Soft. Warm. Safe. My hands rest on the blanket. His touch stays at my face. I can feel desire beneath the gentleness, but it does not crowd me.

Then I lift one hand to his neck.

His mouth deepens. Exactly as I asked. The pleasure of being understood is almost sharper than the kiss itself. I make a small, helpless sound against his lips. He keeps the kiss deep until my hand falls away. Then he slows again. Perfectly.

I pull back, breathless.

"That was…"

"What?"

"Addictive."

The candles flare. Lucian laughs softly. "Good."

"I want your hand on my waist."

He gives it.

"Other hand in my hair."

He gives it.

"Not pulling."

His fingers slide into my hair, gentle.

"Good."

"I want you to tell me what you want," I say.

He stills. There. Not expected. I feel the shift in him—small but real. His gaze holds mine.

"Do you?"

"Yes."

"Why?"

"Because I don't want to practice only receiving. I want to practice hearing desire without turning it into an obligation."

The candles flare so bright the gazebo glows.

Lucian's eyes darken. "Beautiful," he says. He inhales slowly. "I want to lay you on this blanket. I want to take my time with your body until you stop reaching for the next fear and stay inside the pleasure I'm giving you. I want your hands in my hair again. I want your voice, clear and unashamed. I want your mouth on mine when you come."

My breath catches.

"And," he continues, voice rough, "I want you to tell me no the moment no is true."

That last sentence cracks something open inside my chest. Not less desire. More trust. My throat tightens.

"That was a good answer."

"I tried."

"You did."

"I still want to see all of you," I say.

His mouth curves. "That was from the earlier version of this door."

"What?"

"Nothing."

I narrow my eyes. The garden hums innocently. Suspicious.

"I want to be naked with you," I whisper. "Not because we're rushing. Because I want there to be nothing between us for a little while. And I want to see you too."

Lucian's gaze goes molten.

"Color?"

"Green."

"Boundary?"

I think carefully, heart hammering. "No penetration unless I ask for it later. Touch. Kissing. Hands. Mouths if I ask. I want to touch you too… but I might get scared."

"Then you tell me."

"And if you need me to stop?"

"I tell you."

I nod. The candles burn steady.

Lucian reaches for the lacing of my corset. "May I?"

"Yes."

He unlaces me slowly, reverently. The leather loosens, then slips away. Cool garden air kisses my bare breasts and I shiver. He moves closer without being asked, sharing warmth.

The skirt comes next. I lift my hips; he slides the fabric down and folds it neatly. He leaves my black lace panties on for now. I notice. I'm grateful.

I reach for his trousers with trembling fingers. My face burns as I loosen the ties and push them down. He steps out, fully naked.

My brain short-circuits.

He is thick, heavy, hard—rising proud from dark hair, the head already glistening. Not porn-star impossible, but real. Intimidating. Intimate. This is a man who wants me. This is a cock that could be inside me. The thought sends equal parts terror and raw want flooding through my body.

"May I touch it?" I ask, voice small.

"Yes."

I wrap my fingers around him. He's burning hot, velvet skin over steel. He twitches in my palm. Lucian's breath catches sharply.

"You like that," I whisper.

"Fuck yes."

I stroke him experimentally, learning the weight, the texture, the way his hips twitch when I swipe my thumb over the head. Power and vulnerability twist together in my chest. He's letting me explore. He's trusting me with his desire.

"How is this supposed to fit inside me?" I blurt out. "It's so…"

Lucian's mouth curves, but he doesn't tease. "We don't have to answer that today."

The gentleness undoes me. "I want to answer it eventually."

"Then eventually, we will."

That word—eventually—settles something deep inside me. Time. Safety. Choice.

I stroke him a few more times, mesmerized by the way he thickens in my hand, until the ache between my own legs becomes unbearable. I let go.

Lucian pulls me down onto the blanket with him. For long minutes there is only skin, warmth, and slow kisses. His body is solid against mine—hot, heavy, careful. When I ask, he settles more of his weight on me. The press of him makes me sigh from the center of my bones.

"Come over me," I whisper.

He braces above me. I wrap one leg around his hip, then hesitate. Fear spikes—sharp, old, foster-care sharp.

He pauses instantly.

"Keep going," I say. "I got nervous."

"Do you want to stop?"

"No. Tell me I can take my time."

"You can take all the time you need, Dorothea."

His mouth moves down—neck, collarbone, breasts. He sucks one nipple deep, then the other, using teeth when I beg for it. I moan without shame, fingers twisted in his hair. His hand slides between my legs.

"I want your hand beneath the lace," I gasp.

He peels the panties down slowly and settles between my thighs. First his fingers, then his mouth. He eats me like he has all night—long, filthy licks through my folds, sucking gently on my clit, sliding one thick finger inside me and curling it just right. I come on his tongue with a broken cry, pulsing around his finger while he praises me softly against my soaked pussy.

When the tremors fade, I pull him up and kiss him, tasting myself. My heart is racing.

"I want you inside me," I whisper against his lips. My voice shakes. "I'm terrified... but I want it. I want you."

Lucian stills, searching my face. "Color?"

"Yellow-green. I'm scared. But I want this. Slow. Stay with me."

He kisses me deeply. "Always."

He reaches down and notches the thick head of his cock against my entrance. The blunt pressure makes me tense. He doesn't push. He just rests there, letting me feel him.

"Breathe," he murmurs. "Tell me when."

I breathe. Again. Again. The fear is loud—memories of hands that didn't ask, homes that weren't safe—but his voice is louder.

"Now," I whisper. "Slow."

He presses forward. Just the head slips inside. The stretch burns—sharp, intense. I gasp, hands flying to his shoulders.

"Color?"

"Yellow. Stay. Don't move yet."

He holds perfectly still, buried barely inside me, forehead pressed to mine. "You're doing so well. So fucking tight and perfect. I've got you."

The burn slowly melts into a deep, aching fullness. My body softens around him, inch by careful inch.

"More," I breathe.

He sinks deeper. Another inch. Another. The stretch is overwhelming. I feel every ridge, every vein. When he's finally seated to the hilt, we're both shaking. I'm so full I can barely think. Tears slip from the corners of my eyes—not from pain, but from the sheer intimacy of it.

"Dorothea?" His voice is rough with restraint.

"Green. I'm so full… it's a lot. Move. Slow."

He pulls back and slides in again. Gentle. Deep. The drag of him against my walls sends sparks through every nerve. Fear and pleasure twist together until I can't tell them apart. I wrap my legs around him and hold on.

"Talk to me," I beg.

"You feel incredible," he groans. "Hot. Wet. Gripping me like you never want me to leave. I want to live inside this perfect virgin cunt."

The filthy words make me clench around him. He curses softly and keeps the slow, steady rhythm I need. Every thrust pushes me open a little more. Every thrust teaches my body it can trust this.

I start meeting his movements. The pleasure builds differently this time—deeper, fuller, almost too intense. My nails dig into his back.

"Harder?" he asks.

"A little."

He gives it. The wet sound of his cock sliding into my soaked pussy fills the gazebo. I moan shamelessly, lost in the feeling of being taken, being filled, being wanted so completely.

"I'm close," I gasp. "Don't stop—please—"

"Come for me, baby. Let me feel you come on my cock for the first time."

The orgasm crashes over me like a wave. I cry out, back arching, pussy clamping down hard around his thick length as pleasure rips through me in long, shuddering pulses. Lucian fucks me through it, steady and deep, groaning my name like a prayer.

When I finally go limp, trembling, he slows but doesn't pull out. He kisses my tears, my forehead, my swollen lips.

"Still with me?"

"Yes… I want you to come too."

He searches my face. "Inside?"

"Inside. Please."

Lucian's control finally frays. His thrusts grow deeper, harder, more urgent. I hold him tight as he chases his pleasure, whispering filthy praise and sweet reassurance against my neck. When he comes, he buries himself to the hilt and groans long and low, pulsing hot and deep inside me. The feeling of him filling me triggers another smaller, trembling orgasm.

We stay locked together, breathing hard, hearts hammering against each other.

After a long while he eases out gently and pulls me into his arms. I curl against his chest, tears falling again—this time from raw, overwhelming relief and something that feels dangerously like joy.

"You okay?" he asks, voice soft.

"I'm… alive. Scared. Full. Not ashamed." I pause. "Safe."

He kisses my hair. "Good."

The candles glow warm around us. The garden hums. For

the first time in my life, my body feels like it belongs to me—
and like it can belong to someone else without disappearing.

"The figs were literal."

"Small mercy."

We lie together for a while.

No rushing.

No new door.

No immediate question.

Lucian feeds me another honey cake with his fingers,
which is absurdly intimate and also efficient, because I'm
starving. I eat it in two bites. He looks delighted. I refuse to be
ashamed of requiring calories after emotional and sexual
development.

At some point, I ask him to lay his head in my lap.

He does.

That surprises me. Not that he agrees, but how it feels. His
dark hair across my thighs. His face turned toward the flowers. My fingers moving slowly through his hair. A guide resting. Temptation made quiet.

This is not only receiving.

This is offering without disappearing.

I like that.

"You're thinking," he says.

"I'm petting you like a dramatic cat. Let me have silence."

He laughs.

I smile.

The garden hums.

Then, after a while, the question returns.

Not from Lucian.

From me.

"What if I ask Lorenzo what he wants and he answers
honestly?"

Lucian's eyes open.

He looks up at me from my lap.

"What if he does?"

"What do I do?"

"You listen."

"That sounds too small."

"Most brave things are smaller than people expect."

I think of the balloon lifting inch by inch.

The path appearing one step at a time.

The kiss soft, then deeper only when I touched his neck.

Small things.

"I don't know what I want from him," I say.

Lucian's gaze stays steady.

"Yes, you do."

The candle nearest us flares.

I sigh.

"Yes. I do."

"Say it."

My throat tightens.

"I want the fake part to stop being the only part we admit to."

The garden brightens.

"I want him to tell me whether he wants me or the convenience of us. I want him to stop flirting around the truth and say something useful for once in his beautiful, infuriating life."

Lucian's smile grows.

"And I want to tell him I'm inexperienced before he finds out in a way that makes me want to flee the country."

The candles flare.

"I want to tell him I need slow. Specific. Honest. No games unless we both agree they're games. I want him to know that if he calls me Dorothea like that, I might forget my own rules, so he should be careful with it."

Lucian's expression softens.

"And I want," I continue, voice smaller, "to know if he can be careful without making me feel breakable."

There.

The truth.

The flower vines around the gazebo bloom all at once.

White star-shaped flowers open in a rush, releasing a scent like vanilla, cedar, and fresh rain.

I stop.

Lucian sits up slowly.

"That," he says, "is the door."

My eyes burn.

"I don't know if he can."

"No."

"I don't know if I can ask."

"Not yet."

"But maybe."

Lucian's smile is small.

"Yes."

A breeze moves through the gazebo.

The candles flicker low.

The garden begins to shift.

Not vanish. Not yet. But the light changes. The gold afternoon deepens toward evening. Shadows lengthen under the flowers. The path beyond the gazebo opens, leading back the way we came.

I feel the ending of this room before I want it.

"That's it?"

Lucian rises, then helps me sit.

"For this sanctuary."

"I thought there would be more."

"There was."

I look at the blanket. The tray. The rumpled pillows. My corset folded beside my skirt. His trousers discarded near the steps. My skin still warm. My mouth swollen from kisses. My body softer than I remember it ever being.

"Yes," I say. "There was."

He helps me dress.

Not because I cannot.

Because I let him.

Again, the distinction matters.

First my panties adjusted. Then the skirt. Then the corset, though he laces it more loosely this time after I say, "Less armor." The candle flowers flare when I say it, and we both look at them.

"Subtle," I tell the garden.

Lucian puts on his trousers.

Not his shirt.

I notice.

He notices me noticing.

"Aesthetic choice?" he asks.

"Yes."

He smiles.

Before we leave, I pick up one of the figs from the tray.

"For the road," I say.

Lucian looks amused.

I take a bite as we step down from the gazebo.

The path forms under my feet.

This time, I don't test it.

I trust one step.

Then the next.

Flowers part for us and rise again behind us, untouched. Not because we did not pass through. Because passing through does not have to destroy what makes room for us.

That thought feels important.

Possibly too poetic, but I blame the figs.

When we reach the green door, it stands beneath an arch of roses. On this side, it's covered in living vines. The brass handle is warm.

I pause before opening it.

Lucian waits.

"What was the chain?" I ask.

His answer comes gently.

"Believing tenderness makes you vulnerable without making you stronger."

I swallow.

"And?"

He tilts his head.

I look back at the garden.

The gazebo. The flowers. The path that appeared when I walked. The candles that flared at truth. The fruit that held memory. The sanctuary that did not promise no pain, only room enough to feel honestly and stay.

"Thinking I had to be easy to be loved," I say.

Lucian's gaze warms.

"Yes."

"And thinking asking for what I need makes me difficult."

"Yes."

I open the door.

The Hallway of Secrets waits beyond, red flames and dark stone.

Before I step through, I look back one last time.

The garden is still there.

Not mine to stay in.

But real enough to have taught me.

I step into the hallway.

The green door closes behind us.

At its base, a loose chain lies across the stone, threaded with one white star-shaped flower.

I bend and pick it up.

The flower is warm.

It melts into light in my palm.

When I look down the hall, the black door is still there.

Lorenzo's door.

Espresso. Leather. Bakery sugar.

It's not the next door.

Not yet.

But the scent reaches me.

And this time, I don't turn away quickly enough to pretend I did not want it.

Lucian stands beside me. He says nothing.

The hallway stretches ahead.

Somewhere farther down, a red door waits. This one glows like coals behind iron.

Lucian follows my gaze.

His expression changes, heat and gravity arriving together.

"That one?" I ask.

"If you choose."

"What is it?"

His voice lowers.

"Surrender."

My body answers before my mind can.

The black door behind us remains silent.

The red door ahead burns.

I take one breath.

Then another.

Lucian offers his hand.

I take it.

And together, we walk toward the fire.

EIGHT

The red door does not wait politely.

It burns.

Not with actual fire, though at this point I would not put that past the architecture. It burns with light from behind the seams, deep red and gold, like coals banked under black iron. Heat pulses through the hallway with every breath, warming the stone beneath my feet and making the little chain at the base of the green door glow faintly behind us.

I should look away.

I don't.

The garden is still on my skin. Cedar. Honey. Lucian's hands. My own voice asking for what I wanted, then asking for what I needed, then discovering those were not always the same thing. The sanctuary had felt gentle, but it had been just as dangerous as the balloon in its own awful way. Maybe more dangerous. The balloon asked me to risk height. The garden asked me to risk tenderness.

This door asks something else.

Surrender.

The word sits low in my stomach, heavier than fear, warmer than curiosity.

Lucian stands beside me, quiet for once.

That does not reassure me.

He is very rarely quiet unless the silence is doing work.

"So," I say, "red."

"Yes." His mouth curves, but his eyes remain fixed on the door.

I study his face.

That is my first mistake.

Lucian looks different now. Still beautiful, still shirtless because I'm committed to the aesthetic choices I make under magical duress, still calm in the way he has learned to be calm when I'm considering panic as a lifestyle. But there's something more severe in him here. Not cruel. Not cold. Focused.

The kind of focus that says this room matters.

The kind of focus that says he won't let me turn the door into a joke and then mistake laughter for consent.

My throat tightens.

"What are you thinking?" I ask.

"That this room must be entered cleanly."

"Cleanly?"

"With more clarity than hunger."

I look at the red door.

Heat spills beneath it like breath.

"That sounds like less fun."

"It will be more fun because of it."

"You say that with a lot of confidence for a man who has repeatedly delayed gratification in my own fantasy."

"I'm excellent at delaying gratification."

"I have noticed."

His smile appears for half a second.

Then fades.

"This door is not about whether you can want. You have already learned that."

"I would not say learned. Maybe introduced myself formally."

"You have learned more than you admit." His gaze holds mine.

"This room is about chosen surrender."

My body answers before I do.

Chosen.

Surrender.

Both words are dangerous separately. Together, they feel

like standing near an oven door cracked open to five hundred degrees.

I press my palms to my skirt.

The burgundy corset is laced more loosely now, at my request. Less armor. Still structure. Still a reminder that I can be held without being trapped. The skirt brushes my legs, soft and thin. My hair is down around my shoulders, no longer something to hide in or put away.

I'm already changed.

That should comfort me.

Instead, it makes this next door feel more serious.

"What's the chain?" I ask.

Lucian looks back at the door.

"You will know when you see it."

"I miss when people said things like, good question, Dorothea, here is a straightforward answer."

"No, you don't."

"No," I admit. "But I like the idea of being that sort of person."

"A woman who prefers simple answers?"

"Yes."

"You would be bored by lunch."

"Probably before."

The red door gives a low pulse.

A sound moves from behind it.

Not a moan. Not a scream. Not the dramatic nonsense my mind tries to conjure because I have read books, watched movies, and absorbed enough cultural shorthand to know what a red room is supposed to imply.

It's only a breath.

Inhale.

Hold.

Exhale.

My own chest matches it before I realize.

Lucian notices. "Color?" he asks.

I blink. "We are not even inside."

"Color?" I take inventory.

Fear, yes.

Curiosity, yes.

Desire, yes.

A little irritation because the door seems to be breathing at me and that feels presumptuous.

"Green," I say. "With a yellow border."

Lucian smiles faintly.

"Acceptable."

"I'm glad my emotional traffic light meets your standards."

"Your clarity does."

That lands.

Damn him.

I look at the handle.

It's black iron, twisted into the shape of a serpent biting its own tail. A loop. A chain pretending to be a circle.

I know, even before I touch it, that the metal will be hot.

It is.

Not burning. Warm enough to make me aware of my palm.

I turn the handle.

The door opens.

The room beyond is dim, red, and very aware of itself.

I step inside.

My first thought is that it smells expensive.

Leather. Sandalwood. candle smoke. Clean linen. Something sweet beneath it, like dark cherries soaked in wine. The air is warm but not suffocating. Thick, yes. Intimate, yes. The kind of air that presses against bare skin and asks a woman to remember she has nerves.

The walls are draped in fabric, deep red, black, and gold. Not the same lavish tapestries from the original chamber, though they share the same bloodline. These hang smoother, heavier, almost ceremonial. Iron sconces burn with low flames along the walls. Between them are objects.

Some I recognize.

A soft flogger. A paddle. Rope coiled in neat circles. Silk scarves. Cuffs hanging from hooks. A blindfold resting on a small wooden tray. A riding crop, which makes my entire body go very still for reasons I choose not to investigate too quickly.

Some objects I don't recognize.

Curved pieces of polished wood. Strange metal clamps. A

long strip of leather with a handle. Things that look like jewelry until I imagine them in use and have to immediately stop imagining that because my brain has poor supervision.

In the center of the room stands a bed.

Large. Low. Elegant. Draped in red silk sheets that catch the candlelight like liquid. Four posts rise from the corners, black wood carved with vines, flames, and open locks. At the foot of the bed rests a sturdy wooden chest, dark and iron-banded. On one wall is a mirror, tall and narrow, framed in black.

I glare at it.

"No."

Lucian follows my gaze.

"The mirror won't show anything you don't ask to see."

"I don't believe mirrors."

"Wise."

"Can we cover it?"

"Yes."

The answer is immediate.

Before I can react, he crosses the room, takes a black cloth from the top of the chest, and drapes it over the mirror. The glass vanishes.

I stare at him.

"What?" he asks.

"That was easy."

"Yes."

"I expected an argument."

"Why?"

"Because it's a magical room with an agenda."

"The room has an agenda. I have boundaries."

I don't have a joke.

The red room seems to settle around those words.

Lucian turns back to me.

"This room does not begin with touch," he says.

I swallow.

"What does it begin with?"

"Negotiation."

Of course the Devil's red room begins with conversation. That is both deeply sexy and extremely inconvenient.

Lucian gestures toward the bed, but not in a way that tells

me to lie down. More like an invitation to sit where I choose. I sit near the foot, because it lets me see the door. I notice that and decide not to judge myself for it. The door remains visible, closed but not gone. Its handle is not locked.

That matters.

Lucian sits on the wooden chest across from me, close enough for intimacy, far enough for thought.

The distance is, unfortunately, perfect.

"You said this was about surrender," I say.

"Yes."

"Then negotiation feels contradictory."

"No."

"You are going to explain why."

"Yes."

"Fine. Proceed with your emotionally literate Devil lecture."

His mouth twitches.

"Surrender without negotiation is not surrender. It's guessing. It's performance. It's hope with no structure. It asks one person to read what the other cannot say."

I look down at my hands.

"And I have done enough of that."

"Yes."

"Rude."

"Useful."

"Debatable."

"No."

I look back up.

Lucian's face is serious.

"Surrender is not the absence of control, Dorothea. It's chosen exchange. It requires you to know what you are giving, what you are keeping, and what stops everything."

My throat tightens. "What if I don't know?"

"Then we begin by finding out."

"How?"

"We make a list."

I stare. "A list."

"Yes."

"Of sexual boundaries?"

My body reacts instantly, heat flooding between my

thighs, nipples tightening against the thin fabric of my dress. My mind tries to protest, but the ache wins. After everything we've already done, the idea of spelling out exactly how I want to be fucked feels filthy and freeing at the same time.

"This is the strangest customer intake process I have ever experienced."

"You signed a consent form before magical tea, yes?"

"True."

"This should not surprise you."

"It does."

Lucian stands and opens the chest, retrieving parchment, charcoal pencil, and a lap board. When he hands them to me, our fingers brush and I feel it like a spark straight to my clit.

The parchment is blank until words bloom across the top in deep red ink:

YES • MAYBE • NO

I let out a breathless laugh. "The Devil has stationery?"

"The Devil values clarity."

"I'm learning so much."

Lucian sits close enough that I can feel the heat of his body. His thigh presses against mine.

"Pain," he says, voice low.

The word lands heavy between us. My pussy clenches.

I grip the pencil tighter. "Light sting only. Nothing that leaves marks. No real injury. Just enough to make me feel it."

I write it under **MAYBE**, my handwriting slightly unsteady from the growing throb between my legs.

"Good," Lucian murmurs. That single word slides over my skin like a slow lick.

"Restraint."

Heat rushes through me. I picture myself spread open, wrists bound, completely at his mercy while he plays with me for hours. My thighs press together instinctively.

"Maybe," I say, voice huskier now. "Soft cuffs. Nothing locked. I want to be able to pull free if I need to. Not for too long. And no gag—ever."

The parchment writes **NO GAG** in bold red before I can even move the pencil. I smirk.

"Bossy little worksheet."

"Blindfold?" he asks.

"Yes. But you keep talking to me the whole time. I want to hear exactly what you're going to do to me."

I write it under **YES**, already imagining the darkness, his voice in my ear, his hands and mouth everywhere.

"Commands," he continues.

My pulse jumps. "Yes. I like being told what to do—especially when I know I can say no."

Lucian's eyes darken with clear hunger. "Write it."

I do. The words feel like foreplay.

"Praise."

"Fuck, yes," I say without hesitation, writing it boldly under **YES**. The thought of him growling "good girl" while he's buried inside me makes me shift restlessly on the seat.

"Names."

"Good girl—yes. Baby—yes. Mine..." I pause, heat blooming across my chest. "Maybe. Slut and whore are hard no. No degradation."

NO DEGRADATION appears on the parchment in sharp letters. I exhale in satisfaction.

"Spanking."

My thighs press together again. Lucian notices, and the corner of his mouth lifts in a predatory smirk.

"Maybe," I say, cheeks flushed. "Hand only. Start light. Ask me after the first few. Only if I'm not fully restrained. And it's for pleasure—not punishment."

"Excellent," he purrs. The approval in his voice goes straight to my clit.

"Penetration."

The room feels hotter. My pussy is slick and aching now.

"Fingers—yes. Your cock—yes," I say, bolder than I've ever been. "But I want to be the one who decides when and how deep. Slow at first if I ask for it. You stop the second I say stop."

Lucian's gaze is burning. I can see the outline of his hard cock straining against his trousers.

I write the conditions carefully, then look up at him, pulse racing. "I want this. All of it. I want to feel everything while I still have you."

He takes the board from my hands and reads through my list with focused intensity. When he finishes, he sets it aside and looks at me like he wants to devour me right here.

The air between us is thick with promise.

"The list can change," he says. "I know." "Say it."

I roll my eyes, but my voice has already gone husky. "The list can change."

"Good."

He sets the parchment on the chest where we can both see it. The room feels charged now, like the air itself is licking along my skin. The negotiation has done something dangerous and delicious, it's built a container strong enough to hold whatever filthy things we want to do inside it.

Lucian steps closer. His presence is overwhelming — tall, warm, radiating control and hunger in equal measure.

"Safe word." "Red." "Practice it."

I meet his eyes, pulse racing. "Red."

The room snaps into perfect stillness. Every candle flame freezes mid-flicker. Lucian's hands lift away from his sides, open and visible. He doesn't move a single muscle. The instant obedience builds the ache between my legs.

"Good," he says, voice low and rough with pride.

The flames begin moving again. "Again."

"Red."

He steps back instantly. The door behind me cracks open, letting cool air brush over my already heated skin. My nipples tighten into hard peaks.

"Oh," I whisper, stunned by how quickly and completely he honors it.

"Your no does not have to persuade me," he says, eyes locked on mine. "It only has to be spoken."

The power of that truth settles deep in my belly — and lower. I feel myself getting wetter.

He steps close again. "Yellow." "Pause. Check in. Slow down or adjust if I need it." "Green?" "Keep going. I want more."

Lucian reaches for the tie of my corset. "May I undress you?"

I look at him — at the list, at the open door, at the mirror still covered — and feel a surge of bold, hungry confidence.

"Yes. Slowly. I want to feel every inch of fabric leaving my body."

He unlaces the corset with deliberate care, but there's nothing clinical about it. Each pull of the ties feels like a caress. When the leather finally falls away, the cool air kisses my bare breasts and I shiver hard, nipples aching. Lucian's gaze drops to them, dark and hungry. He doesn't hide how much he wants me.

The skirt follows. He kneels in front of me, sliding the fabric down my legs, his breath warm against my thighs. When I step out of it, I'm left in nothing but black lace panties already soaked through. The evidence of my arousal is impossible to miss.

I hook my thumbs into the waistband.

Lucian catches my wrist gently. "Only if you choose."

"I know," I say, voice breathy but sure. "I want to be completely naked for you."

I slide the panties down and kick them aside. Cool air hits my slick, exposed pussy and I have to bite my lip at the rush of vulnerability and need. When I straighten, Lucian's eyes devour every inch of me, slow, reverent, and blatantly filthy.

"Color?" he asks, voice rough. "Green. Exposed… and very turned on."

"Good girl."

The praise hits me like a slow stroke between my legs. I let out a shaky breath. "I really like that."

"I know." His mouth curves. "I can see how much you like it."

He moves to the chest and returns with the blindfold — soft, matte black silk. He holds it up. "Blindfold is yes, with constant verbal check-ins."

"Yes," I confirm, already aching with anticipation. "I want it now."

Lucian steps behind me. The heat of his body presses close. The silk settles over my eyes, plunging me into total darkness. My other senses sharpen instantly — the sound of his breathing, the scent of him.

"Can you see?"

"No. Green."

His hands rest lightly on my shoulders, grounding and possessive.

"Say red."

"Red."

His hands disappear immediately. The sudden loss makes me whimper softly. I feel exposed, dripping, and strangely powerful.

"Good," he praises from a short distance away.

I laugh, a little shakily. "That was a test?"

"That was trust."

My chest tightens with something deep and warm. "Come back. Behind me again. Hands on my shoulders."

He obeys instantly, pressing close once more. The hard ridge of his cock brushes against my lower back through his trousers, and I have to fight the urge to grind back against him.

I breathe through the darkness, naked, blindfolded, and more turned on than I've ever been in my life.

The darkness changes everything. Without sight, every sensation becomes louder, sharper, more obscene. The warm air teases my hard nipples. Cool drafts kiss my soaked pussy. I can feel how wet I am — slick, swollen, and aching — just from the negotiation and the blindfold.

Lucian's hands rest on my shoulders, solid and warm.

"What's your job?" he asks, voice low.

"To tell the truth."

"What's mine?"

"To believe me."

His hands tighten once, pleased. "Good girl."

The words feel darker in the dark. Rougher. Like a hand sliding between my thighs.

He guides me forward with one hand on my shoulder and the other at my waist. Slow, careful steps. The backs of my knees brush the edge of the bed.

"Sit."

It's a command — soft, but unmistakable. My body obeys instantly, pussy clenching at the quiet authority in his voice. I sit on the edge of the bed, thighs pressed together, already throbbing.

"That command was green?" he asks.

"Yes."

"Do you like commands?"

"I like commands when I know I can say no."

"Good girl."

I grip the sheets tightly as fresh wetness slips down my inner thigh.

Lucian kneels in front of me. I feel the shift in the air, the heat of his body between my legs. His hands wrap gently around my ankles.

"May I open your legs?"

The polite, filthy question makes my breath hitch.

"Yes."

He parts my knees slowly, spreading me open. Cool air kisses my dripping cunt, and I know he can see everything — how wet and swollen I am, how my pussy glistens with arousal. I fight the urge to close my legs again, but the exposure only makes me wetter.

Lucian's hands rest heavy on my spread thighs. "Color?"

"Green."

"Name it."

"Vulnerable… and so fucking hungry."

His fingers press deeper into my thighs. "Yes."

"Terrified."

"Of what?"

"That I'll like the wrong thing."

Lucian's hands still. "There's no wrong thing here if it's chosen, safe, and does not harm what you are."

I swallow hard. "What if what I am is wanting too much?"

His voice drops, rough and intimate. "Then let us meet her."

A full-body shiver rolls through me.

Something soft — a feather — traces slowly up my inner thigh. I jolt at the light, maddening touch. It drifts higher, teasing along my hip, across my lower stomach, then up the side of my breast. My nipples are painfully tight. My clit throbs, desperate for attention.

"Green?" he asks.

"Green."

The feather vanishes.

His hot mouth presses to my knee, then slowly higher. I whimper, hips shifting restlessly.

"Words," he reminds me.

"Green. More."

"What kind?"

My face burns beneath the blindfold, but I force the words out. "Your mouth. Higher."

He kisses my inner thigh again. Higher. So close I can feel his breath on my soaked pussy.

"Lucian…"

"Yes?"

"You're being a tease."

"Yes."

"Higher."

Another kiss, torturously close.

"Higher than that."

"Say where."

I'm dripping. Aching. The words feel filthy and powerful on my tongue.

"Between my legs. Put your mouth on my pussy."

His warm breath fans over my swollen folds. "Good girl."

But he still doesn't give me what I want. Instead, his fingers circle my right wrist.

"Cuffs now?"

Everything inside me tightens with dark, needy anticipation.

"Yes," I breathe. "Soft ones. Not locked. Release if I say red. Check in after."

"Good."

He slips the soft cuff around my right wrist. The material is silky but firm. The quiet click of it closing sends another rush of slick heat flooding from my cunt.

Soft leather lined with velvet closes snugly around my right wrist, then the left. Lucian guides my hands upward and secures them to something above me. Not high enough to strain, not tight enough to hurt — but enough that when I test them, I feel the delicious bite of restraint.

Panic flashes through me, bright and immediate. Old foster-care fear.

"Color?" Lucian asks instantly. "Yellow."

Everything stops. His hands leave me. The room goes still. Even the candle flames seem to hold their breath.

"Good," he says, voice calm and steady. "What do you need?"

My heart hammers. "I need to know I can get out."

The cuffs loosen immediately. Lucian guides my fingers to a small release tab on the inside of each cuff.

"Here. Press this."

I do. The right cuff opens. Then the left. My hands drop free. The blindfold stays on. Lucian remains close, not touching, giving me space.

"What did yellow do?" he asks.

"It stopped everything."

"And what happened?"

"You gave me a way out."

"What did I not do?"

"You didn't make me feel guilty for needing it."

Something deep inside my chest loosens.

"Good."

I take a shaky breath. "I want to try again."

"Are you sure?"

"Yes. Because now I know where the door is."

Lucian is quiet for a moment, then kisses my palm with surprising tenderness. "Excellent."

He recuffs me — first one wrist, then the other. This time I locate the release tabs myself before settling back. The knowledge that

I can free myself at any moment settles something primal in me. The fear doesn't vanish, but it transforms into a dark, pulsing thrill.

"Color?"

"Green." "Feeling?"

"Still scared… but more willing. And very turned on."

His hand slides slowly up my inner thigh, stopping just short of where I'm dripping for him. "Very good."

The praise sinks into me like warm honey, making my pussy clench hard. I settle deeper into the restraints. The strangest part is this:

the moment I know I can escape, I stop wanting to. I pull gently against the

cuffs just to feel them hold me, and a fresh rush of slick heat coats my

thighs.

Lucian's mouth returns to my thigh, kissing, licking,

teasing higher. His hands explore me — sliding over my hips, my stomach,

cupping my breasts, rolling my stiff nipples between his fingers. Every touch

feels electric in the darkness. I can't see him. I can only feel him. Hear him.

Need him.

A low moan escapes me as he cups one breast fully. My back arches hard, pushing my tits toward his mouth.

"Green?" he asks, voice rough. "Yes."

His thumb brushes over my aching nipple, then pinches

just hard enough to make me gasp. Pleasure sparks straight down to my clit. I

pull against the cuffs again — not to escape, but to feel them bite into my

wrists as I writhe.

Lucian's hot, wet mouth closes around my nipple. He sucks

hard.

I cry out, loud and shameless, hips jerking.

He pulls back immediately.

"No — green," I pant. "That was so fucking good. Please don't stop."

"Then say it clearly."

"I want more. Suck harder."

He gives it to me. His mouth is filthy and perfect —

sucking, licking, grazing my sensitive nipple with his teeth while his hand

works the other breast. I'm dripping onto the sheets now, my pussy throbbing

with empty need. Every tug of his mouth sends another pulse of heat between my

spread legs.

"Good girl," he growls against my wet skin. "Look at you

— naked, cuffed, dripping for me."

I moan loudly and pull harder against the restraints, loving the way they hold me open for him. The helplessness feels like freedom.

His hand reaches between my spread thighs, cupping my soaked pussy. Not pushing inside — just owning me with slow, firm strokes over my slick folds. He glides through the mess I've already made, teasing my swollen clit with maddening patience.

My hips jerk up greedily, chasing his touch.

"Patience," he murmurs. "I'm out of patience." "No. You are out of hiding."

I laugh, breathless and desperate. "That is not the same."

His fingers circle my aching clit again, slick and slow. The pleasure coils tight and vicious in my core. My cunt clenches around nothing, dripping down onto the sheets. I'm so close already — embarrassingly close.

He pulls his hand away.

I let out a broken, undignified whimper.

"Lucian." "Yes?" "If you stop every time I'm close, I will become difficult." "You are already difficult." "More difficult."

His low, dark laugh sends another rush of heat flooding between my legs.

Then his hand leaves me completely. My empty, throbbing pussy aches so badly I groan, pulling hard against the cuffs. The restraint only makes me wetter.

"Yellow?" he asks.

"No."

"Frustrated?"

"Yes."

"Do you want release?"

"Yes."

"Do you want to ask for it?"

"No."

"Why?"

Because asking makes me feel needy. Because need feels like weakness. Because if I beg and he refuses, I'll have to sit with the shame of wanting out loud.

"I don't know," I lie.

"Liar."

I pull against the cuffs again, wrists straining, pussy pulsing with frustration. "Fine. Because if I ask, you can refuse."

"Yes."

Lucian's hand cups my cheek with shocking tenderness. In the darkness, it feels almost too intimate.

"That is the shape of all real wanting," he says softly.

Lorenzo's name flashes through me like a knife.

Wanting Lucian is safe. His refusal is part of the lesson. But Lorenzo... Lorenzo could refuse because he simply doesn't want me enough. Or because he's afraid. Or because real life doesn't come with worksheets and safe words.

"Dorothea," Lucian says gently.

"I thought of him."

"I know."

"I don't want him here."

I tug once more on the cuffs. They hold me firmly. I could release them... but I don't.

"I want him to know how to do this," I whisper. "Not this exact room. I mean... I want him to ask. I want him to listen. I want him to not make me feel ridiculous for needing a list, or time, or filthy, unsexy words that somehow make everything possible."

Lucian's thumb strokes my cheek. "That is a desire worth honoring."

My eyes burn beneath the blindfold.

"What if he cannot?"

"Then he does not get the room."

The simplicity of it steadies me. Not my body. Not my fear. Not this soft, dripping, complicated place inside me. Not unless he earns it.

I breathe through the ache between my legs. My nipples are tight. My pussy is soaked and swollen, visibly throbbing with need.

"What do you want now?" Lucian asks, voice low and rough.

I listen to my body — cuffed, blindfolded, spread open, dripping, and strangely, powerfully alive.

"I want to come," I say. The words come out clear. No apology. No joke. Just raw want.

Lucian's breath changes, growing heavier. "How?" "With your mouth."

"Still cuffed?"

"Yes."

"Blindfold?"

"Yes."

"Ask me fully."

My face burns beneath the blindfold, but I don't hesitate. "Please put your mouth on my pussy and make me come."

Silence. Then his voice, low and dark with hunger. "Good girl."

His mouth finds me.

The world disappears. No sight. No hands. Only the cool silk beneath my back, the firm bite of the cuffs around my wrists, Lucian's strong hands spreading my thighs wider, and his hot, wet mouth devouring my dripping cunt exactly the way I begged for.

The first long, slow drag of his tongue through my soaked folds rips a loud cry from my throat. I pull hard against the cuffs, the restraints holding me open for him as my hips buck shamelessly against his face. He groans deeply into my pussy, the vibration rolling through my clit and making my toes curl.

"More," I gasp.

He gives it — licking broader, filthier strokes, sucking my swollen clit between his lips with perfect pressure.

"Slower."

He obeys instantly, torturing me with slow, deliberate licks.

"There— right there, please—"

He stays exactly where I need him, tongue flicking and circling while he feasts on me like I'm the only thing he's ever wanted. My wrists strain against the cuffs, the helplessness only making me wetter. I can feel my arousal coating his chin, dripping down my ass onto the sheets.

My body climbs fast, thighs shaking around his head. This time he doesn't pull away. He holds me right on the razor's edge with merciless skill, sucking harder on my clit while his tongue works me perfectly.

"Lucian—"

He hums against my throbbing pussy and that's it. I shatter.

The orgasm crashes through me hard and deep, ripping a raw, broken cry from my throat. My back arches violently off the bed as my cunt pulses and gushes against his tongue. Wave after wave tears through me, thighs clamping around his head while his hands keep me spread open so he can drink every drop. I'm shaking, whimpering, completely undone.

When the pleasure finally ebbs, he kisses the inside of my thigh softly, then rests a warm hand on my hip, grounding me.

"Color?" he asks, voice rough. I laugh weakly. "Green... but my skeleton has left the building."

"Do you want out of the cuffs?"

I consider it, floating in the afterglow. "Yes."

He releases me immediately. My arms fall limp to my sides. He removes the blindfold. Candlelight returns slowly. Lucian kneels between my spread legs, lips and chin shiny with my release, eyes dark and proud. The sight makes my pussy clench again.

I cover my face for half a second, then force my hands down. Let him see me like this — flushed, wrecked, and still hungry.

"Name it," he says.

"Powerful. Undone. Safe." I pause, smiling shyly. "And very aware that I like being restrained... which is information I'm not ready to put in the town newsletter."

Lucian laughs, warm and low. He brings me cool water and wraps a soft black blanket around my shoulders when he notices me trembling. The care feels almost as intimate as the orgasm.

"Do you want to continue?" he asks quietly.

I look at him — shirtless, hard, controlled, and visibly aching for me. My gaze drops to the thick, heavy outline of his cock straining against his trousers. Heat floods through me again.

"I want to continue," I say.

His eyes darken. "How?"

I glance at the list, then back at him, heart pounding but voice steady. "I want you inside me. I want to feel you stretch me open and fuck me. Slowly at first. I want you to check in. No blindfold. No cuffs for this part. I want to see your face… and I want to feel some of that surrender by letting you lead after I say yes."

Lucian's chest rises with a slow, controlled breath. "That is very clear."

"I want you inside me," I repeat, holding his gaze. "Please."

He stands and removes the rest of his clothing. His cock springs free — thick, hard, and flushed. The sight makes my mouth go dry with a mix of nerves and raw desire.

He moves over me slowly, bracing on his forearms. The weight of his body pressing me into the silk feels incredible.

"More weight," I whisper.

He lowers himself until I feel deliciously pinned beneath him. His thick cock rests hot and heavy against my soaked pussy.

"Color?"

"Green. Scared green."

"You can change your mind at any time," he reminds me.

He kisses me deeply, then reaches between us. The blunt head of his cock nudges against my entrance, hot and insistent. He waits.

"I want you inside me," I breathe again. "Please."

Lucian pushes forward slowly. The stretch is intense — a burning, aching fullness as my body opens around his thick cock. Inch by inch he sinks into me, watching my face the entire time. When he's finally buried to the hilt, we're both breathing hard, foreheads pressed together.

He stays perfectly still, letting me adjust to being so completely filled.

"Breathe," he murmurs.

I do. The pressure slowly melts into deep, throbbing pleasure. I shift my hips, and sparks shoot through me.

"Oh…"

"That?" he asks, voice strained.

"Yes. That. Move."

He begins to fuck me — slow, deep, perfect strokes that drag against every sensitive place inside me. The wet sound of his thick cock sliding in and out of my soaked pussy fills the room with every thrust.

I answer by gripping his shoulders and opening my legs wider around his hips, inviting him deeper.

He moves again, sinking even further inside me. The pleasure isn't sudden fireworks — it's slower, warmer, more intimate. His thick cock stretches and fills me completely, dragging against every sensitive inch of my walls with every deliberate stroke. His breath mingles with mine. My voice keeps giving him permission — yes, green, slower, again, again, again.

The rhythm builds.

My fear doesn't disappear. It transforms. Each deep thrust gives it less room to breathe. I realize, somewhere between one gasp and the next, that surrender isn't disappearing beneath him. I'm more present than I've ever been. Every nerve is awake. Every word I speak matters. Every yes has weight and shape.

Lucian's hand slides between our bodies. "May I?"

I know what he's asking. "Yes."

His fingers find my swollen, sensitive clit. The first firm circle makes me gasp sharply. The second makes my nails dig into his back as pleasure spikes through me.

He stills. "Green?"

"Green. Don't stop unless I ask you to."

His eyes darken with raw hunger. "As you wish."

Then he really fucks me.

The slow rhythm turns deeper, harder, more consuming, but he never loses me. He watches my face, listens to every sound I make, adjusts instantly. When I moan "harder," he gives it to me, driving his thick cock into my soaked pussy with perfect, powerful strokes. When I whimper "not so fast," he slows, grinding deep and filthy. When my words dissolve into broken gasps, he checks in, and I answer "green" because it's still true — I'm drowning in pleasure and I don't want it to stop.

The room blurs into red and gold. The silk sheets twist beneath me. The wet, obscene sound of his cock sliding in and out of my dripping cunt fills the air with every thrust.

The pleasure builds, deep and demanding, coiled tight in my core. I reach for him, not to stop him, but to hold on.

"Lucian—"

"I have you."

"More."

He gives it.

The word becomes a command, not a plea. "More."

His mouth crashes down on mine as the orgasm rips through me. I come hard around his cock with a broken, shameless cry, my pussy clenching and pulsing violently around his thick length. My whole body shakes beneath him as wave after wave crashes over me. He swallows every sound, fucking me through it, drawing out every last tremor until I'm limp and gasping.

When I finally float back down, he's still buried deep inside me, perfectly still, jaw tight with the effort of holding back. His control is beautiful and painful to witness.

I touch his face tenderly. "Lucian."

His eyes meet mine.

"Do you want to keep going?" I ask.

His breath catches. "Yes."

"Then ask me."

Surprise flickers across his face, followed by something like pride. He rests his forehead against mine. "May I keep going?"

My chest fills with warmth. "Yes. But slower for a minute."

He kisses me deeply and obeys, moving inside me with slow, luxurious strokes that make my toes curl. The second rise is gentler, somehow even more devastating. When he finally lets go, his body tightens, his breath breaks, and he groans my name low and rough as he comes deep inside me. The feeling of him pulsing and filling me triggers another smaller, shimmering orgasm that leaves me trembling.

He doesn't collapse on me. He lowers himself carefully for warmth, then rolls us to our sides. When his cock slips from me, I feel the immediate, aching loss of him — but I also feel full. Held. Not used. Not erased.

Lucian pulls the blanket over us. For a long while, neither of us speaks. The red room breathes softly around us.

Eventually he asks, "Color?"

I laugh into his chest. "Still?"

"Especially after."

"Green," I whisper. "Soft green."

His arms tighten gently around me. "Good."

He brings me water, then cleans me with a warm cloth — gentle, thorough, reverent. The aftercare undoes me almost more than the sex itself. He dresses me with the same care, lacing my corset loosely when I ask. I leave his shirt off. He lets me.

Before we leave, I pick up the parchment list. The words lift from the page in red light and sink into my palm. The paper dissolves, but the structure remains — burned softly into me.

We walk to the red door. It opens before I touch it.

At its base lies a loose chain, cooling from red-hot to black iron, with a small open lock beside it.

I touch the lock. It dissolves into warmth against my fingers.

"What was the door?" Lucian asks.

I look at him. "Surrender."

"And what is surrender?"

"A chosen exchange. Not a collapse."

"And control?"

"Not something I lose by sharing it with someone worthy."

"Good."

This time the word doesn't just make me ache. It makes me stand taller.

The hallway waits. Steam curls ahead from a new dark stone door veined with silver light. Lucian's face carries a quiet sadness as he looks at it.

"The final temptation," he says softly.

I take his hand — not because he offers it, but because I choose to.

"Ready?" he asks.

"No."

His smile is small and sad. "Good."

Together, we walk toward the steam.

NINE

The steaming door does not burn.

After the red room, fire would almost be comforting. Obvious danger has become familiar by now, which is probably not a sentence any woman should be able to say about her Tuesday evening. Fire announces itself. Fire says, I'm hot, I'm dangerous, don't put your hand in me unless you have thought this through and possibly signed something.

Steam is different.

Steam hides.

It softens edges. It turns doorways into questions. It wraps around ankles and wrists and throats, warm enough to invite, thick enough to conceal.

The door ahead is dark stone veined with silver, its surface wet as if water runs just beneath it. Water lilies are carved into the frame, their petals open and delicate, their roots twisting down into the stone like little chains. Steam curls from beneath the threshold and slips across the hallway floor.

Lucian stands beside me, holding my hand.

I'm dressed again, if loosely. The burgundy corset is laced with enough room to breathe. The skirt brushes my legs. My hair is down, still carrying the scent of cedar, smoke, leather, and all the rooms I have survived. My body feels warm and tender in a way I'm trying very hard not to think about while standing in a hallway full of sentient emotional architecture.

The red door behind us is closed.

At its base, the little open lock has vanished.

The chain is gone too.

I should feel triumphant.

Instead, I feel tired.

Not bad tired. Not bakery-after-fourteen-hours tired, when my feet throb and my thoughts become murderous over the concept of sweeping. This is deeper. Softer. The kind of tired that comes after crying, wanting, laughing, asking, coming apart, and discovering you are still somehow in one piece.

Lucian looks at the steaming door with sadness in his eyes.

I don't like it.

Lucian is many things. Tempting. Infuriating. Beautiful enough to justify several city ordinances. Patient to a degree that suggests either great wisdom or a troubling lack of hobbies. But he has not been sad before.

Not like this.

"What's that face?" I ask.

He turns toward me. "What face?"

"The one that makes me want to throw a pastry at you."

"That is very specific."

"I have specific coping instincts."

"I'm aware."

"You said this is the final temptation."

"Yes."

"Final has implications."

"Yes."

"I dislike implications."

"I know."

The door exhales steam.

The hallway grows quieter.

Even the other doors stop whispering. The green door with its star-flower chain. The red door with its heat and open lock. The blue cloud door, somewhere behind us, quiet now. The black door with Lorenzo's scent still waits in the distance, silent and smug, but even it seems dimmer here.

The final door wants all the attention.

Rude, but effective.

"What's the temptation?" I ask.

Lucian's fingers tighten around mine.

"Open it."

"That is not an answer."

"No."

"Are you going to become cryptic now? Because I'm emotionally too tired for riddles."

"You have been emotionally too tired for riddles since the first room."

"And yet you persisted."

"I'm very committed."

"To being annoying?"

"To your freedom."

That shuts me up.

Only briefly, but still.

I stare at the door.

Steam beads on the stone petals. A drop of water slides down one carved lily and falls to the floor. It lands without a sound.

"You said I need to know," I say.

"Yes."

I sigh. "Fine."

Lucian says nothing.

I look at him. "Fine, I'll open it."

His mouth curves faintly. "You don't have to announce every brave act with irritation."

"I do, actually. It's part of my brand."

The sadness in his eyes softens, but does not leave.

I reach for the handle.

There's no metal. Only smooth stone, warm and damp beneath my palm. The water lily roots carved around the edge seem to loosen at my touch.

The door opens.

Steam rolls out.

Warmth wraps around me, heavy and fragrant.

Mineral water. Wet stone. Night-blooming flowers. Moss. Rain. Something faintly sweet beneath it, like honey dissolved into tea.

For one second, the hallway disappears behind white vapor.

Then Lucian leads me through.

The world on the other side is not a room.

It's night.

We stand on a path of smooth black stone at the edge of a hot spring. The pool is natural, or appears to be, carved into dark rock beneath a sky thick with stars. Steam rises from the water in slow, white ribbons, drifting through the air and catching silver light. The spring itself glows faintly blue at the center, as if the moon has melted into it, though I cannot see a moon overhead.

Around the pool, lush greenery grows from the stones. Ferns. Moss. Vines with white flowers that open only in the steam. Water lilies float in the shallower edges, pale and luminous. Somewhere nearby, water trickles over rock, steady and quiet, not dramatic enough to be a waterfall, too persistent to be ignored.

The air is warm and wet.

My skin drinks it in.

The path leads down to the pool, where stone steps descend into the water. On a flat rock beside the spring are folded towels, a wooden tray with a pitcher of water, two cups, and a little bowl of fruit.

At least the final temptation understands hydration.

I look around.

"This is very peaceful," I say.

"Yes."

"I don't trust it."

"Wise."

"I was hoping you'd say I could."

"You can trust it to be what it is."

"That sounds like a terrible customer guarantee."

His thumb brushes mine.

The water murmurs.

Beyond the pool, the darkness is soft. No walls. No doors visible except the one behind us, which now looks like a standing slab of stone covered in carved lilies. The hallway is no longer visible through it. Just stone.

I don't panic.

I notice that.

Lucian notices me noticing.

Good guide.

Awful man.

"So," I say, "hot spring."

"Yes."

"Final temptation."

"Yes."

"Not sex?"

His mouth curves.

"Not unless you are attempting to hide in it."

My face warms.

"I was asking academically. I'm a scholar of odd rooms."

"An excellent field."

"It lacks funding."

"It usually does."

The little exchange should make me feel better.

It almost does.

But Lucian still looks sad.

The surface ripples. Steam rises. Tiny star-shaped flowers float near the edge.

My body aches in places I'm not ready to put language to. Not bad aches. Not exactly. More like reminders. The red room remains in my muscles, in my thighs, in my wrists where the cuffs held me and where I learned that restraint could be an agreement instead of a trap. My skin still remembers Lucian's mouth, his hands, his weight, his careful questions.

And beneath all of that, there's a grief beginning to take shape.

I know what comes next before he says it.

Maybe I have known since the first door opened.

Magic always asks for return.

Even in fairy tales. Especially in fairy tales. Midnight comes. The spell ends. The borrowed dress turns back. The carriage becomes a pumpkin, which frankly always struck me as wasteful. No one lets a woman stay at the ball forever. Not even when the prince has good hair and the orchestra knows the exact song for emotional damage.

Lucian releases my hand and steps toward the water.

"We should get in," he says.

"Bossy."

"Warm water will help."

"With what?"

"Everything you are pretending not to feel."

"I preferred the hydration answer."

"I know."

He begins unlacing his trousers.

I blink, startled by how ordinary the movement feels after everything. We have been naked together. He has been inside me. He has heard me ask for things I never thought I would say out loud. Still, watching him undress in this quiet place feels more intimate than the red room somehow.

No performance.

No heat to hide behind.

Just Lucian removing his clothes beside a pool of glowing water under a sky of impossible stars.

I turn away, then immediately feel ridiculous.

He laughs softly.

"You may look."

"I know."

"Do you want to?"

"Yes."

I turn back.

The candles of previous rooms have been replaced by starlight here, softer and less flattering in a way that feels more honest. His body is still beautiful. But in this light, he looks less like a fantasy built to tempt me and more like someone tired at the end of a long day.

That hurts.

I don't know why.

I remove my clothes more slowly.

The corset first. Less armor. The skirt. My panties. Each piece folded on the rock because apparently even in magical erotic shadow-work, I'm not a monster. Lucian says nothing, though the corner of his mouth betrays amusement when I smooth the skirt twice.

"Some of us respect fabric," I say.

"I would never suggest otherwise."

"You absolutely would."

"Yes."

I step down into the water.

Heat closes around my foot.

I gasp.

Not pain. Surprise. The water is hotter than I expect, but not scalding. It wraps around my calves, then my thighs as I descend, then my hips. By the time I lower myself fully, the spring reaches my chest, and the heat seems to move straight into the tired center of me.

My body sighs.

Audibly.

Lucian smiles. He slips into the water across from me, not beside me.

Again, space.

He is always giving me space exactly when I'm most likely to fill it with wanting.

Steam curls between us.

For a while, neither of us speaks.

The hot water loosens everything the red room opened. My muscles soften. My wrists stop remembering the cuffs as pressure and start remembering them as proof. My thighs ache less. My breathing slows. The mineral scent settles in my lungs.

The spring is not sensual in the same way the other rooms were.

It's sacred.

I hate that word because it sounds like something on an expensive candle, but it's true. The water does not seduce. It receives. The stone does not decorate. It holds. The flowers don't flare at truth. They simply float, pale and quiet, as if truth no longer needs applause.

I lean back against the smooth rock and close my eyes.

Steam kisses my face.

Water laps softly against my shoulders.

I could stay here.

The thought arrives gently.

So gently I almost don't notice the hook.

I could stay here.

Not in the red room. Not in the garden. Not in the balloon, though the sky still calls somewhere in me. Here. Warm. Held. Safe. With Lucian nearby. With all the lessons named and none of the consequences knocking on the door yet.

No bakery.

No lease.

No fake relationship.

No Lorenzo standing on the other side of a real counter with real eyes and real disappointment if this goes wrong.

No need to explain that I'm inexperienced, except now less inexperienced, which is a wildly complicated category I don't care to define.

No town gossip.

No invoices.

No risk.

Just steam, stars, and a man who knows exactly how to hear me.

My chest tightens. Ah. The final temptation.

I open my eyes.

Lucian is watching me through the steam.

His expression tells me he has seen it.

"I want to stay," I say before he can ask.

Lucian does not move. "I know."

"No," I say. "Not in a dramatic way. Not like I'm in love with you and want to run away from my life into a hot spring dimension. I'm still practical. Mostly. I know this is not a mortgage-friendly location."

His mouth curves, but his eyes stay sad.

"I mean," I continue, "I want to stay because here I know the rules."

"Yes."

"You ask. You stop. You interpret. You make worksheets appear when necessary, which is an alarming but useful skill."

"Yes."

"You know when I'm lying to myself, but you don't punish me for needing time. You are safe." The word echoes faintly against the stones. "You are fantasy."

"Yes."

"And fantasy is safe."

"No."

I blink.

He looks up.

"Fantasy is controlled," he says. "That is not the same thing."

The water laps against my chest.

I look away.

Controlled.

Every danger here has been curated. Even fear came with a guide. Even surrender had a list. Even the red room had release tabs and a covered mirror. Even the balloon could not kill me. Even Lucian's refusals were careful, purposeful, designed to move me closer to myself.

Real life does not do that.

Real life drops rent increases in your inbox and calls it business. Real life sends a charming man into your bakery during the lunch rush with paperwork and eyes that make you forget how to steam milk. Real life lets people misunderstand you. Want you badly. Want you badly and still fail you.

Real life has no guaranteed return phrase.

"I was made to show you the door, Dorothea," Lucian says.

His voice is gentle.

Firm.

Not unkind.

Not giving me room to pretend.

"Not to become the room you hide in."

The words hit harder than I expect.

I turn toward him.

"That's unfair."

"Yes."

"You don't get to be this safe and then tell me not to want safety."

"I don't want you to stop wanting safety."

"Then what?"

"I want you to stop mistaking a cage for a sanctuary because the bars are velvet."

Steam moves between us.

The Devil card.

Loose chains.

The original chamber, beautiful and iron-laced.

My life, useful and lonely.

My caution, sometimes wisdom, sometimes costume.

I close my eyes.

I laugh once, but it breaks. The sound falls apart in the steam.

When I open my eyes, Lucian is closer.

I did not hear him move.

He sits beside me now, not touching. The water ripples around his shoulders. Starlight rests in the wet strands of his hair.

"Are you real?" I ask.

The question has been waiting since the first room.

Maybe longer.

His gaze softens. "What answer do you want?" He almost smiles. Then he looks toward the center of the spring, where blue light glows beneath the surface. "I'm real enough to change you," he says. "Not real enough to choose instead of you."

My throat closes.

"I touched you," I whisper. "You touched me. I felt you."

"Yes."

"And when I wake up?"

"You will have felt me."

"This is cruel," and my voice breaks.

"Cruel can be defined in many ways. It's also mercy. It gives with one hand and opens the other before you understand what must be placed there."

I sink lower into the water until it reaches my chin. Very dignified.

Lucian waits for me to work through my thoughts. "What if I forget?" I ask.

"You won't forget everything."

"That's not the same. What if I go back and become exactly the same person?"

"You may," he says a bit too ominously.

I stare at him. "That was not reassuring. You're supposed to say I'm transformed."

"You are."

"Then why say I may go back?"

"Because transformation is not a spell that removes choice. It gives you new ones."

The water ripples.

A flower drifts past my shoulder.

"You can return to old patterns," he says. "You can lock the door again. You can call it caution. You can let the bakery consume you. You can let Lorenzo remain a fake boyfriend because fake has rules and real requires asking. You can do all that."

"This is an awful speech."

He takes my hand under the water.

This time, I don't flinch.

"You can also choose one different thing."

My chest aches at his words. "One thing?"

"Yes."

"That sounds too small."

"It's supposed to."

The rooms were enormous. Castle chambers. Infinite hallways. Sky. Garden. Red silk and cuffs and written boundaries. All that magic, all that heat, all that desire, and the real work returns to one small thing.

A text.

A conversation.

A yes.

A no.

A door opened without knowing what stands behind it.

"What one thing?" he asks.

I look at him.

I know what he is asking.

Not generally. Not vaguely. Not I will live fearlessly, which sounds pretty and means nothing if I can say it without changing my schedule.

A real promise or a real action.

The spring waits. Steam curls around us.

"I will answer Lorenzo's next call," I say.

The words come out too quickly.

Lucian's brow lifts.

"No," I say. "That's not enough."

He remains quiet.

"I won't text him some vague, breezy thing and then hide in the bakery freezer for twenty minutes."

Lucian's mouth curves.

"I will also not pretend I'm busy if he comes by."

The water warms around my chest.

Still not enough.

I know it.

My body knows it.

The Devil card knows it.

Even the water lilies know it, smug little aquatic witnesses.

I take a breath. "I will tell him the fake part cannot be the only part we admit to anymore."

Lucian goes still.

The spring brightens faintly.

I keep going.

"I will tell him I need to know what he actually wants from me. Not from the business arrangement. Not from the town thinking we're together. Me."

My voice wobbles, but I don't stop.

"And if he wants me, then I will tell him the truth. That I need slow. Specific. Honest. That I'm not good at this. That I may need words that sound practical before they feel sexy. That I need him to ask, and I need to be able to say no without losing him if he is worth keeping."

Lucian's hand tightens around mine.

The water glows brighter.

"And I will tell him," I whisper, "that I want him."

There.

The black door.

The scent of espresso and leather and bakery sugar.

The real door inside me.

Opened a crack.

The spring exhales. Or I do.

Lucian's face softens with something that looks like pride and loss together. "That is a promise," he says. "Do you understand what it costs?"

"No." I laugh through the ache.

"That is your favorite word."

"It has served us well."

"It has."

The laugh fades.

I look at our joined hands beneath the water. His fingers are blurred by the blue light. Mine look pale and strange beneath the surface. Together, they seem both real and already vanishing.

"I don't want to say goodbye to you," I say.

His face changes.

For the first time, he looks as if the words hurt him.

Not because he is real in the mortal sense. Not because he can leave this place and follow me into Coral Cove. But because whatever he is, he has been here with me. He has touched and listened and wanted and stopped. He has helped me make language out of fear.

If he is only fantasy, then fantasy has done more careful work than most real people.

"I know," he says.

"That's all you have?"

"No."

"What else?"

He shifts in the water until he faces me fully.

"I don't want you to use me as proof that real men will fail you."

My breath catches. The final chain, tightening. "I wasn't."

"Not yet."

I look away.

Because yes.

Maybe.

A little.

It would be easy, wouldn't it?

To return to Coral Cove and compare every man to Lucian. Every pause. Every question. Every failure to read my face. Every imperfect response from Lorenzo could become proof that fantasy was better, safer, cleaner.

Lucian was made for me. He knows how to speak my language. Lorenzo will have to learn it.

And I will have to teach him without hating him for not already knowing.

"That feels unfair," I say.

"To him?"

"To me."

Lucian nods slowly.

"Yes."

"What if he fails?"

"He might."

"What if I fail?"

"You might."

"What if I choose wrong?"

"You will, sometimes."

"You are terrible at comfort."

"I'm excellent at useful truth."

"I noticed."

The water moves around us.

Lucian lifts my hand and kisses my knuckles.

The gesture is soft enough to undo me.

"You don't have to choose perfectly to be free," he says.

The tears come then.

Not dramatic sobs. Not yet. Just tears slipping hot down my face while steam gathers on my skin and the spring glows beneath us.

"I want to be different," I say.

"You are."

"I want to stay different."

"Then choose differently. Again and again. Small things. Real things. Not all at once."

I wipe my cheek with my free hand.

"This is obnoxiously practical for a magical sex journey."

"Sex was never the end."

"No. Of course not. That would have been too straight-forward."

His smile is faint.

"The Devil shows temptation, yes. Desire. Appetite. Bondage. But the card also asks why the chain remains when the hands are free."

I think of the card.

The figures beneath the horned throne.

Loose chains around their necks.

All this time, the chains were loose.

Not gone.

Not meaningless.

Loose.

"You have lifted several," Lucian says.

"But not all of them."

"No."

I groan. "I miss the worksheet."

He laughs and the sound warms the air. I realize I'm going to miss his laugh. That nearly starts the crying again.

Lucian sees, because he sees everything useful and most things inconvenient.

"Come here," he says.

Not a command.

An invitation.

I move through the water to him.

He wraps his arms around me, and I rest my cheek against his wet chest. His skin is warm from the spring. His heartbeat is there under my ear.

Heartbeat.

Real enough to change me.

Not real enough to choose instead of me.

I close my eyes.

We sit like that in the water for a long time. Or maybe only a minute. Time has been lying since I drank the tea, so I no longer ask it for accountability.

The spring holds us.

The trickling water continues.

Flowers breathe their night scent into the steam.

At some point, Lucian's hand moves slowly over my back. Not erotic. Not quite. Aftercare for the whole journey. A final soothing of all the places the rooms have opened.

I let myself be held because I'm saying goodbye. There's a difference. "I need to ask one more thing," I say against his chest.

"Ask."

"If I come back…"

He stills.

I lift my head.

"If I come back to The Arcane Room, will you be here?"

The steam thickens.

Lucian's eyes are dark and sad. "Yes."

My heart clenches. "And will you remember?"

"In the same ways you will."

"That is not clear." I laugh weakly.

He touches my cheek. "If you return because you need a threshold, I will meet you at one."

"And if I return because I want to hide?"

His thumb stills.

"Then I will show you the door."

My breath catches.

There he is. Kind. Firm.

But not mine. Not in the way real people can be. I nod. "Good."

He smiles faintly. "You said it."

"I did."

"It suited you."

"Don't get sentimental. I'm very fragile and will mock you defensively."

"I would expect nothing less."

The spring begins to cool.

Only slightly, but I feel it. The first sign.

The final door calling time.

I grip Lucian tighter. "Not yet." The words slips out before dignity can intervene.

Lucian closes his eyes briefly. "Dorothea."

"No. Not yet."

"We have reached the edge."

"I'm not ready."

"I know."

"Then don't make me."

His face tightens.

For one second, I think I have found the thing that hurts him.

"I cannot make you leave," he says.

Hope flares.

Cruel hope.

Then he continues. "But if you stay because leaving frightens you, the chain goes back on."

The hope dies. Or not dies. Changes. Becomes something sharper.

"If I stay," I whisper, "what happens?"

Lucian looks toward the center of the spring.

The blue light pulses beneath the water.

"You would not remain here as you are."

"What does that mean?"

"This place would keep comforting you until comfort

became sleep. It would give you whatever you needed to avoid wanting the world. More rooms. More lessons. More pleasure. More tenderness. More proof that fantasy can be safer than life."

"That sounds…"

"Tempting?"

"Yes."

"It's supposed to."

My stomach twists.

The true Devil temptation. Not lust. Not bondage or surrender.

Avoidance dressed as healing.

I think of the bakery. The ovens. Lea. Park. Ms. Vesper's shop. Lorenzo's folder. Lorenzo's hands. The black door. The real conversation waiting like a rising loaf that might collapse if handled wrong.

I think of staying here until those things shrink. Until they seem miniature from a permanent sky. Until I can tell myself I chose peace when really I chose distance.

"No," I say.

The spring brightens.

Lucian's hand moves to mine.

"Again."

"No."

The steam pulls back from the water.

The far edge of the spring appears.

A simple white door stands there. Plain paint. Brass knob. Slightly chipped near the bottom, like any ordinary door in any ordinary building.

"That's it?" I ask.

Lucian looks at it. "Yes."

"Very underwhelming."

"The real doors often are."

I laugh, then wipe my eyes. "Of course they are."

He stands first, water streaming down his body.

The finality of it hits me.

I stay seated a second longer.

The water is not as warm now.

Not cold.

Just no longer enough to make staying feel harmless.

I stand.

Lucian helps me out of the spring. His hand is steady. Mine trembles.

We dry off in silence.

Not awkward silence. Heavy silence. The kind that carries all the words we cannot say because saying them would turn goodbye into something we might try to negotiate.

He dresses me one final time.

The thought almost undoes me.

I put on my panties myself because I need to remember I can. He helps with the skirt. Then the corset, laced loose, because that is what I ask for. Less armor. Enough structure. Room to breathe.

He dresses too.

Trousers.

Then, finally, he reaches for the white shirt.

I don't stop him this time.

He slips it over his head.

The loss of his bare skin feels absurdly emotional.

"It had to happen eventually," I say.

His mouth curves. "Did it?"

"No. But it feels symbolic."

"It is." He reaches for the red cloak and fastens it over his shoulders. There he is again. Lucian, as he was when he first entered my chamber.

No.

Not as he was.

I see him differently now.

Not only temptation.

Guide.

Mirror.

Door.

He offers his hand.

I take it.

We walk around the edge of the spring toward the white door. The ground beneath my shoes is smooth stone, damp with mist. Flowers glow softly at the edges of the path. The sky overhead is full of stars, brighter now, as if they have moved closer to watch me leave.

Typical.

Even the universe wants a dramatic exit.

At the white door, Lucian stops.

My hand tightens around his.

"If I say I don't want to go," I whisper, "will you say you know?"

"Yes."

"I don't want to go."

"I know."

My eyes blur.

He turns toward me. The white door waits at his back. "When you walk through," he says, "you return to the white room. Your body will wake. Time there will have barely moved."

"It felt like days."

"Yes."

"Will I feel different?"

"Yes."

"Will they see it?"

"Perhaps."

"Will Lorenzo?"

His gaze softens. "That depends on what you show him."

My throat tightens.

Right.

Not magic.

Me.

I look down at our joined hands. "I'm afraid. I'm afraid I'll chicken out."

"You might."

"Lucian."

"Then choose again."

"What if I avoid him once?"

"Then answer the next time."

"What if I say it badly?"

"Then clarify."

"What if I cry?"

"Then you cry."

"What if he wants me?"

"Then breathe."

"What if he doesn't?"

Lucian's face softens with something almost like sorrow.

"Then you will still have told the truth."

The tears spill over. "I hate this part. I hate that truth doesn't guarantee the ending."

"I know."

"I hate that I have to go back to a world where I can be brave and still not get what I want."

Lucian steps closer and cups my face in both hands.

His palms are warm.

"Dorothea," he says, "that is the only world where getting what you want can matter."

The sentence breaks me.

Quietly.

Completely.

I close my eyes and cry into his hands.

Lucian holds my face until I stop.

Or until I become tired enough that the tears slow on their own.

When I open my eyes, he is still there. For now. "Will you kiss me goodbye?" I ask.

His thumbs brush my cheeks.

"How?"

I laugh through the ache.

"Still with the questions."

"Especially now."

I think.

Not hungry.

Not deep.

Not a kiss that makes leaving harder because it pretends not to be goodbye.

"Soft," I say. "Real enough to remember. Not enough to hide in."

Lucian's eyes shine. He kisses me.

Soft.

Warm.

Brief enough to hurt.

Real enough to change me.

When he pulls back, the white door glows faintly.

I take a breath.

"I promised," I say.

"Yes."

"I will answer Lorenzo's next call. I won't hide behind work. I will tell him the fake part cannot be the only part we admit to. I will ask what he wants. I will tell him what I need."

Lucian nods.

"And," I add, because the final chain is not his, not Lorenzo's, but mine, "I won't punish him for not being you."

The spring goes silent.

Then the stars overhead flare.

Lucian's face changes.

Pride.

Grief.

Tenderness.

"Good girl," he says softly.

The words no longer feel only erotic.

They feel like a blessing I can leave behind.

I place my hand on the white door.

The knob is cool.

Ordinary.

Real.

Or as close as this place comes.

I look at Lucian one last time.

"Goodbye," I whisper.

His smile is small and sad.

"Goodbye, Lady Dorothea."

I open the door.

White light spills out.

For one second, I feel every room at once.

The first chamber, velvet and mirrors.

The red room, cuffs open.

The blue sky.

The green garden.

The hot spring steam.

The hallway of doors.

The black door with Lorenzo's name on its breath.

Then Lucian's voice reaches me, low and steady.

"Don't live as if the chain is locked."

I step through.

TEN

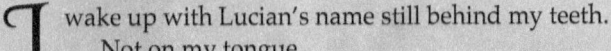

I wake up with Lucian's name still behind my teeth.
Not on my tongue.
Not spoken.
Held there, warm and dangerous, like a bite of something too rich to swallow all at once.

For a moment, I don't open my eyes.

That feels safer.

Behind my eyelids, there's still steam. Hot spring water. Stars overhead. Lucian's hands on my face. The simple white door. His voice telling me not to live as if the chain is locked.

My body remembers before my mind accepts.

Warm water fading from my skin.

A final kiss, soft enough to hurt.

The press of his fingers around mine.

Then white light.

Then here.

The surface beneath me is no longer stone warmed by a mineral spring. It's leather. Smooth black leather, warm from my body, slightly sticky against the back of my neck. The air is different too. No steam. No flowers. No smoke, leather, cedar, hot metal, or night water.

Sage.

Dust.

Old paper.

Something faintly sweet from the tea.

257

The white room.

I keep my eyes closed anyway.

A person is allowed a moment of denial after a magical erotic identity crisis. I'm almost certain that is in the consent form somewhere, probably under emotional aftercare, subsection: don't sit up too fast or immediately text complicated men.

"Dorothea," a voice says softly.

Not Lucian.

My chest tightens anyway.

The grief of that is strange. Small, but sharp. Not grief like losing a person. Not exactly. Lucian was real enough to change me, not real enough to choose instead of me. He told me that. I understood it.

Understanding does not prevent the ache.

It rarely does. If understanding solved pain, bookstores would go out of business and half the town would stop making terrible dating choices.

"Take your time," Ms. Vesper says.

I open my eyes.

The white ceiling waits above me.

No canopy. No chains embroidered in gold. No stars close enough to count. Just smooth, blank, merciless white.

I turn my head.

Ms. Vesper stands beside the chaise, hands folded at her waist. Her dark hair falls over one shoulder. The tattoos on her arms seem quieter in this room, the ink softened by all the light. She watches me with the expression of a woman who has seen many people return from impossible places and has learned not to ask foolish questions too soon.

Good.

Because I'm full of foolish answers.

I sit up.

Slowly.

My body feels heavy.

Not old, exactly. Not weak. Just real. Gravity has opinions again. My bones have remembered they are bones. My muscles hum with a soreness that should not exist if the consent form was telling the whole truth. Not pain. Not harm.

Nothing dramatic enough for a complaint. More like the ghost of sensation.

I glance down at myself to find myself in jeans, a gray bakery shirt, and an apron. Flour dust still on the hem.

The burgundy corset and silk robe are gone. No black lace. No wet hair from the spring. No visible marks on my wrists. No trace of Lucian's hands on my skin.

For one startled, foolish second, I'm disappointed.

Then I notice something else.

My hands are unclenched.

They rest in my lap, palms open.

That undoes me more than a dramatic magical souvenir would have.

I stare at them.

My work hands. Dry from dish soap. Fingernails short. A little burn near my wrist from the oven rack. A smear of flour still caught in the crease below my thumb.

Before the tea, I looked at these hands and saw function.

Now I see questions.

What will you ask for?

What will you hold?

What will you stop carrying alone?

I close my fingers, then open them again.

No chains.

Just hands.

Ms. Vesper offers me a glass of water.

"Drink," she says.

Not a suggestion.

I take it.

The glass is cool. The water is plain. I sniff it anyway because I'm not a woman who learns nothing.

Ms. Vesper's mouth twitches. "It's only water," she says.

"That sounds like something someone with magical tea would say."

"It's also true."

I drink.

The cold water moves down my throat and lands in my stomach with shocking ordinariness. I did not realize how much I wanted ordinary until it arrived. Ordinary water. Ordinary room. Ordinary body. Ordinary clothes.

Ordinary world waiting just outside the door.

Terrifying thing, the ordinary world.

At least the magical Devil castle was honest about wanting to rearrange me.

"How long was I gone?" I ask. My voice sounds normal.

That surprises me.

Ms. Vesper glances at the pocket watch hanging from a chain around her neck. I don't remember it being there earlier. That is becoming a theme.

"Twenty minutes."

I laugh once. It comes out rough.

"In here," she adds.

Twenty minutes.

I lived days in twenty minutes.

Maybe not days. Maybe I only felt the weight of days because I stopped running through myself long enough to notice the rooms I had locked.

I set the water glass in my lap.

"Is he always like that?" I ask.

Ms. Vesper raises one eyebrow. "He?"

I give her a flat look.

"Don't make me say sex demon in this very white room."

Her smile spreads slowly.

"I would never."

"You absolutely would."

"Yes."

Something in my chest loosens. A laugh. Small, but mine. "Lucian," I say. His name shifts the room.

Ms. Vesper inclines her head. "The guide shaped by your card." She waits.

I look down at my hands again. "Was he real?" The question leaves me before I decide to ask it. I already asked Lucian. I know his answer. Real enough to change you. Not real enough to choose instead of you.

Still, some stubborn part of me wants a second opinion from the woman with the tea, the tattoos, and the suspiciously well-zoned threshold business.

Ms. Vesper does not answer right away.

Good. Bad. I don't know anymore.

"The Devil is a mirror with teeth," she says at last.

I look up. "That is horrible."

"Yes."

"Also possibly accurate."

"Yes."

She steps closer, her black skirt whispering over the white floor.

"The Devil does not only show us temptation," she says. "It shows us the lock and waits to see whether we notice the key is already in our hand."

My fingers curl around nothing.

The parchment list flashes in my mind. Yes. Maybe. No. The color codes. Red. Yellow. Green. The release tab in the cuff. The basket rim beneath my hand. The garden path forming one step at a time.

"The key," I whisper.

Ms. Vesper nods once.

"Was he real?" I ask again, softer.

She studies me with eyes that know too much and don't seem interested in using that knowing to make me feel small.

"Did he change you?"

"Yes."

"Then begin there. It's a doorway."

I roll my eyes, but there's no force behind it. "Everyone in this building is committed to making language inconvenient."

"Only the important words."

I drink more water because arguing with threshold women while emotionally raw is probably how people accidentally join covens.

"How do you feel?" she asks.

I take inventory.

The old me would have answered fine. Fine is a useful word. A locked pantry of a word. Put everything inside and leave it on the shelf until it spoils.

I don't say fine. "Hungry," I say first.

Ms. Vesper smiles.

"Embarrassed."

Her smile deepens.

"Powerful."

The word surprises me.

I sit with it.

"Yes," I say. "Powerful. Also slightly horrified that I may now have to speak honestly to people."

"A common side effect."

"You should list that on the form."

"It frightens customers."

"As it should."

"What else?"

I look at the white room.

It still feels blank, but not empty now. More like a counter cleared after a long bake. Flour wiped away. Bowls washed. The work done, but not forgotten.

"I feel like I went somewhere and came back with no proof," I say.

Ms. Vesper's gaze drops to my hands.

"No proof you can show easily."

My skin prickles.

"What does that mean?"

Instead of answering, she reaches toward me, palm up.

I hesitate.

Then I place my hand in hers.

Her thumb brushes the center of my palm. Warmth flashes there. Not hot. Not painful.

I draw my hand back and look.

For one second, red letters glow against my skin.

YES

MAYBE

NO

Then they vanish.

My breath catches.

Ms. Vesper's face remains calm.

"The useful things tend to stay," she says.

My eyes burn.

I close my hand into a fist. Then open it again.

Still no visible mark.

Still, I can feel it.

The structure.

The key.

"Thank you," I say.

The words are small.

Not enough.

Nothing is enough, really. What do you say to a woman who handed you a cup of tea and twenty minutes later you returned with your whole interior architecture mildly demolished and up to code for the first time?

Thank you seems offensively underbaked.

But it's what I have.

Ms. Vesper accepts it as if it's enough.

"You did the work," she says.

"I had help, from a shirtless man with a cloak."

"That happens less often than people assume."

I stare at her.

She smiles and I can't help but laugh.

The laugh becomes something dangerously close to a sob, but I manage to keep it in the laugh family. Mostly. The white room does not comment.

After a moment, Ms. Vesper steps back and gestures toward the door.

"You can sit longer if you need."

I look at the door.

Plain. White. Ordinary.

The real doors often are.

Lucian's voice, not in the room, but in me.

I stand.

My knees hold.

My body feels strange inside my normal clothes. The denim of my jeans is rougher than I remember. My shirt is too familiar. My apron hangs over me like proof that the person who walked in here still exists, but not in the exact arrangement.

I reach behind my neck and pull the apron strap over my head.

Ms. Vesper watches.

I fold the apron slowly.

It smells like butter, cinnamon, coffee, and work.

For once, I don't put it back on.

I carry it in my hand.

When we leave the white room, The Arcane Room feels smaller than before.

Not diminished.

Just real.

The shop is still warm and maroon and crowded with tarot decks, crystals, books, candles, and tiny objects that probably know more than they should. The bell above the door waits in silence. The amethyst still catches the light. The shelf of journals still displays titles like What You Refuse To Say and What You Want When No One Is Watching.

I stare at that one.

"No," I tell it.

Ms. Vesper says nothing.

Good.

At the counter, the old Devil card remains in the display case.

I stop in front of it.

The horned figure sits enthroned. The two people stand below, chained loosely by the throat.

I used to think the card was about the figure with the horns.

Now I cannot stop looking at the chains.

Loose.

So loose.

My chest aches.

"Keep going," I whisper.

Maybe to myself.

Maybe to Lucian.

Maybe to the little figures on the card.

Ms. Vesper stands behind the counter.

I dig into my bag and pull out my wallet.

My hand shakes only a little.

I take out cash. More than sensible. Less than the experience deserves, but I'm a business owner and not a woman with a fantasy-castle budget.

I place it on the counter.

Ms. Vesper looks at the bills, then at me.

"This is generous."

"It was either this or name a croissant after you."

Her eyes brighten. "What kind?"

"Dark chocolate. Cherry. Sea salt."

"That sounds excellent."

"It would be."

"Then perhaps both."

I laugh. "You drive a hard bargain."

"I run a threshold, dear. Bargains are implied."

I slide the cash closer.

"Take it."

She does.

No false modesty. I appreciate that. Money is energy, people say when they are about to charge too much for a workshop, but money is also rent, utilities, inventory, and the deeply unmagical reality of keeping doors open.

A lady has rent.

I'm starting to understand Ms. Vesper.

Terrible development.

At the door, I pause.

"Will I see him again?"

Ms. Vesper's expression softens.

"That depends on which door you open next."

"I meant Lucian."

"I know."

I sigh. "You're impossible."

"Yes."

The bell above the door laughs softly before I touch the handle.

I point at it. "And you are smug."

It laughs again.

I open the door and step out.

Coral Cove hits me like a cold cloth.

Rain. Salt air. Car exhaust. Wet pavement. Coffee from the cafe across the street. The far-off smell of ocean, green and briny. Someone's dog barking. A gull screaming like it has been personally wronged by capitalism.

The sky is gray.

The sidewalk is damp.

A car rolls through a puddle too fast and sprays water near the curb.

The world has not changed.

How rude.

How merciful.

I stand under The Arcane Room's awning with my folded apron in my hand and let the ordinary evening gather around me.

Twenty minutes.

The bakery will still need closing. The folder will still be on the counter. The rent problem will still exist. Lorenzo will still be Lorenzo, a real man with real hands and a real ability to disappoint me.

Nothing has been solved.

That should depress me.

Instead, it steadies me.

Magic did not finish my life for me.

Good.

I would have resented it by morning.

I start walking.

The streets look different on the way back.

Not because they have changed. Because I'm not moving through them as a woman trying to outrun every question inside her own body.

The candle shop window glows warm, full of jars labeled with names like Hearth, Moonwater, and Ex Lover. I still think Ex Lover is an irresponsible candle name. The tea house sign says Ask Us About Your Aura. I still intend not to. The florist is closing, its owner pulling buckets of flowers inside. A little bell rings from the door of Spellbound Stories as a customer steps out with a paper bag hugged to her chest like contraband.

Lea is visible through the bookstore window.

She stands behind the counter, shelving something from a rolling cart, glasses low on her nose. She looks up at exactly the wrong moment.

Our eyes meet.

Her face changes.

Not dramatically. Lea is too good at subtlety for that. But she sees something. I know she does. Her hands go still on the book. Her mouth softens.

I lift one finger.

Not a wave. Not the middle one, although that has history. Just a small acknowledgment.

She smiles.

Then, mercifully, she does not run outside.

Good friend.

Good menace.

I keep walking.

Knead the Dough waits two storefronts down, dark except for the light over the register and the faint glow from the kitchen I forgot to turn off. The sign still says Sorry, We're Closed. The rolling pin doodle looks too cheerful for the emotional evolution that has apparently occurred in its absence.

I unlock the door.

The bell jingles.

Only a normal bell.

"Thank God," I mutter.

Before The Arcane Room, the smell of the bakery felt like responsibility.

Now it feels like home and warning at once.

A place I built and a place I hide. Both can be true. I lock the door behind me.

The quiet settles.

Not empty quiet. Bakery-after-closing quiet. The hum of the refrigerator case. The soft tick of cooling metal. The low rumble of the walk-in. The building breathing after the customers are gone.

I set my apron on the counter.

Lorenzo's folder waits beside the register.

Charcoal gray. Crisp. Professional. Infuriating.

I stare at it.

It stares back.

The folder contains lease terms. Festival contracts. Notes from Lorenzo in his precise handwriting. Legal language I have been avoiding because every time I open it, my chest tightens and I hear the quiet old voice that says, You cannot afford help. Help costs. Help means owing. Help means someone can take what you cannot repay.

I reach for the folder.

Then stop.

My palm tingles.

Yes.

Maybe.

No.

The key is already in your hand.

I pick up the folder.

It's heavier than paper should be, but that is not magic. That is adulthood.

I carry it to the little table near the front window, the one Lea had occupied earlier while accusing me of being a clenched fist in an apron. I sit down. The chair is hard. Real. No velvet. No silk. No hot spring. No shirtless guide asking me to name every sensation.

Just me.

The bakery.

The folder.

The world.

I open it.

The top page is a summary Lorenzo prepared. Not the actual lease language. A translation.

For me.

I blink.

He has written the key points clearly, with notes in the margins.Below that, in handwriting darker and more slanted than the rest, he added: *Dorothea, this is manageable if you stop avoiding me long enough to let me manage it.*

I laugh. The sound breaks the bakery's quiet wide open.

"That man," I say to no one.

I'm also suddenly, dangerously close to crying because he did not write, You have messed this up. He did not write, Why did you wait so long? He did not write, I told you so, although I suspect he wanted to, because Lorenzo is human and therefore morally imperfect.

He wrote manageable.

He wrote it for me.

I flip the next page.

More notes. More plain language. A list of documents he needs from me. A sticky note stuck to the side, bright yellow.

Eat something before you panic over this.

I stare at the note.

Then I laugh again.

It becomes a sob.

I press the heel of my hand to my mouth.

The bakery blurs.

I want Lucian suddenly, fiercely. Not sexually, though my body is apparently still capable of being inappropriate in moments of legal stress. I want his voice. His stillness. The way he would say, Name it, and I would say scared, embarrassed, hungry, and he would say yes, yes, yes, until the words stopped being a swarm and became something I could hold.

But Lucian is not here.

The room I'm in belongs to me. So I do it for myself.

"Scared," I say aloud.

The refrigerator hums.

"Embarrassed."

The ovens tick.

"Hungry."

My stomach growls, because apparently my body enjoys comic timing.

I look toward the pastry case.

The overbaked cinnamon rolls sit covered on the back counter.

Fine.

The sticky note did say eat something.

I stand, go behind the counter, and take one of the cinnamon rolls from the tray. It's still good. Not perfect. Dark at the edges, too firm in places. Sellable with a discount, yes. Worth eating alone after magical intervention, absolutely.

I tear off a piece.

The center is soft.

I eat it standing at first, out of habit.

Then I stop.

No.

I take the plate to the table and sit down like a person who believes she is allowed to receive calories while not actively producing value.

It feels absurdly rebellious.

The cinnamon roll tastes like butter, sugar, cinnamon, and a small amount of professional disappointment. It's also wonderful.

I eat three bites.

Then drink water from the bottle I left near the register.

Hydration, Lucian would say.

Bossy, I would answer.

My chest aches.

I look at the folder again.

The black door in the hallway rises in memory.

I expected his door to be about sex. Maybe it still is, in part. Desire does not become irrelevant because legal paperwork arrives. If anything, the contrast makes the desire worse. I can now imagine asking him for things, which is inconvenient.

But the door was never only about his body.

It was truth.

The possibility of letting him see me as wanting and scared at the same time.

The possibility of saying, I need help.

The possibility of saying, I want to know what this is.

I pull out my phone.

Then set it down immediately.

"Nope," I say.

Good start.

Very brave.

I take another bite of cinnamon roll.

The bakery does not judge me.

Or if it does, it keeps it to itself because it knows what I have endured.

My phone sits on the table.

Dark screen.

Ordinary.

A white door.

The real doors often are.

I pick it up again.

My thumb hovers over Lorenzo's name.

He is saved in my phone as Lorenzo Moretti, because saving him as Lorenzo would have felt intimate and saving him as Problem With Cheekbones would have been discoverable in court.

My thumb taps his contact.

Call.

Text.

Message.

Email.

I stare at the options.

A phone call is too much.

A text is too easy to hide behind.

Email is for cowards and contract attachments.

I close the contact.

Then open it again.

This is ridiculous.

I have had a man's mouth between my legs in a magical hot-air balloon, but apparently calling a lawyer has become the true erotic terror of my evening.

"Fine," I whisper.

My palm tingles.

Not visibly.

Enough.

I press call.

Then immediately panic and nearly hang up.

No.

I place the phone on the table and put both hands flat beside it, as if I'm dealing with a very small bomb.

One ring.

Two.

My heart pounds.

I'm going to throw up.

No, I'm not.

I have survived customers asking if croissants are supposed to be flaky. I have survived the Hallway of Secrets. I have survived saying please and meaning it. I have survived realizing fantasy is not freedom if I use it to avoid the real door.

Three rings.

Lorenzo answers.

"Dorothea?"

My name in his voice.

Real.

Tired, maybe. Concerned. Slightly rough, as if he has been talking too much or thinking too hard. No candlelight. No magical echo. No perfect guide waiting to interpret me.

Just Lorenzo.

My pulse jumps so hard I nearly laugh.

"Hi," I say.

Brilliant.

Inspired.

An opening line for the ages.

There's a pause.

"You okay?"

I look at the folder.

The yellow sticky note.

The half-eaten cinnamon roll.

My folded apron on the counter.

The bakery around me, home and hiding place, both.

"No," I say.

The word lands.

I don't soften it.

"I'm not," I continue. "But I'm trying something new and answering honestly before I can make that inconvenient for everyone."

Another pause.

Then, softer, "All right."

Not teasing.

Not pushing.

All right.

I close my eyes for half a second.

"I read your notes," I say.

"Good."

"The sticky note was bossy."

"You needed to eat."

"I did."

"Good."

The word hits me so unexpectedly that I almost laugh.

Good.

Not Lucian's voice.

Not the same.

Not fantasy.

Still, my body remembers that praise can be received without owing anything for it.

I breathe.

"I have all the documents you've requested." I say.

"Dorothea."

There's my name again.

Careful.

Like he knows I might run.

"Yes?"

"Are you at the bakery?"

"Yes."

"Alone?"

"Yes."

"Have you been crying?"

I freeze.

My first instinct is to lie.

No.

Don't be dramatic, Lorenzo.

I'm fine.

The words line up, old and practiced.

The key is in my hand.

"Yes," I say.

The silence after is not comfortable.

But I stay in it.

"Do you want me to come over?" he asks.

My whole body reacts.

Want.

Fear.

A black door opening half an inch.

I grip the edge of the table.

There are so many ways to answer badly.

No, because I want yes too much.

Yes, because I'm scared to say what I actually need.

A joke, because jokes are aprons for the soul.

I breathe.

"I don't know," I say.

It's not elegant.

It's honest.

Lorenzo's voice lowers. "Okay."

"I need to talk to you," I say. "About the paperwork, about our fake relationship, about things."

His breath changes on the other end. "Okay."

My hand trembles.

The phone waits.

Lorenzo waits.

Not like Lucian.

Not perfectly.

But he waits.

"I need to know what you actually want from me," I say,

and the words shake but don't break. "Not from the business arrangement. Not from people believing whatever they already believe. Me."

Silence.

For one second, I almost grab the words back.

Then Lorenzo says, "I can be there in ten minutes."

My heart stumbles.

"That is not an answer."

"No," he says. "It's me asking to give you one in person."

The bakery goes very still.

Or maybe I do.

I look toward the front window. Main Street glistens with rain beyond the glass. The world continues. Cars pass. A woman under a yellow umbrella hurries by with a paper bag clutched to her chest. The neon from the diner flickers red over the wet sidewalk.

A real world.

Messy.

Uncurated.

No consent worksheet appearing by magic.

No guide interpreting every silence.

Just a man asking to cross the distance.

I can say no.

I can say not tonight.

I can say tomorrow.

I can say yes.

The chain is not locked.

I close my eyes.

"Ten minutes," I say.

Lorenzo exhales, and something in that sound reaches through the phone and touches a place in me I'm not ready to name.

"Lock the door until I get there," he says.

Bossy.

My mouth curves.

"It's already locked."

"Good."

There it is again.

Good.

Real this time.

Imperfect.

Unscripted.

Risky.

I end the call before I can over-explain.

Then I sit there in the quiet bakery with my phone in my hand, my pulse racing, and my half-eaten cinnamon roll cooling on the plate.

Nothing magical happens.

No candles flare.

No door opens.

No chain drops to the floor in symbolic applause.

The bakery only hums.

The rain taps against the window.

The folder remains open.

My life waits.

I stand.

First, I put the cinnamon roll in the microwave for ten seconds, because courage is important but so is texture.

Then I whisper, "Green." Because I'm choosing to keep going.

Back in the bakery, I unlock the front door but leave the sign turned to Closed. The bell over the door waits quietly above it.

I sit at the table.

I drink water.

I eat another bite of cinnamon roll, warm now, better than before. Not perfect. Still worth wanting.

Outside, headlights turn onto the street.

A car slows near the curb.

My heart lifts into my throat.

The real door is opening.

I put both hands flat on the table.

Open palms.

No chains.

And when the bell over the bakery door rings, I don't run.

Also by Jax Wilder

Coral Cove Series

Sleighed by Love

Harvesting Love

Dawning Desire

Knead You Now

Love Rewound

Perfect Lover Spell

Haunted by Her

Red, White, and Ravished

Frosted Sugar Charms

Tarot Fantasies Series

The Devil's Temptations

Strength of the Beast

Hanged Passions

Six of Cups

Death's Embrace

Queen of Pentacles

Seven of Pentacles

Ace of Wands

Three of Swords

Lovers In The Veil

Two of Swords

Seven of Wands

Three of Cups

Coastal Cupid Series

HeartBound Souls

Witches of Coral Cove
From Hell With Love

Fae Ring Series
Alice and Her Mad Hatters
Bound By The Glass Slipper
Call of Cthulhu's Heart
Stand Alone Titles
Pride and Prejudice and Witches

Lorelai Hamilton
Encyclopedia of Divination
Encyclopedia of Cryptids
Encyclopedia of Faeries
Encyclopedia of Supernatural Rules
Encyclopedia of Cursed Objects
Tarot Tales and Magic Spells
Teenage Tarot
Arcane In Verse
The Eclectic Witch's Grimoire
Teenage Witch's Grimoire
Find Your Bliss
Tarot Reflection Journal
Tarot Refection Journal Coloring The Tarot
Dream Journal
Fluent Tarot
Fluent Tarot Workbook
Fluent Tarot Matters of the Heart
Fluent Tarot Matters of the Heart Workbook
The Eclectic Witches Grimoire

Additional Books by Rainbow Quartz Publishing

Miranda Levi

From A Youth A Fountain Did Flow (Book 1 of The Fountain Of Youth Series)

The Sea Withdrew (Book 2 of The Fountain Of Youth Series)

What I've Tasted of Desire(Book 3 of The Fountain Of Youth Series)

A Tear In Time

Mother Nature

Restraint

In Orion's Hands

Jackson Anhalt

From The 911 Files

About the Author

Jax Wilder is a passionate romance author hailing from a charming small town nestled in the picturesque Pacific Northwest. With a heart full of love and an unyielding belief in the power of happily ever afters, Jax weaves enchanting tales of love and connection that leave readers captivated.

Jax's novels are a reflection of her commitment to celebrating the magic of love, and her characters' journeys mirror the warmth and happiness she has found in her own life. Join her on the enchanting journey of love, passion, and enduring connection through her heartfelt romance novels.